Bruce Hill

FULL CIRCLE

Bruce Hill is a retired translator. His work covered almost any sphere, from the translation of serious medical studies and legal documents to translations of hospitality brochures via innovative IT texts, operator manuals and company press releases, the latter couched in technical phraseology or business jargon. He wished, at last, to distance himself from the world of commercial profit and write for his own pleasure and possibly for the pleasure of others.

J. Farady (a friend)

Edition: BoD - Books on Demand,
12/14 rond-point des Champs-Élysées, 75008 Paris
Printing: BoD - Books on Demand, Norderstedt, Germany
ISBN: 9782322380411
Legal deposit: August 2021

BOOK I

CHAPTER 1

A terrible wind was blowing, cold and penetrating, down from the Massif Central. The tall leafless trees were bending under the weight of the gale and from time to time old, sapless twigs and small branches would come flying across the field where Charles with the constant and uniform help of Mardi the Percheron was ploughing the 5 hectare stubble field from the previous year's harvest. He had abandoned his cap which was now tucked into his belt as the wind blowing at some 50 km/hr was indeed fierce. As a result, his fair hair which he refused to have cut short, unlike most young men of his age, kept blowing into his face and making him swear. However, when he reached the headland he halted Mardi, gave him a handful of grass to munch and sought and found some tough, flexible but thin twigs from a bush growing there and twisted them into a rough rope to tie his hair back. That done, he took hold of the plough handles again and manoeuvred the horse and plough to the furrow to be turned over in the opposite direction. It was November and the field had to be finished before the first snowfalls and frosts. He could be described as being completely resigned to his life of farmer's son, thought nothing of rising very early in the morning and bedding down early in the evening, just like his parents. There was a difference though and that was that his mind had been nurtured and his intellect encouraged to blossom through the attentiveness and devotional care of the local priest or *curé* who had taken him under his wing at an early age. Could he have been five years old? This had not been without a certain amount of opposition from his parents who feared that there would be no successor to take over the running of the farm later on. The *curé* reassured the parents to some degree by emphasizing that any instruction he gave their son would be based on the bible and the music he taught would be put to good use in the parish church on the organ. He did indeed teach Charles the rudiments of the Old and New Testaments together with the catechism that was more or less mandatory at that time and the musical training he received was put to good use after he had reached the age of fifteen by accompanying the choir and parishioners for the different parts of the mass – Offertory, Kyrie, Gloria – and for the hymns. However, the musical instruction, unknown to the parents went far beyond that and he succeeded in instilling in the lad a love of classical music and also simple country music. Idem for classical writings over and beyond the sacred works encouraged by the Church of the day. The *curé* was in fact an enlightened person and although he was a true believer in the Almighty he was also a believer in Man and being of an extremely generous nature he sought to bring out the best in his parishioners and had spotted young Charles at an early age when he left the church with his parents on a Sunday after the mass. The young lad had questioned him about his sermon asking for instance how the sea had parted into two to allow the Jews to escape the Egyptians. He had put further questions, like the seven loaves and seven fish, which the priest had answered evasively always putting the 'will of God' to the fore. It was precisely these questions that made the latter feel strongly that Charles was intelligent and was not to be put off by vague, imprecise replies, exactly like himself, he mused. So, once a week in the morning when he was still very young and then in the evening when he had reached the age of helping his father actively on the farm he was taught history, literature and music at a level far above the level of the compulsory education administered by the local elementary, then secondary school. Strange to say he knew so much more than his contemporary pupils at all stages that he had to appear to be a little dull-witted not to draw the attention of the teachers and above all of his friends. It did show through though sometimes and when he became a little too inspired by some literary work, for instance, or when he started to quote some poet, he suddenly realized what he was doing and shut up like a clam. His school mates frankly could not understand his behaviour especially as he played the rough and tumble games with them just like all of them. The teachers were not naive and realized they did not have to worry about his education. Even though he kept a very low profile they could see he was well beyond the others as far reading and writing were concerned. They rarely asked him questions, except for mathematics, not wishing to make him feel superior to his class mates. This might be thought to be very advanced for the period, but not really. It simply meant that practically speaking they had one less child to educate!

So he developed a true love of literature, for Voltaire, de Lamartine, de la Fontaine (for his fables) and for many others and would spend as much time as possible reading works and memorizing poems. In respect of the music the *curé* taught him, he would spend much time in the church on the organ but also with a guitar that his guide and mentor lent him and eventually gave him, unknown to his parents. He learned the true facts about Napoleon, his conquests, defeats and final banishment and in so doing learned something about other European countries and especially England. He would not be long in knowing a little more about England but from another source!

The ploughing job he was engaged in was passing quite rapidly because although it looked a dull, repetitive job to an onlooker, it made Charles feel close to Nature. There were birds pecking at the worms in the turned slices of land and rabbits, squirrels and other animals about their business around the field and in the boundary trees but most of all he enjoyed the company of the percheron, Mardi. He was firm but gentle with the horse, often patted his flanks, stroked his head, gave him grass to munch. Ploughing with the horse was real teamwork, the animal encouraging the man and vice versa. When a field was eventually ploughed, Charles looked at it in the same way a painter might glance at his latest work. A satisfied feeling of work well done. Not only that, but he would sing sacred solo parts of the mass he found attractive or even local country music. A passerby in the lane adjoining one side of the field might stop and listen to his melodious voice in the still air accompanied by the sound of the metal plough share hitting stones although not in time with the song!

He felt it was time to eat his ploughman's lunch made up by his mother in a no-nonsense way. There was almost a whole baguette with a large piece of goat cheese made on the farm, a half bottle of some unknown red wine, the same of spring water, some walnuts, an apple and a large wad of his mother's cake. It was very wholesome and when he had devoured it he settled down in a trimmed ditch out of the wind but with sun shining on his face from time to time, to take a nap. The horse was unhitched and eating its own 'lunch' in the hedgerow accompanied by half a wine cask filled with water to slake its thirst. This was as near to happiness Charles would ever get – a pity he did not realize it.

He was just rubbing his eyes after his nap when he heard the muffled sound of hoofs from the unpaved lane. Standing up he could see his mentor and now friend (one could say) trotting slowly down the lane, longish hair floating in the wind and round, empathetic face with large lips and deep brown eyes smiling almost fiendishly astride his sturdy, nicely brushed mare. The *curé* raised his hand in welcome and Charles pushed through the hedgerow to be able without shouting to say a few words."Good afternoon, Père Farnault, how are you on this brisk November morning?"

"I'm fine, Charles, just trotting my horse and enjoying the sunshine while trying to devise a theme for next Sunday's sermon. As you know, I want to introduce Christian values into people's lives without thrusting religion as such down their throats. It's not so easy." All this in his deep, rounded, magnetic voice.

"Oh yes, Père, I've noticed that you avoid reference to hell's fires and even to eternal bliss and prefer talking about the worthwhile aspects of the here and now, even going as far as saying that to relax and enjoy your life is not negative as long as it hurts no-one. I've taken your advice to heart and I frequently find certain aspects of my life not too tedious. Of course I love reading, as you know, and I love playing and listening to music, as you know, too. But I have come to enjoy things I would only have considered as hard work before and what I am doing today is one such task. I suddenly realized this morning that ploughing this field with my old friend Amber (a small chuckle) is a pleasure – quite hard work, of course, but when I look upon the achieved job, I can actually feel happy."

Still seated on his saddle, "Don't get me wrong, Charles, I believe there is a force out there somewhere and that force we Christians call God but I am not sure that that force is counting points – in one column for unpleasant deeds or words and in another for good deeds or words – to see whether we end up there (he pointed upwards) or there (downwards). I feel that we are all responsible to some extent for what we do in life but confined to certain limits. For example, it would be difficult for a baker's son, or daughter for that matter, to become a doctor or lawyer. Your position on the other hand is somewhat different in that you are destined to become a farmer but that due to your intelligence and perhaps a little tuition I have given you, you could do something else with your life. However, you have just said, more or less, that you are satisfied with your life and even happy, so it's not for me to persuade you to change direction." All this was said slowly but with a twinkle in his eye. "I know I'm a bit nosy but can you tell me what you are reading at the moment?"

"Well, I heard some people at the town hall talking enthusiastically about a book and as it was available I borrowed it but I only have 2 weeks to read it. It's quite long. It's called Marion Lescaut by Antoine François Prévost. It's difficult to put down - not at all stodgy. Do you know it, Père?"

"Oh, yes, indeed. The version available today has been revised because nearly a century ago the book was condemned to be burned. It treated subjects that people were not allowed even to think about at that time. Luckily things have changed and those poor women of ill-fame are now at least allowed to change their lives if they can. The Church would say that they would have to repent. But you know all that. I believe that it is not always possible to change one's life and many of these women are in their position through no fault of their own. Anyway, it's true the story takes you up and carries you along with it. Yes, I read it some time ago at a time I should not have - at the seminary in fact. Gosh, if the Father Superior had known I would have been thrown out! Read it, enjoy the good parts and let me know what you think about it afterwards but don't let it encourage you to do anything untoward. I must be on my way." A huge wink and off he went, clippety clop.

Charles smiled enormously. The *curé* always did him a lot of good but he could not have told you why.

The conversation that had been punctuated by pauses where each man looked the other in the eye before replying had delayed Charles' work and he could see he was going to be late returning to the farmhouse for there were other tasks awaiting him, not least the feeding of the farm animals. However, he kept going for another three hours but as the evenings were short and vision was becoming a problem he decided to call it a day, unhitched the wheeled plough from Mardi, patted and stroked the horse for his good work and climbed up onto his back to ride slowly but saddle-less to the stable almost a kilometer away in distance. They (Charles and Mardi) were just leaving the rough entrance between two hedges to the field that entailed a short descent when from the corner of his eye he noticed but could not yet hear a white clad figure on what looked like a fine chestnut thoroughbred trotting with apparent ease down the lane towards him. Had he seen the figure before, that he now saw was a woman, he would have let her pass before leaving the field but as it was he had no choice but to wait and stop in the lane, pulling Mardi to one side allowing the horsewoman to pass with plenty of room to spare. It was obvious that the woman, now seen to be young, had come from the white painted but slightly tarnished manor house to be seen on the hilltop facing the field Charles had been ploughing. This was surprising because Charles and his parents assumed that the house that he seemed to remember was ironically called "Beau Repaire" (built one hundred years before on the site of a highwayman's cottage) was empty and had been for many years.

"Oh, thank you so much," she said with a strong accent - Germanic, or was it English? "You are so, how do you say, chivalrous!" With this phrase which it was obvious gave her pleasure to utter she smiled a highly enticing smile, enhanced undoubtedly by her playful green/hazelnut eyes and fairly wide mouth.

Charles saw she was young and noticed her long auburn hair tied very fashionably with bright ribbons. He also noticed her hands that were not the hands of someone who was unused to manual work but bore long, tough fingers that were not gloved nor did they look as if they were manicured. She was obviously quite tall judging by the stirrups and carried no excess weight. All this he took in at a glance.

These observations of the young woman were reciprocated by her for Charles saw her eyes sweep over his person to take in his height (a little above average) his angular but not lean face, the intense expression emanating from his dark brown eyes and his long hair, still tied back rustically behind his head. She must have seen that his body was lean and muscular.

Charles, having been brought up to respect the gentry (although often combined with a certain disdain) expected the young lady to trot away from him without another word but this was not to be so. Instead, she turned her horse round so that she was face to face with Charles and asked. "Is your farm far from here and what will you be sowing in this field I see you have so neatly ploughed?" All this in her quaint foreign accent but with no faults of grammar or syntax.

"Well, he replied, it will take me 20 minutes or so to reach home on Amber (he patted his Percheron on the neck) and as for the field, I think my father has decided to sow winter oats in this field." He did his best to put on a natural voice although he tried to cut out any rustic words or accents. He wanted to be up to the mark although he knew in advance that that could not be. How could he, a mere country lad, be at the same educational and cultural level as someone like this newcomer before him? "By the way, my name is Charles Berger and my parents' farm is called La Rouarniere."

"I'll never be able to remember the name of your farm, but can I call you Charles or must I call you Mr Berger?" she said, a twinkle in her eye. "My name is Priscilla, Priscilla Grafton, and you will have guessed that I am English."

"Funny to see a noblewoman in this neck of the woods, but yes, I did guess you might be English or German. Is your family staying in ... in ... the white hilltop manor?" He laughed a little awkwardly after posing the question.

"Yes indeed. She smiled very reassuringly. My father is a diplomat and has received an appointment at Clermont Ferrand following the fall of Napoleon. I do not know what his job is exactly but he decided to rent a property of standing not too far from his posting, so here we are. Now tell me about this land you're working. Does it belong to your family, and when will you be sowing the oats?"

"There's quite a lot of work to do before we can sow. The land must be harrowed after ploughing, then sown, rolled and fertilizer spread."

"That's interesting but I know nothing about farming. What's this term "fertilizer? I have never heard of that before now," and he briefly explained the new technique.

"Perhaps I will have the opportunity of hearing more about your modern ways of farming, she said amiably, but there will be a lot of repair work and painting to do at the house before we can receive guests although that should only take a few weeks but when that's done – here she hesitated a second or two before resuming - I'm sure you will be seeing more of us, Mr Berger. *Au revoir*" She laughed tantalizingly. And off she trotted.

Charles took a deep breath but kept Amber at a standstill until Priscilla was out of sight. He was astonished by the way she addressed him because the only person above his station who talked to him in such a friendly way was the priest. He could not imagine the local marquis or marchioness even smiling at him let alone talking to him as an equal as she had done. But when she had said "more of us" did she mean her family or herself alone? A conundrum that only time would unravel but he thought it improbable that his parents and hers' could mix. No, he would have to get her out of his mind.

CHAPTER 2

The Bishop of Clermond Ferrand was unlike many of his rank in the ecclesiastical hierarchy, that is, he had never pushed to be in the position he now enjoyed but had reached it by dint of hard work and good example. Most people in the Western World might associate bishops with pomp and think of them perhaps as well established clerical "civil" servants with nothing much better to do than sign clerical papers and ordain priests!

Not so, our bishop who thought it his duty, with a pinch of pleasure, to visit the parishes in his bishopric on a routine basis.

It was thus the turn of the commune and parish of St Germain de la Montagne to welcome His Excellency some two weeks or so after the encounter of Charles with Priscilla. *Père* (Father) Farnault had been informed of the date of the visit some time previously and was prepared. Being quite a good musician himself he had often rewritten musical scores of masses by eminent composers to suit the limited musical resources of his parish. In the present instance he could however count on Charles to play the small organ and a lady whose husband was a successful lawyer would play the violin. That was it for instruments but the choir also was limited in number. There were five or six women and an equal number of men. Farnault had rewritten the scores of a mass by Vivaldi for two voices – mezzo soprano and baritone – which simplified matters. The result was not at all bad at the last rehearsal and in the small mediaeval church with its more than adequate acoustics the sound was quite uplifting. All concerned in the musical rendition of the mass were looking forward to the bishop's visit. *Père* Farnault would conduct the musical endeavour while the bishop himself would say the mass.

An hour before the mass was due to start Fr Farnault carried out an ultimate rehearsal of parts of the mass, especially the Gloria, that were fairly difficult – a sudden change of tempo, for example, or a pause after which it was imperative to find the right note. One could now hear the parishioners arriving and they settled into their customary although not obligatory seats. Some were chatting together discreetly while others, mostly women, were on their knees. The mass was due to start at 11 a.m. and towards 10.45 a carriage could be heard pulling up before the entrance to the little church. Yes, it was His Excellency dressed as it behoves a bishop in his purple cassock but smiling gently and patting children's heads while chatting pleasantly with parishioners. He was accompanied by the deacon who had replaced the parish priest during the rehearsal. The deacon preceded the bishop to the sacristy to enable the latter to dress in alb, stole and chasuble to say the mass and chat for a few minutes with the *curé*. All was in place when just before the hour struck in the steeple the small choir, musicians and choirmaster took their places before the altar. Then it was the turn of the bishop, followed by the deacon in his liturgical attire and two altar boys.

There was a pause for a few minutes while Charles played some pleasant background music on the organ. The mass then proper began with the Kyrie and the small choir started to put up a valiant performance backed by the two musical instruments.

They had sung the first Kyrie Eleison and were ready to embark on the Christe Eleison when a loud sound of hoofs could be heard arriving before the church. There were almost certainly two horses to make such a clatter. The main door of the church opened and who could be seen to arrive but Priscilla and her (it would seem) father. All heads including the bishop's now turned towards the distraction. The father, strikingly different from most of the parishioners present, wore a tail coat and breeches and held his top hat in his hand. He looked frankly foreign but very much at ease and with no difficulty found the seats reserved for him and his daughter in the front row. Priscilla wore a long hooded cloak hiding her dark blue full length dress to a large extent. They settled down as comfortably as the wooden benches would allow.

The Kyrie was now almost over and Priscilla was glancing around the quaint church and at its occupants. She saw the bishop now before the altar and the deacon and two altar boys who were serving him and behind them Father Farnault's back, the small choir neatly spaced apart with the violinist to one side but the organist could not be seen. The organ was two meters or so behind the musical gathering and it was only when one or other member of the choir moved position slightly could he be seen and of course he had his back to the congregation. But that was enough to arouse her interest because Charles's long fair hair was to say the least unusual in such a formal setting. She did not of course recognize him for a long time, for who would expect a farmer's son to be sitting at an organ and playing so delicately. But at the end of the mass which had unfolded without a hitch and quite successfully the bishop turned to Fr Farnault and he, in turn, beckoned the choir, violinist and organist to the foot of the altar, bowed to the congregation inviting his singers and musicians to do likewise. People almost wanted to clap but at that time it was not the done thing. However, one could hear murmurs of appreciation emanating from the congregation and the bishop, after thanking the parishioners for their goodwill and wishing them a joyous and holy Sunday, said how much he had liked the mass adorned with such beautiful and happy music and pointed out that the parish priest had been to great pains to put it together so wonderfully. Being slightly non-conformist he said. "If you so wish, you can clap discreetly" which caused almost a gasp but clap they did.

The people were now starting to gather up their missals, gloves and hats and were very slowly filing out of the church. All this while Fr Farnault was talking to the bishop but then introduced Sir Adam Grafton, Priscilla's father and Priscilla herself to His Excellency and the four of them chatted pleasantly for ten minutes or so. Priscilla, however, seemed a little distracted and was trying to keep her eye on Charles who was shuffling about, darting a few words to members of the choir and violinist, trying to look occupied but whose real attention was focused on Sir Spencer's daughter. At one moment the two young people's glances intercepted each other and if you had been close to one or the other you would have seen them blush fairly profusely. But then suddenly they, both of them, found something extraordinarily interesting in what their interlocutors were saying! Could Cupid's arrows have found their targets? That's to be seen. For the moment the great day's event, yes, the mass, had come to a close and nothing more would happen except that the *curé* invited his stalwart choir and musicians to the presbytery to drink the health of the bishop, and why not? the health of everyone. Unfortunately, there was no good reason to invite Sir Spencer and his daughter to this minor festivity so after saying "au revoir" to the latter, the bishop and priest led the choir and musicians out of the church and to the presbytery.

CHAPTER 3

Charles was this Monday back in the same field as the previous week. He and Amber were plodding up and down the furrows letting the slices of earth fall over gently to be worked by the sun, rain, wind and insects for sowing the barley in a few weeks. He was singing parts of the Gloria or Kyrie from the eve's performance or sometimes whistling. He felt fine but just a little disappointed that nothing had subsequently happened after he had seen Priscilla in the church but he thought, "it was not to be, is not to be and never was to be ..."

He had ploughed four furrows in the two parallel directions which had taken some 20 minutes when having started to plough a fifth time in the direction of the parkland opposite with its slight rise and the large house sitting smugly on it, he saw in the middle distance a figure dressed in a dark cloak slowly descending the incline on a black horse. Charles continued to the headland nearest the parkland and pretended not to notice the person now coming plainly into view. He raised the plough and he and the Percheron took their time to move purposefully over to the furrow that would take them in the direction of the wood, away from the lane, the parkland and the person who Charles now saw, from her build and her way of holding herself in the saddle, was clearly Priscilla. Ploughing in the two directions, towards the wood and then towards the lane was a task of some ten minutes and Charles was certain at first that the English gentleman's daughter would continue her ride taking no notice of the farmer's son labouring in the field. Imagine his surprise when, ploughing now towards the lane and parkland, he saw from the corner of his eye, for he kept his gaze downwards towards the plough share, that the young lady had mounted the slight rise of the entrance to the field and was sitting there motionless waiting for him to arrive.

"Good day, Mr Berger, Mr Charles Berger, is it not?"

"Yes, indeed, Miss Grafton, Miss Priscilla Grafton?"

"Oh that's lovely, Mr Berger. I love your sense of humour and I love your organ playing. That was a great surprise to see you seated there in front of the instrument and playing so sensitively. I felt I had to meet you properly. Have you ten minutes to spare?" She had pushed the hood away from her cloak to reveal her auburn hair. It was parted in the middle and both sides arranged with hair clasps leaving the wind to play with the ends which were free.

"Yes, Miss Grafton, "Charles said hesitatingly, "ten minutes is permissible but my father is a hard taskmaster and he wants me to finish this field this week."

"Well, Mr Berger, I am very curious to know how you came to play the organ. After all, it's not an easy instrument to play with its different keyboards – it's difficult enough playing the piano which I do, though not very well."

"Let's not exaggerate, Miss Grafton. My teacher has been the *curé* for the last five years or so and a very good teacher he is – patient and methodical. I have learned a lot from him. You might have noticed, he's not a stuffy spouter of morality and eternal damnation. He's very human and a good laugh, too."

"As you undoubtedly know, the English are not Roman Catholic but mostly Church of England which however bases its rules and liturgy on the Roman church, which means that if I come to hear the priest's amusing sermons and your music at the Sunday mass I will not be able to receive your Communion. Does that matter?"

"Not at all. I know it's heretical to say it in this day and age but for me the Church liturgy and lots of its teaching is mumbo jumbo. Perhaps I believe in a god but I mostly believe in the goodwill of men – and women, of course," he chuckled. "People might look at you and be astonished that you do not receive communion but word will get round that you are a convert in the making and they will all be pleased! Anyway, they are all good people, so don't take any notice."

"Very well, I will bear your advice in mind. Will I have the opportunity of talking to you after the mass. I think we have things in common. What do you think?"

"Well, I don't know about that. Do you really think we have things to talk about? You are a young woman of the world. You are used to meeting grand people and know a great deal about the politics of both England and France. I know practically nothing except from what I pick up from old discarded newspapers. Of course we have music (some music or all music?) in common, but what else? Do you know what it's like to work on a farm, the sheer grind sometimes?"

"Not really, but come off it, I'm not interested in politics and not at all in politicians, who are all men of course. On the other hand, to answer your question, I have to clear out the stables and load the manure on carts that a neighbouring farmer takes away to be spread on his fields. That's the arrangement with my father for having a horse. Also, I love using my body to keep in good physical health – unlike most women. For example, and don't tell my father this, I enjoy rock climbing which I do with a small group of men and one other woman. I feel as if I have achieved something when I reach the summit. For the moment we climb small outcrops of rock here and there but even that is exciting and we have plans to climb Snowdon in England but my father must definitely not learn about that!"

"Well, you surprise me in no small way", said Charles, hands on hips and looking at Priscilla in a different way. "I had never even thought of that as a pastime."

"The idea came to me when I learned that seven Italian climbers went up the south side of Monte Rosa in the Alps to seek a mythical lost valley - and that was some forty years ago. I just love clambering up rocks. Of course we are all made secure with ropes between us and we carry sorts of hooks to get a grip on the rock where there is no hold."

"Perhaps we have some things to talk about, after all," Charles said amusedly, "but I'm sorry, I must get on with this ploughing job otherwise my father will get in a state. The farm to him is his life."

"Right, said Priscilla, but there must be a way of talking together leisurely in some place, at some time. After all, you are not a slave, or are you?" She laughed out loud and Charles joined in.

He had begun to enjoy their conversation discovering that she was not at all the unreachable, arrogant, aristocrat-like person he had imagined. "I will see what I can invent to satisfy my father and perhaps I will see you here again, say Thursday, which is the day the field should be finished."

"Yes, I will be back. *Au revoir*," and Priscilla trotted off leaving Charles nonplussed.

She had not gone far when a man's irate voice could be heard above the sound of Priscilla's horse's hoofs. He heard "where" and "late" and "who was that you were talking to?" much louder. Then the sounds of muffled voices and hoofs faded away by degrees. Charles could see nothing so presumed the man had arrived from the direction of the parkland, like Priscilla, and had been behind the high, overgrown hedge at its boundary. He then thought no more about it and concentrated on ploughing the field as fast as he could. The lunch break would be shorter than usual but the price was well worth paying for the pleasure he had experienced in talking to Priscilla. However, on considering their different social orders could he expect any sort of result from their almost furtive efforts at communication? This he doubted very much. He must drum it into his head that she was way out of his orbit. That's funny, where did he get that word from and what does it mean? Oh yes, the curé uses it quite a bit –something to do with astrology, no, astronomy! I'm so ignorant. How would Priscilla react to conversing with a nincompoop like me, not to mention her parents. They would be appalled to hear me speak, except of course that they are not fully fluent in French. Well, anyway, get her out of your mind, he thought as convincingly as possible. Alright now, she's gone from my mind. Ouf! Thirty seconds later, strangely enough, she popped up again!

So the day plodded on, just like Charles and Mardi plodding in the field, and was concluded in his rather dark bedroom after supper with his parents (some sort of soup, goat's cheese and bread). He noticed that his parents gave him puzzled looks when he retired to his attic much earlier than they as he did most days although he made a point of remaining with them a while on Sunday evenings. He loved his parents as would do any dutiful son or daughter but their conversation, always focused on crops, farm animals and sometimes cooking, made him feel uneasy. He knew he was being unreasonable. But how could they discuss anything else? They were tied day and night to the farm and the only education they had received allowed them to read basic documents only and prayers, of course, and to add and subtract. He himself needed more and that "more" he found in books. He was able to read books and outdated newspapers with the help of an oil lamp. He finally settled down to a good night's sleep at around 10 p.m.

The next day followed the course of the previous day's routine. With the cows, calves, goats and other animals including Mardi to be fed before anything else, then a cold shower under a makeshift affair he had contrived himself in an outbuilding, breakfast prepared by Charles's mother was served and gladly welcomed. It was basically made up of fried stale bread soaked in milk and battered egg with sugar shaken on it. Coffee with milk accompanied the nourishing meal. Then off to the stable again to harness his companion Mardi and the longish trek to the field which had to be finished, according to his father, at the latest on the morrow. His mother gave him a quick peck on the cheek but nothing from his father who was getting ready to carry out other tasks on the farm – probably fencing or hedging.

Arriving at around 8.30 a.m. he was more than amazed to see Priscilla in the field he had come to plough, sitting on a large boulder near the entrance to the field holding the reins of her stallion and looking at him fixedly as if he had no excuse for arriving so late!

"Well, this is the biggest surprise I've had for a long time. What on earth are you doing here so early. I half expected to see you, but only half (with a wry chuckle), later on in the morning or this afternoon. What is happening? I hardly know you …"

Priscilla, her hair a little dishevelled and looking unlike her usual composed and calm self, stood up, shook the particles of farmland dust and vegetation from her cloak, placed her left hand to her brow to prevent the sun shining directly on her face and said. "Please, can I call you Charles? I would very much like that. I will call you Mr Berger in front of other people, of course." Charles nodded his head in assent but on his face could be seen a large question mark in the form of a narrowing of the eyes, his eyebrows approaching each other and his pursed lips.

"Charles, I haven't much time as I'm supposed to be driving into Clermont Ferrand for lunch with a would-be future husband, his family and my father." She was now looking very upset as if she expected a figurative slap in the face from Charles and dismissal from his life. "I don't know what to do. The chap is alright, his family is rich so I suppose he is too, but I have everything I need in life and he doesn't interest me in the least. He's arrogant and thinks he can do as he pleases. He has manipulated my father with his smiles and wealth and thinks that that is the end of the matter. The lunch today for him, his parents and my father is a sort of betrothal ceremony, a promise of marriage sealed with a glass of champagne. For me, it's like being condemned to a life in prison."

"Christ Almighty – oh, sorry for that, muttered Charles, it looks as if you have no option but to attend the so-called lunch. I would advise you to play the innocent, thank the hosts, including this man, for their hospitality and like in a duel, make any direct aims – I mean allusions to marriage and suchlike – slide off you and make it apparent that to you the lunch is just an enjoyable moment to be in the company of delightful people (lay it on a little but not too much!) and to be able to discuss this and that with your friend – be careful that you insist on calling him your friend and not your betrothed. Smile a lot, do not look awkward and let them only half believe you have understood the whys and wherefores of the lunch. If you go for a walk with your friend afterwards, make it plain that you like the man, his company and his family but that that you had no idea he was seeking you as a wife. Obviously it's up to you to decide, if after due reflection, you wish him to be your husband."

"Oh, Charles, you make it seem so easy. You know, you are not at all like my so-called friend, Henri-François, and I so wish I was having a meal with you and your family rather than his! I must be off now. When can I see you again? Sunday perhaps, after the mass?" With that she gathered up her skirts jumped up with ease into her saddle and sped off looking quite a different young woman. She waved joyously while turning round to give Charles a wonderful open and charm-laden smile.

Charles had to stop a moment to recover his spirits after such an unexpected turn of events. It seemed now fairly certain that she was waiting for something from him. Surely it could not just be good advice. He liked her a great deal – she was everything that he could have imagined an intelligent, attractive young woman could be – but he had assumed from the first meeting that she was out of his range of possibilities. She was just too good for him. He knew that he himself was not daft and that young ladies in his restricted social circle were not indifferent to him. He knew also that his view on things political and social in this very difficult post-revolution age was different from that of his parents and that of many people he occasionally met in the course of his life, barring Fr Farnault. The latter, to Charles, was exceptional from many points of view. Could he possibly broach the subject with the *curé*? For the moment he had to get on with ploughing the field so he gave Mardi a little flick on the flank with a thin supple stick he had cut from the hedge to encourage a little more speed from the faithful animal, more to appease his father than from a personal appetite to work faster!

CHAPTER 4

The field was now ploughed, the week had come and gone and with it, Priscilla. The weekend was over and apart from Charles's stint on the organ for Sunday mass nothing had changed. Nobody special came to the mass – just the usual parishioners including his parents – so Charles was somewhat disappointed. "Well, he had said to himself, that was almost bound to happen, or not happen, depending on the way one looked at it!" He had had to laugh to himself as he always had done in like circumstances, refusing to take things too seriously.

But now, there were serious jobs to be done in the same field he had ploughed the week before. The first was to break down the soil into a seedbed. This was to be done by means of harrows that had been loaded onto a cart at the farm and hauled to the field by Mardi. The work would probably only take one day as the soil was fairly dry and of a type easily broken down. Charles got everything ready that Monday morning and started out methodically harrowing back and forth across the field including the headlands that he had ploughed last thing the Thursday before. He succeeded in reaching the halfway point by about 12.30 p.m. and detached Mardi from the harrows and set him loose to browse for suitable herbage. He himself settled down in the same ditch as before out of the wind and hopefully to enjoy a little sunshine if it chose to shine spasmodically from time to time. His mother had prepared as usual, when he was unable to eat with his parents, a fresh baguette, cheese, walnuts and an apple together with half a bottle of homemade wine and some spring water.

He had just finished his "harrowman's" lunch when he heard the steady plodding of horse's hoofs coming down the lane and guessed it was the *curé*. Too bad for the nap which he had been looking forward to. However, this might be the opportunity of talking about Priscilla and picking the churchman's brains. Why not?

"Hello, young Charles. What, sleeping again? This does not behove a budding farmer. There's work to be done!" The two of them laughed long and loud. "What would your father say? But I have something quite serious to talk about and I'm fairly sure you are involved. Tell me, have you met the daughter of the new owner of the house on the hill? You have, I see. Now, I have no right to say anything about the visit of Mr and Miss Grafton the other day but I will because of something very strange, to me at least. They came to see me at the behest of the father to arrange the marriage of Priscilla - I think that's her name – to a young landed gent who resides not far from here. Well, and here's the part that concerns you, as we were talking, a man who apparently works closely with Mr Grafton arrived posthaste with a missive for his employer. Mr Grafton turned away apologetically, excused himself to read the letter and give instructions to the man but imagine my surprise when Priscilla took advantage of the interruption, approached me and uttered in a secretive fashion, almost in my ear, that she had met you and that you had talked of me. She seemed distraught and said – 'I don't want to marry that man' – and then admitted to liking you a lot and wondered if I could arrange a meeting between you. What do you think of that?"

Charles was absolutely flabbergasted and realized that his advice to Priscilla for the lunch at Clermont had either not been followed or had gone unheeded. "Fr Farnault, yes, I have met her three times now but briefly each time and every time in this field! I had an idea she liked me and I can tell you very honestly that I like her very much. I even had the idea of talking to you about her, but here you are almost as if you had heard my wish."

"Listen, Charles, this is going to be difficult. Knowing you as I do, I would imagine that you think you would have no chance of becoming engaged to Priscilla. You might even think that she is, not to put too fine a point on it, too good for you. Am I right?"

A nod from Charles.

"A priest is not a judge of character, he is concerned with the soul, but I have seen the young gent talking to various people after mass and frankly I would not want my daughter (if I had one!) to marry him. I would say that he does not converse but puts forward his point of view as if it were law not giving his interlocutor time to reply. I would tend to agree with Priscilla. However, I would be almost certainly defrocked if anyone got to hear about our conversation. It is most important that you tell no-one, not even Priscilla if you see her. Another problem is that the man's family – the Verron family - are quite generous with their alms for the poor. So, any move I make has got to be done carefully and neutrally, if you see what I mean. Still, we have moved away from the Middle Ages which means that she cannot be forced to marry someone she does not love even if it displeases her father. Of course, there are all sorts of ways of manipulating people so we must keep ears and eyes open. By the way, as you know there is a *bal de village* (outdoor village ball) in 2 weeks. Did I not hear you say that you were playing the guitar on that occasion?"

"That's true, Father, but I'm not at all sure that Priscilla would know about it and where would she stay for the night? As you know the *bal* continues late into the night, sometimes until 1 a.m."

"Listen, Charles, I have an idea. I plan to pay a surprise visit to the Grafton house next week to see if we can induce them to participate in Church events. I know they are Church of England but there is little real difference between the two religions (although the pope would firmly disagree!). I will mention the village *bal* and try to persuade the parents to let their daughter attend it. She would be able to be put up at the village inn. They could themselves come if they wanted to but I doubt if that would interest them. They have their own circle of acquaintances but I will try to persuade them that it is in the interest of the young lady's general culture to enjoy herself with the village people and in any case I will be there to keep an eye on things." In saying this he gave Charles a large wink and was quickly understood by the latter. "There will be an accordionist playing most of the time quite obviously (what's a *bal* without an accordion?) so you should find time to converse with whom you wish but I hope that I will not be ignored!" Another large wink.

You will be playing your guitar only from time to time I would imagine and most probably when your parents will have left. It's probably still too soon to let them know you are acquainted with that string instrument. By the way, the leading soprano in our church choir has agreed to sing some local songs and she would like to be accompanied by the guitar. Could you do that? If so, you will have to carry out one or two rehearsals. Can you come to the presbytery during the week, say Tuesday of next week. You agree? Good, I will let Marie-Thérèse know. And with that he was off.

CHAPTER 5

It was now the day of the *bal*, a Saturday, which meant that Charles had little farm work to do apart from feeding the livestock. His mother had got his breeches, jacket and waistcoat washed and ironed and he himself had polished his shoes. His mother had also cut his hair a little so that even if it was still long, it was at least tidy and it is true he cut a very manly but interesting figure. His short, neat beard was also trimmed. His parents sorely wished he would meet and marry some nice girl of his same station so went out of their way to let it come about.

The *bal* was due to start at around 8.30 p.m. so Charles wandered over to the makeshift rostrum and placed his guitar in its case carefully under a length of tarpaulin for safe keeping. The accordionist was already in position and beaming while holding a large glass of some alcoholic liquid in his hand. Charles and he exchanged a few amicable words but then he was surprised to see a violin case on a chair next to the accordionist's and raised his eyebrows. Jean, the accordionist was watching Charles and said. "Yes, the lady violinist who played at the mass when the bishop came agreed to join us."

The various refreshments stands were now receiving their first customers, chandeliers had been lighted in most corners of the village square and the decorations mostly in the form of paper chains looked bright and joyous. The villagers were now arriving in some number colourfully dressed, for the women and girls, in their long bright dresses and lovely ribboned hair or wearing flowery hats. The men were decked out, like Charles, in their best breeches, shirts and waistcoats. Luckily, the square was not very spacious so the dancing when it got going would be fairly concentrated in a small area. Jean had now taken up his instrument and was starting to play a lively tune. Charles wandered around the square having a word here and there with those he knew which was practically everyone. His parents were chatting with another farmer and his wife so Charles shook their hands as he passed. Several young women noticed him and he either gave them a quick peck on each cheek if he knew them well or a brief *"bonjour"* if not. All this time he was searching for Priscilla or the *curé* or both together and his gaze rested a moment on the inn, the Crested Eagle, where Priscilla would have spent the night if Fr Farnault had succeeded in his mission of persuasion with the Grafton parents. It was now 9 p.m. and the *bal* was in full swing with Jean and the violinist taking turns, or sometimes together, more or less successfully, to turn out the melodies. Half a dozen couples were dancing the waltz, French countryside version, and there was a contented buzz of conversation emanating from all parts of the square. Charles had just turned his head away from the direction of the inn and was wandering disconsolately towards the musicians and wondering if he would ask a village girl to dance with him when he heard, above the general hum of voices and music, a deep, melodious voice from the direction of the inn.

"So, you choose to ignore me, I suppose," followed by a guffaw.

Turning his head he immediately recognized the *curé* and waved his hand in acknowledgement. He naturally then moved towards the speaker and the two men, linked by friendship, by indebtedness (Charles), by philanthropy (Fr Farnault) and now by a natural concordance of minds, flung their arms around each other. They were at that moment behind a large plane tree so no-one would have seen them but if they had, they would have been surprised to see a usually quiet but empathetic priest showing affection for a mere farmer's son!

"There will be a surprise for you in a little while – well, a half surprise, shall we say. Anyway, how are you faring? Have you finished harrowing?"

There was then a detailed agricultural discussion between the two men – Charles who knew his job back to front and the priest who was well acquainted with the world of farming, the village being situated in an area where farming represented some 80% of all occupations.

"I know you would like to have some news of Priscilla and if you will give me five minutes or so I will relate how my visit to Manoir de Brion unfolded. Naturally, Mrs Grafton was very surprised to see me and of course I did not introduce the subject of their daughter straightaway. Mr Grafton was absent and still is as far as I know. I was told he had to return to

England for work purposes. Over tea in the English tradition – milk before the tea was poured! - I asked how they had settled down in St Germain de la Montagne and she reassured me that they had been warmly welcomed not only by other landed gentry of the area but by the village people themselves. A girl from the village carried out the domestic tasks with method and enthusiasm apparently. I also talked about the church services and the difference between RC and C of E. We had quite a good laugh about that. She said she was quite happy to attend mass and seemed to appreciate my sermons that she said were human-being oriented and not too obsessed with hellfire and not at all depressing. I then broached the subject of their daughter. It appears Priscilla is studying to be a doctor. Did you know that? That's very pioneering – a woman doctor! I was very impressed. Then I mentioned the village *bal* and suggested it would do her daughter good to meet the local people if she could attend, dance with the local lads and generally enjoy herself. She told me about her hopes of finding a well-off gentleman from the region but the man they had found for her did not suit her at all although the young man was confident, a little arrogantly, I thought, that he could win her over. She agreed that if her daughter wanted to visit the village dance she was welcome to, as long as I kept my eye on her. So she rode over this afternoon from Beau Repaire (I think that's what their house is called) and we arranged stabling for her horse and a nice quiet, very clean bedroom for her. I should think she will come down very soon now. Look, there she is."

Charles had been listening to the priest and trying to concentrate while all his thoughts and attention were focused on the village inn but he did manage to break into the monologue edgewise although mostly with phrases like, "yes, thank you, but ..." or similar. It was obvious that Fr Farnault was almost as excited as Charles at his success in enabling Priscilla to be present at the village *bal* but he was overjoyed at allowing Charles the possibility of, as it were, rising above his station and developing a relationship with this ravishing young English lady.

Priscilla was dressed in a way Charles had never seen before. She had obviously wanted to merge with the village folk by dressing in a similar fashion although it was quite obvious that the stuff of the cotton and silk she wore was of good quality but she managed to look the part with a large brimmed hat boasting feathers, an outer garment worn over a long blue dress and delicate shoes. One could just see her ankles. Even wearing this somewhat voluminous clothing one could see she carried no unwelcome flesh and that she was in very good health. She looked very happy, too. "Good evening, Mr Berger, or can I call you Charles?" She was looking simultaneously at the priest and Charles as she asked the question.

Fr Farnault said. "Call the young man Charles but make it discreet."

Both Priscilla and Charles looked at each other with, it would seem, a glow in their eyes. They shook hands and walked over to the rostrum with the priest who greeted the two musicians and talked to the woman who would be singing solo when Charles would eventually be able to play his guitar (when his parents would have left). A young man Charles knew quite well perceived Priscilla and asked her to dance. She looked at Charles first, simply nodded to the young man whom Charles knew very well from his childhood who then led her to that part of the square in front of the rostrum where all the dancers were concentrated. They danced together or rather swirled around together with the other couples, the women in their long dresses whirling with the movement and showing off their plunging necklines just about covered by shawls or jackets. Quite a sight but Charles was patient knowing that Priscilla wanted very much to be his partner and no-one else's. However, discretion was the leitmotif of the evening and he 'allowed' her to dance with other young fellows most of whom he knew quite well before finally pushing himself forward to claim her arms and her regard.

She looked so thankful to be with him. "They are very nice young men and very respectful and dance quite well on the whole but I am here to dance with you, and you know it," she declared and from her eyes flowed intense tenderness and was it not combined with a hint of desire directed towards the overjoyed Charles who had started dancing with her as attentively and as gracefully as he knew how?

"Your friend, the *Père Farnault,* is quite remarkable. You should have seen how he twisted my mother round his little finger. I was listening behind the door. I must give him a discreet hug as soon as possible." Their laughter was contagious and a few people nearby looked at them with interest.

They were able to dance for some time before Charles noticed that his parents were preparing to leave. The latter were moving in the direction of Charles and Priscilla just at the moment he surrendered his partner to the arms of another young man having explained to her that he had promised to play his guitar to accompany Adèle the singer when his parents had left but that it would not last long. His parents kissed him briefly on the cheek, told him, as if he was a small boy, not to return home late and left him. They had noticed nothing untoward in his behaviour especially as he was now dancing with a village maiden, Priscilla being at some distance from them.

When that particular dance was over, Charles thanked the girl he was dancing with and moved over to the rostrum where the soprano from the church choir was waiting for him. One great song writer of the period was Charles Cros and his song *"Mille étés mille hivers"* (a thousand summers, a thousand winters) was the first Charles and Adèle had practiced. This song was mostly accompanied by the piano, so Charles had had to adapt the score to suit his instrument. He had more or less taught himself musical composition (with lots of help from the *curé* at first) and was keen to see the public's reaction to this well-known ditty. Charles took his instrument, found middle C with the help of Adèle who had the gift of perfect pitch and started the introduction.

Immediately, the small crowd of villagers and farming folk moved towards the rostrum as they realized that a different sort of music was about to be heard and perhaps enjoyed. It should be realized that the vast majority only had access to music on occasions like this popular *bal* and of course at the Sunday mass - of a less pleasurable kind perhaps!

Adèle now started singing and the lovely, lilting tune got people swaying and even holding hands. It's true, she had a lovely voice and the resulting effect was spell-binding. There was one person, in particular, who was completely mesmerized by this entirely unexpected performance. This was of course Priscilla who came as close as possible to the rostrum and was gazing at both the musician and singer in wonder. Charles looked down at her several times and was delighted to see that she looked, shall we say, happy. Fr Farfault was also delighted, as the guitar had belonged to him, and one could say that he had himself fashioned to a large extent this very beautiful rendition of the song. There were other songs by Charles Cros but the gathering requested the Summer/Winter song several times much to the amusement of Charles and Adèle.

The performance lasted some thirty minutes after which the violinist and accordionist once more sprang into life playing at a fast tempo in contrast to what had just been heard and the people in their turn were once more dancing joyously and vigorously.

Charles and Adèle, after mutually thanking each other by a cheek to cheek embrace, parted company and Charles, making a discreet sign to Priscilla, disappeared behind the tarpaulin covered rostrum where she followed him to within its shadow. They held each other for a few seconds not really wanting to do anything, either of them, but kiss and caress.

"Your music is really lovely and the girl's singing was heavenly, too. I'm so amazed, you are so cultivated and manly as well. I have never seen a man like you, either in England or in France. I do really want to know you better but I don't know how. My parents want me to marry into high society but quite frankly I cannot stand most of the men I have been introduced to and they are practically insisting that I marry this Verron man and he, too, thinks it's a bygone conclusion. I mean, he's wealthy, good-looking and is probably everything any other girl might want in a man but he's so arrogant and sure of himself. If only he had a little consideration for others and a little intelligence. Of course he's had an excellent education and has read all the great authors from the Greek civilization down to our days but his opinions are those of his parents – monarchical really – but it's impossible to have a good conversation with him, he is against women in power and like many men (and many women) think that women are inferior to men in most respects. There, that's it. I could go on but it must be very boring to you. But you, you are really different. At first sight a young hard-working country man but I know now that that is illusory. You respect women, you have a good knowledge of music, have read a lot and love your work. Incredible, really!"

They were now looking at each other face to face, each holding the other's arms fondly by his or her elbows.

"Let's not exaggerate, I was more or less nurtured in music and in literature by Fr Farfault. He is clever, you know, and don't be beguiled by his clerical stance. He uses his post to show love and commiseration to people and never insists on the Church's teachings. You will never hear him mention Hell and even Heaven has an ambiguous significance! I must admit that before meeting you I was much at a loss as to how I could meet a nice girl who would have similar interests to mine. And yes, it's true, I love all the things you mentioned but the countryside with its bird and animal life, not to mention the trees and plants, has a special interest for me. I don't know how I will be able to fit all I love into my life and still find the perfect wife! Any ideas?" Here, his eyes narrowed to slits causing Priscilla to laugh.

"Oh, you are being ingenuous. You have that person before you! It's getting a little chilly. Shall we take a stroll?" She slipped her arm gently but firmly through Charles's and led him away from the music, dancing and excited voices into a narrow cobbled street where there was no sign of life. There was little light, it was in fact almost dark except for moonlight filtered by some patchy cloud. At this point the inevitable happened – a long, persuasive and ardent kiss that caused both of them to practically reel. This was real contact but neither of them had expected, until now, that their distant, occasional and potentially disturbing relationship could so quickly become present, overpowering and urgent. After what they were later to describe as a truly unique and incredible kiss they simply held each other tightly and gazed as far as the light allowed, into each other's eyes.

It was at this point that they heard the shuffling of feet and saw a lantern coming into view and a voice calling, "Priscilla, Charles" and they recognized the voice of Fr Farfault.

"Oh, thank God I've found you. I was beginning, just beginning, mind you, to get worried. I see that you have begun to get to know each other a little better (a slight chuckle, his smile could hardly be seen) and so much the better but if you want your 'friendship' (change of tone on this word) to last and last in a decent way, you must return to the ball and dance with other young people – but don't go together. You will arrange other ways of seeing each other, I'm sure, but if I can help you by passing messages from one to the other, you can trust me. I am really happy to see two young people who are so obviously fond of each other have the possibility of building a lasting relationship. But off you go now, slide into the crowd discreetly from opposite ends and only dance once or twice together to avoid any tongue-wagging."

Priscilla gave the priest a quick hug and a "Thank you" charged with emotion and gratitude and stole away to the *bal.*

Charles also gave a show of gratitude by clasping both hands of his mentor's hands and the two of them walked slowly back to the square. Then, as agreed, both Charles and Priscilla danced with partners that they would not have necessarily chosen but who were the means of their showing their continued status of unattached young people. Most people at the *bal* had no idea who Priscilla was especially as she had adopted the attire of village women, clothes of good quality but very ordinary in appearance. No-one but Fr Farfault knew that there was an aspiring groom in the name of Verron never very far away. However, they managed to dance together twice and in so doing to arrange a meeting in a secluded spot for the following week. This would be in a barn on Mr Berger Senior's land. There was access to the barn from one side of the farm so Priscilla would have no trouble finding it during the course of a ride on her horse. Charles described in detail the route she had to take and made her repeat it to him. She seemed happy when eventually she went back to the inn after once again thanking the *curé*.

CHAPTER 6

One of Charles's tasks was to fetch hay from the barn where he and Priscilla had arranged to meet on the Tuesday following the *bal* and quite luckily it was a day without rain and with occasional bright periods. They had agreed 3 p.m. would be the best time. This would be a time when no-one – that is, especially his father - would wonder what he was doing. They would assume that he was about his daily farm routine. For Priscilla it was the same. Her parents had no real authority over her as she was 21 years old (in the year 1817 AD) but they liked to know what she was doing if only from a safety point of view. The horse ride from the Grafton's manor house would only take about 20 minutes so she got her horse ready for the ride with the help of the groom-cum-gardener and when all was ready she heaved herself into her saddle and started out on her pleasant amble to the barn. She did not ride side saddle (*amazone*) which was unusual, but she was an unusual young woman and was wearing a riding habit over a less voluminous than usual dress.

Mrs Grafton was doing her daily piano practice when Priscilla set off and was concentrating hard on trying to achieve a good rendition of Beethoven's Moonlight Serenade and was succeeding quite well when she heard the sound of hoofs from the direction of the drive at right angles to the wing where she was playing. She got up from her instrument, left the room and walked up the short corridor that led to a rarely used salon and gazed out of the large window that gave onto the drive. She now saw as he disappeared behind the house to place his horse in the care of the groom that it was the would-be suitor Verron and she quickly coiffed her hair, shook her dress, looked at herself in a mirror and returned to her piano as if nothing was amiss. She had not been sitting on her piano stool for more than two minutes when the maid, Honorine, opened the door of the music room and announced the arrival of Mr Verron. The aspect of his handsome face with its slightly aquiline nose, sharp greenish-blue eyes, his hair cut short, moustache and small nicely trimmed beard was somewhat spoiled by his manner which, while remaining polite, revealed a bad temper barely repressed.

"I'm sorry to burst in on you in this way but I have no news of your daughter. I wrote to her twice when I was in Paris but have received no reply. I believe you yourself are in favour of our marriage and that she can be won over with a little help from you and your husband. Is it possible to speak with her? There will be quite a lot of arrangements to be made but I thought the ceremony could be held in Clermont Ferrand in the early Spring."

"Certainly, Mr Verron that sounds wonderful but I do think that Priscilla must give her full assent. I will of course speak to her again about it and when my husband comes back from England or wherever he has gone on diplomatic business, we will have a chat all three of us. You are well suited as far as rank, resources and good looks (here, the suspicion of a smile) are concerned, so we shall have to see ..." Mrs Grafton was in two minds about Mr Verron. He presented well, was rich, good looking, had good manners, was a well-accomplished sportsman as a dueler so of course he fitted the bill as a good spouse for her daughter but there was something about him that reined in her enthusiasm for such a match. Frankly, she did not like the man and was not surprised that her daughter did not either. This sentiment did not last. She pushed these negative ideas from her head as she was completely immersed in the customs of the time which left no hesitations to be considered – money, rank in society, respectability, a good appearance and social niceties were the only characteristics that counted

"By the way, Priscilla has gone out riding. She left about one hour ago but I cannot tell you where. You can remain here until she comes back or you can, if you wish, try to find her. You know, she loves outdoor activities and would not agree to having the role of 'lady of the house'. That, you must realize. She's not like many young women of her age and education. But, to return to the subject of finding her, If you go down the lane that leads to the farm by the name of La Rouarniere you might find her. I have seen her riding in that direction several times. She goes that way because the lane is well kept and it's easier on the horses. I don't know where she goes after the farm but you can try that or, as I said, you could wait here. I shall be having tea very soon, so you can join me and tell me something of your family and occupation."

"Thank you, Mrs Grafton for your kindness but I think I will try to find her. There is such a lot to talk about. I will see you soon, I hope. Good Day, Mrs Grafton," and he swept out with a graceful bow.

After pulling on his cloak once more and seeking his horse in the stables at the back of the house, he remounted his steed and set off downhill across the parkland, toward its boundary, then along the lane, passing the place where Priscilla and Charles had met, making his way leisurely but determinedly in the direction of La Rouarniere. He was sure he was going to meet her. In this surmise he was not mistaken.

Verron had passed the entry to the farm, gazing as he did at the quaint, mostly ground floor house, well-built but in need of painting, situated at some hundred meters from the lane and continued along a track that had been worn by the hoofs of cattle and sheep over the decades. He was now thinking that he must have been mistaken in coming this way when before him at the top of a knoll appeared the mounted figure of Priscilla. They would have to meet.

Seeing Verron was a shock to Priscilla but she was an English lady of much inner control and did nothing more than just smile at the man seated arrogantly on his steed.

"Oh Good Day, Mr Verron, what good fortune to meet you here in such an out-of-the-way place. I have had a wonderful ride today and have found many new paths suitable for riding at an amble in spite of the weather. What about you, What brings you here?" she said, still exhibiting what most people would have interpreted as a friendly smile.

It could not be said that the man was smiling. He was rather showing a grimace he was trying to convert, not at all successfully, into a smile. "Well, I returned from my business in Paris just yesterday and expected to see a reply to the missives I sent you but there was nothing, so having nothing of great importance to do today I passed by your house, saw you mother who told me where I might find you. I have no need to tell you, of course, why I need to see you."

Priscilla adopted a puzzled expression. One could almost say her face was made up of question marks. "And pray what would that be?"

"You know, very well Priscilla, that we are all but betrothed. All that lacks is a meeting between our families, a proper celebration dinner and all will go according to plan. And, Priscilla, please do not call me Mr Verron. We are on Christian name terms, so you must address me as Hugo." Here, a false, almost self-satisfied smile was pasted on his face as though everything in respect of their future marriage was going according to plan.

"Mr ..., sorry, Hugo, I have to disagree with you about a future marriage. You are a fine young man with many accomplishments in both war and peace and very much at ease financially – everything a young woman might expect of a man – and of course I like you, but I cannot agree to a marriage without being first convinced that it offers the best future for me and being convinced I love the man and that the feeling is mutual. As you know and as my accent tells you, I am English and today in England there is a strong movement afoot allowing women greater freedom and giving them the choice of whom they marry. As I understand it, this is not yet the case in France. Will you come back to our house for refreshments?" She did not change the tone of her voice from start to finish showing no sign of exasperation nor even of annoyance. This did nothing to quell the bad temper of the man – Priscilla had had him summed up for some time and felt reasonably at ease in the situation and of course her seemingly kind but firm stance was further shored up by the existence of Charles ...

She had spent about one hour with Charles in the barn and although nothing intimate had taken place their feelings one for the other had undoubtedly grown stronger. They had spent much of the time gazing at each other lulled by a feeling that they were somehow meant for each other – rather banal, one might say – but although in both their circles, especially in Priscilla's, this expression, "being meant for each other," was treated with some disdain because nearly everything in their lives was arranged and they simply did not believe it could ever happen, one could always hope, *n'est ce pas*? So, they kissed unrestrainedly and fervently, holding each other tightly so that each could feel the other's salient bodily features. But their educations forbade them to go any further and in any case time was at a premium so they simply agreed to meet at the same place, the barn, at the same time the following week.

But Verron was so impregnated with the customs and beliefs of the day, especially when they were in his favour, that he was in no way put off by Priscilla's short discourse but was all the same a little suspicious as to her availability for marriage especially as he had seen with a quick glance a shred of straw on her riding habit. He wondered a moment and then pushed aside any potential complication. He would, he thought, follow her on the next occasion to see if she had any liaison although instinctively he was convinced she must be free. She had noticed his gaze and had briefly flicked the straw to the ground but said nothing.

CHAPTER 7

The following Tuesday had now arrived so after her luncheon with her mother she prepared herself for her second visit to the barn. The time arranged for the meeting with Charles was the same as before which was a pity as we shall see. She set off wearing clothing that was not at all constraining but warm all the same. Her auburn hair under her hood was fabulous and her green-hazelnut eyes shone with intensity. It was now mid-December and although temperatures were well above freezing, the air was chilly. She wore low-heeled black shoes that were well lined with some woollen material and with her dark coloured dress also of wool, her beige cloak and ribboned bonnet she looked, well, to say the least, dashing.

Unfortunately, Hugo Verron, as he had done every day since the day he had accompanied Priscilla back to her house, was taking an afternoon horse ride in the vicinity of the Grafton house on the off chance of seeing her set out for an assumed liaison because he had almost convinced himself that she indeed had a 'lover' although he was far from sure. He was wearing his military sword in case he felt he owed it to himself to be persuasive. That day, the Tuesday following the above incident, he was intrigued to see her setting off at a trot, looking very comely but apparently tense in some way or could it be that she was excited. His blood was now up but he managed to remain discreet, following her at a distance where, even if she turned her head, she would not have recognized him. The trot lasted some twenty minutes through some almost wild countryside but following a path roughly worn by hoofs. He then lost sight of her as she had turned off the track unseen by him, either to the left or to the right. Arriving approximately at the place where she had disappeared he noticed that the vegetation to the left of the track at right angles had been trodden down very recently so he slowly rode in that direction. He had ridden for two or three minutes only when he saw a barn about half a mile away and he lost sight of Priscilla once more as she was either entering or riding around the further side of the farm building. He decided to ride nearer the barn, tether his horse behind a clump of small trees and walk to the barn to see what, if anything, was going on inside. He looked decidedly out of place on this tract of farmland in his riding jacket, breeches and above all with his sword clasped to his side.

He moved to the right-hand side of the barn and sidled along its exterior wall until he came to the front face of the barn where he stopped for several seconds trying to catch the sound of any voices. His ears were finally rewarded by a subdued whispering and sighing sound. That, he now realized, was Priscilla in a state he never could have imagined heretofore. His blood was now indeed racing and the belligerent side of his character, the side that would allow of no rival, was surfacing rapidly. He unsheathed his sword, opened one of the two none too rigid doors of the barn and entered holding his weapon before him at an angle of 45 degrees before storming across the inside of the building to find Priscilla in the process of pulling herself away from a person who he could only describe as a country dweller or farm worker which to him, of course, was beyond the pale. How could she find herself in the presence of such a person when he himself with his wealth, position and good looks was available to her? These thoughts raced through his madly jealous mind in just a few seconds and then he was there before the more than surprised couple brandishing his sword in the direction of Charles and almost screaming, "I've got you, you scoundrel, how dare you steal my promised wife. You will not get away with this. You will pay with your life."

One must realize of course that he had been reared in the type of environment where only the best succeeded and where dominance was ensured by the might of attack, weapons or the mere threat of same. His was a military upbringing, one could say, and typical of the upper classes of the period.

Charles was wearing a long, loose linen shirt, a waistcoat, a cape, breeches and socks to the knee – a stark contrast to Hugo's rich frock coat and breeches of very superior cloth. It was obvious that he was inferior in rank to Hugo but was in no way cowered by his aggressive stance and stood tall and bold even with the tip of the sword almost touching his chest.

"Oh yes, and how, pray?" said Charles in a voice without a waver.

During this brittle exchange Priscilla had pulled away from the two men and was gazing upon the scene in horror. She was certain for a moment that Hugo would kill Charles at one fell swoop.

"Hugo, what does this mean? You deliberately followed me here. That is in no way to your credit. It's shameful and I have made it plain to you that you would need to exert a great deal of persuasion to make me change my mind." She looked dashing in her cloak over her long loose dress and her bonnet set firmly on her head wherefrom long meshes of auburn hair curled at their ends pushed out. She was angry, too, and this trait of character was utterly unknown to Charles, although that was hardly surprising since their "friendship" was relatively recent.

"I am determined to marry you, Priscilla. Your parents will it and you will not be disappointed in years to come. I can offer you many advantages which as a woman you could not contemplate with this mere ..., this mere ... cowhand."

Charles. "Don't you call me a mere cowhand. It's true I tend to livestock but I run a farm and that is far from easy. I think I am your equal at almost anything and if Priscilla wishes to visit me she is free to do so."

"We'll see about that," retorted Hugo curtly and nastily. He clearly thought that he was a cut above Charles in almost any respect. "To see if you really are my equal in anything, I propose a sword duel with you. He who lives after the duel, will marry Priscilla." This he said with great defiance, arrogance and certitude. He just knew in his inner self that Charles would be no match for him. A surprise was shortly to come but before the surprise, Priscilla pleaded with Charles. "You cannot have a swordfight with Hugo. He has practiced duelling with a sword since he was young and is usually victorious. I believe he killed one or two adversaries during the last successful Napoleonic campaign. He will kill you, too. Please, Charles, do not accept. We shall find a peaceful solution to this problem, shan't we...?"

Hugo, now looking smug and self-satisfied. "That's true. You will have no chance against me."

"That's to be seen," responded Charles with a gleam in his greenish blue eyes that suggested he wanted to rise to the challenge. "I am ready to face you. Don't be too sure you will be victorious. By the way, don't bother about seconds. My sword will not be the equal of yours for its lethalness but will be just as effective. I am ready to face you when you wish." He said this without any animosity at all and surprised both Hugo and Priscilla by his calmness and apparent serenity. They could not believe their ears.

"Charles, no," almost shouted Priscilla but Hugo, slightly taken aback by Charles's reaction, simply nodded.

Charles then declared that as he was at a disadvantage as regards weapon, he would have the advantage of deciding the time and place of the duel and suggested the barn as the terrain of the duel and the time, a week from that day soon after sunrise, at 8.30 a.m. Hugo said he had no choice but to agree especially as the location would make no difference to him, he would be the victor.

Priscilla simply hung her head in grief knowing that the only man she had ever loved would be the victim of this other man, a man she increasingly detested.

"Priscilla, you must be getting home. Your mother will be wondering where you have got to. You, the farm hand, I will see you here next week soon after dawn. Good Day, Sir," and he bowed with a flourish of his hat, facetiously and mockingly.

"I have no option, Charles, but to follow him. I'm sorry, I really am. I am the cause of all this. You really must not fight him. You will be massacred. Please think again." She was crying now but was at the same time gathering her clothes around her and making for her horse that was peacefully munching hay at the other end of the barn.

CHAPTER 8

We are now at a decisive moment in the story. The time has come for the duel but there are a few details to be noted before assuming that Charles was seeking to deliberately shorten his own life for whatever motivation might come to mind. No, and No, again. In fact, he had been at great pains to oblige Hugo to agree to a week's delay for the battle for one simple reason. As we have already insisted, Charles was no swordsman and had in fact never held a sword in his life. However, he was more than adept at manipulating a baton which he had done from a very early age to fight his comrades who, like him, took on the role of mediaeval knights. The baton became the sword and the village and country boys spent much time manipulating their weapons against each other much to the dislike of their mothers. Charles had returned home many times as a small boy and then as an adolescent with bruises all over the top of his body and especially on his head with more than once a splendid black eye. His mother nursed him, if not tenderly, then at least with efficacy. His father, on seeing these war wounds, would just laugh and tell him to let his opponents receive the same treatment. He was secretly proud of his son because he had spied on him several times when he was in full battle mode and saw that he was very capable of defending himself.

But a boy's baton was one thing and a sword another. He knew he was deft enough to counter the thrust of any sword even with a baton but the latter had to have certain properties to be effective. It had to have the length of a sword's blade taken with its handle but it also had to be slightly flexible and possess a characteristic that would enable it to stun an opponent on contact. So, during that week when he had time Charles wandered around the farm looking for a long, flexible piece of live wood with a knot of very hard wood attached to its extremity. It took him two or three days to find but a very old oak not far from the farmhouse itself offered the possibilities he was looking for. He fetched a ladder and climbed up into the lower branches of the tree holding a saw and small axe. He felt in his pocket for his mother's measuring tape and marked out 35 inches from the knot in the wood to the point where he would cut it. It was very quickly cut and he was soon down at the foot of the tree. He now studied his 'weapon', found it to his liking and brandished it aggressively against a non-existent opponent. He then took his knife to remove the bark and then polish it a little with a clean rag and smooth its end and the knot with a file. Another task was to attach some sort of handle to the baton so that it could be wielded with ease. He found what he needed among his father's tools – the handle of some special long shears used to lop branches off trees – fixing it on securely with a couple of screws. This done, he again brandished it, testing its flexibility – it was just what he had aimed at – and then tested the hitting power of the knot at the end of the baton. This, he found satisfactory. It had to be big enough to inflict injury but small and light enough to be rapid and dexterous in the handling.

Charles, as we have seen, now in his twenties, was a calm and peace-loving individual. Violence was contrary to his ethics but he would not hesitate to use his strength to protect anyone who was being maltreated. In his adolescent years he was reckoned to be the local champion of these "sword fights". He was very quick to react and often saw his opponent's move before even the opponent knew what he himself was doing. It was impossible to guess he was so skilful and efficacious, so calm, attentive and careful he looked. However, he would never inflict more than a light blow to his opponent and was thus known to be a generous and indulgent victor. Even faced with the sheer hatred and almost brutality of Hugo, even if he got the upper hand which was by no means certain, he did not at any moment contemplate killing the man although he knew that the sentiment was in no way reciprocal.

It is now 8.20 a.m. on the appointed day of the duel. Charles had, much to the surprise of his father, already fed and watered the animals and milked the few cows. He is now in the barn waiting for the arrival of Hugo. There are usually seconds present for a duel whose role is to check that all is correctly prepared for the person they represent, that there are no advantages for one or other of the duellists and that all is fair and above board. A few minutes before the agreed time he could hear the sound of hoofs, the hoofs of more than one horse, approaching the barn and there he was, the great fighter in full combatant's regalia, in cape, cap, breeches and polished shoes. The two men jumped off their horses smiling hugely and the second asked to see the weapon Charles would be wielding and when he showed him his baton or oak stick the man said. "No, I didn't ask you with what stick you herded your cows into the meadow but the weapon you will be using to combat Mr Verron." Huge peals of laughter from the two men. "You know, you're asking to be slaughtered, because I know Mr Verron does not appreciate your initiatives with Miss Grafton."

"Don't you worry about me, Dear Sir, rather worry about Mr Verron and offer him advice when necessary."

This sally was equally greeted by guffaws. They clearly thought, both of them, that Charles was making a suicide bid and could not wait for it to happen so that they could return to wherever they had come and above all, so that Hugo could claim the hand of Priscilla as his wife.

"And where pray, My Dear Mr Berger, is your second?"

"I have none, but I am perfectly sure that Mr Verron is a man of honour and would do nothing to upset that reputation. I see his sword complies with conventions and that he is dressed as is proper. I see nothing untoward. I am ready to fight him as well I can without the assent of a second."

The second then asked to inspect Charles's weapon and the latter duly handed it over for verification. "Well, I see nothing here that could harm anyone. Let's start but I doubt if the duel will last more than two or three minutes."

With that the opponents took up position some three or four meters apart, Hugo with his sword pointing upwards at 90°, Charles simply holding his weapon in front of him. Now Hugo, it should be pointed out, was something of a champion and had won many cups during his military service and later in civilian life. However, his style was rigidly traditional learnt in the best schools of the day but he had never come up against anyone who had not been through the same process so he would be completely surprised by Charles's style. Charles had decided that his best stratagem was to pretend to be vulnerable, a question of bluff, and await events. Hugo, on the other hand, so sure he could not lose and wondering whether he would really kill his opponent as he had threatened or just leave him wounded, thought he could make offensive lunges from the start. He had the mentality of a conqueror.

The second dropped his hand, the sign that the battle could start. Charles just stood there with his left foot before his right foot waiting for the first attack. It was not long in coming. Charles was not wearing anything special for the duel except that his cloak was fairly old and bulky and he intended to use it as a sort of decoy. He intended it to be torn by Hugo's sword to make the latter feel sure of himself. This tactic was already paying off as Hugo made a fast lunge and Charles sidestepped and the sword duly slashed through his cloak.

A cry almost of triumph. "Ah, ha!"

Another lunge but this time Charles had seen it coming even before Hugo had started his execution of the move and the sword simply glanced off the baton much to the surprise of Hugo.

"Oh, so you think you can hoodwink me. Well, we'll see about that!" He lunged again but with a little less assurance and Charles was able to parry the thrust and instantaneously inflict a mild blow to Hugo's right shoulder with the knot at the end of his baton. It should be said that his boyhood and adolescent battle experience had given him a sort of premonition of any opponent's moves. One could say it was almost innate and was a huge advantage in any situation like the one he now found himself in. He let Hugo take the initiative once again and allowed him to rip his cloak a little more. It could be said that Charles, although during the days previous to the fight had been really apprehensive about the coming encounter and had not been completely sure of his ability to defend himself, was now feeling more at ease as he could almost see into the mind of Hugo and knew practically a micro-second before the latter what move he was going to make. The battle continued in this way, neither making any great headway to the detriment of the other but it could honestly be said that Hugo was expending a great deal more energy than Charles. This also was Charles's ploy, to tire out his opponent into making errors that could easily be parried and turned to his advantage. After some ten minutes of dueling, Hugo's cheeks and forehead were beginning to take on a colour, something between red and black and he was manifestly perspiring profusely. Charles was likewise hot in the face but he had not lost his composure and whereas Hugo would be darting from right to left and back again with speed trying to surprise his adversary, Charles was content to stand his guard, left foot before his right and to counter the frequent and now savage attacks made by Hugo by simply stepping aside at the last instant and letting the steel sword glance off his baton, stick or pole, whatever you would like to call it. Once or twice Hugo lost his balance when he trod on an uneven part of the beaten earth floor and a ruthless assailant could have inflicted great injury on him. Charles had no intention of doing anything more than teach Hugo a lesson and in any case what could a wooden stick do against a warrior's weapon?

So now, Hugo was trying desperately to find a way of breaking down Charles's defense but that was not going to be easy seeing that in all his dueling career he had never met with an adversary using, to him, such unknown tactics. This was almost the moment Charles had been waiting for. He could see that Hugo did not seem to be able to continue his adopted role of dominant force he had assumed until then and almost felt sorry for him! Once more, when he made a particularly vicious lunge towards Charles's body, Charles stepped nimbly aside, parried the sword's forward movement so that it simply cut through the air two feet from his shoulder making a whooshing sound. When the sword glanced off his baton, Charles immediately struck Hugo in the face. His weapon looked fairly ineffective but it was light and just flexible enough to almost double the force of the blow it could exert. Hugo put his hand to his face and howled in pain. A nice black eye was beginning to form.

"You blackguard, scoundrel of a farmhand. You think you can do that to me?"

He got into such a state that Charles had no difficulty whatever in evading his lunges and even returned his forays with several more or less forceful taps on the body. On receiving one of these bruise-inflicting blows to his right upper arm he tripped and Charles, with all the muscular power of his right leg, pushed him to the ground, the sword leaving his assailant's grasp and falling some feet away. Hugo was now lying on the ground with Charles astride him, holding the knot of his baton to his breast.

"Well, kill me now," whimpered Hugo.

"You forget, my Dear Mr Verron, that I do not possess a sword so it is impossible. I have no intention of killing you and I would not want to waste my time doing so. I know now that you are not the man you pretend to be so I think we can call the joust over. But one thing, you will now leave Priscilla alone and allow her to make up her own mind as to her future. I will not force her hand as you were trying to do. There are now two conditions to be fulfilled. Your second – oh there you are – will now declare that I am the winner and that you, Mr Verron, will henceforth leave Priscilla free to make her own choices. Please go ahead Mr …, never mind your name!" and the second solemnly proceeded to declare what Charles had ordained but with obvious reluctance since he himself was now in just as ludicrous a position as Hugo.

Charles now pulled Hugo to his feet, brushed the dirt from his clothing and said, quite simply. "You must go home now and treat your eye. It's nothing, you know, and in a week there will be no sign of it. Thank you for the duel. It's given me good practice and I might even take up sword fighting as a sport."

Hugo said nothing, just glowered at him in pure humiliation. He and his second then mounted their horses and trotted off slowly without saying a word.

CHAPTER 9

Charles received no news from Priscilla for many days and had decided that he had to free his mind of her permanent presence. He continued his work and now management of the farm – the latter because he had started reading various manuals by experts and he wanted his parents to bear the fruit of any improvements he could make as to the running of the family venture. The most important aspect was the recent introduction in farming of basic fertilizers which handsomely increased the yields of cereals coupled with a tendency to reduce the acreage of grassland for stock breeding. So here he was again in the same field with the same horse, Mardi, spreading fertilizer using an implement he had persuaded his father to borrow from a neighbour. It was mid-afternoon and he had already made many runs across the field when he heard a familiar sound from the lane. He looked over the hedge to see his dear friend Fr Farfault trotting peacefully down the lane but wearing a particularly sparkling and almost mischievous smile.

"Hello there, my hero!" he exclaimed with no detour.

"Why do you say that? You're certainly poking fun at me. I'm no hero – just a poor farmer's son," retorted Charles shaking his head but now smiling, too, rising to the bait.

"Well, I have just come from the Grafton's house to seek some news of Priscilla and also asking whether any of the family might be interested in joining our church choir. As you know, we need a tenor and a mezzo-soprano. I saw Priscilla and she is very worried about you. I think she imagined you dead or something. She muttered something about a duel and how she feared for your life. Apparently, you had accepted a duel by sword with our famous Mr Verron. But how could you accept, knowing that you possess no sword, unless I'm mistaken, of course. Well, I must say you look anything but dead. You look extraordinarily well, to my mind. I suppose in the end you had to accept defeat but that does not explain why she has had no news either from you or from Mr Verron. Knowing this gentleman to some extent, I would have expected him to carry her off, so to speak, straight to the altar if he had won a combat with you or if you had renounced the duel. Explain, young man!"

"To tell you the truth, Father, I imagined that she had chosen Mr Verron and had no intention of seeing me again. As I was working when you arrived I had decided to put her firmly out of my mind but I admit that that is far from easy."

"Yes, I understand that, Charles, but what on earth happened to put her in that state?"

"We-ell, the duel did take place, in our barn, and I - well I managed to give him a black eye. He was not at all pleased ..."

"But how did you do that? He is known to be a good fighter, I've heard more than once about his achievements, but you, Charles. You have no experience and above all, no sword. How did you do it?"

Charles then explained his search for a wand, stick, baton, pole, whatever and its required shape with the knot at its end. He reminded Fr Farfault of the battles he had always fought and usually won with boys and youths of his age across his early years. The *curé* nodded as the memories of the fights Charles had engaged in came back to mind and he then smiled.

"So the upshot of all this is that you with your stick beat a champion with a sword. That is absolutely astounding. Mr Vennor would be a laughing stock if it got around what happened. Knowing you, though, I'm sure no-one knows anything about it – not even Priscilla!"

"I deducted that Priscilla had been told by Verron, albeit in a roundabout way – for example, that he decided that the marriage, on further thought, could not go forward for one good reason or another. I know he would not have said that had he been beaten. He is too proud a man."

"Well, listen Charles, I will trot right back to the Grafton's and ask to see Priscilla on behalf of a certain gentleman. Her mother and her father, if at home, will presume I am talking about Mr Verron so there should be no difficulty and in any case I imagine that you would not like these incredible circumstances to be proclaimed aloud from the rooftops so it's best that I see her alone."

"That is really wonderful of you, Fr, I can't thank you enough. Goodness gracious, it's going to be difficult to finish the work now."

"Well, work quickly because I'm sure she will be down here with you in no time!" and at this he trotted off, patting both his horse and his hands in time as if to music.

The task of spreading fertilizer was fairly fast compared with most jobs related to growing cereals - ploughing, tilling and sowing - so Charles was just completing the last run towards the lane when sure enough, he heard a horse that was moving at a fairly respectable pace down the lane from the parkland and knew without even looking up that it was Priscilla just as the *curé* had forecast.

"Charles, Charles, oh Charles, how glad I am to see you well and uninjured. I wasn't sure whether you were alive, injured or dead. Verron said he would kill you if he could but it looks as if he has fallen short. What happened? He has not contacted me at all. I was really worried. I even imagined he had killed you and was keeping well out of the way of the gendarmes."

So he recounted the duel once more without relating the preparations he had made in respect of his weapon – he did not know whether Priscilla knew that he had no sword - but was very prosaic about the whole affair and said nothing in respect of Hugo's villainous moods, his savage attacks and finally his badly accepted defeat and humiliation. He simply said that after the combat the second had solemnly agreed that Verron would make no more overtures towards Priscilla. This then meant that Charles was now free to woo the lady! He did insist however that she should not relate the defeat of Verron either to her parents or to anyone else. He was, it could be argued, more than fair in his attitude to the man. Priscilla naturally enough agreed to this.

She then flung her arms around him placing her head against his shoulder while uttering gentle words of love. Kisses there were in abundance. The scene is not difficult to imagine.

It was now late afternoon and the sky had darkened so the two had to part. Before doing so it was agreed that Priscilla would explain to her parents that Verron had finally decided to back away from marriage for reasons only he could provide. She would wait a week or so and then persuade her parents to invite Charles, his parents and Fr Farfault to a luncheon. She intended to talk very frankly beforehand with her mother and possibly her father as to her feelings for Charles and their possible future together. She knew that they had no great esteem for Verron and respected him more for what he could have provided their daughter than for his character. However, in her enthusiasm she forgot that until her meeting with Charles she also, while being of an independent character, was kept hemmed in as were nearly all women, by Society's conservatism. She suddenly realized that her parents in no way deviated from that sense of values based on power, rank and money. Women, although treated as vital to the continuation of the lives of families and sometimes idealized for their beauty or position or both, were always assumed to be inferior to men in matters of judgment, intellect, art and music and that their opinions, hers included, could never bear weight against that sheer mass of centuries of civilization. A huge persuasive reason would have to be brandished to bring them round to her way of thinking. In fact, hardly knowing her father as he was almost always absent she did not really know what he would have said but she assumed that her mother could not but share the same views as her father and uphold the generally accepted norms of social practices of the day, both in England and in France.

Priscilla left her new, can we call him her new 'suitor'? to return home in a more than light-hearted mood, albeit punctuated by down-to-earth realism while Charles gathered up his implements and tools and returned to La Rouarniere, he also more than happy. He stowed away the fertilizer distributing implement, stabled and watered Mardi and entered the farmhouse kitchen to the sound of pots and pans and the smell of some lovely soup. His father was sitting at the table studying various bills. Charles now sat down at the table opposite his father who was looking very tired and worried. It was always the same – low income and high costs even though Charles was unpaid. They talked agriculture, costs and receipts for a while and then chatted about nothing in particular, the three of them together, after Mrs Berger had served the soup. It must have been early evening – 6.30 or 7 p.m. when there was a loud knock on the door.

"Now who the hell is that?" cried Mr Berger, or similar who was in no mood for visitors. If it's that Marcelline again looking for alms, you can just tell her that it's not the right day." He said this as Mrs Berger was making her way to the main door that gave directly onto the kitchen.

"Oh, Good Evening, Father, please come in. Would you like a bowl of soup? I have just made it. "No?" as the *curé* shook his head. "Well, what can we do for you?" She said this kindly although it could be seen that she was just a little annoyed to be disturbed at the only moment in the day when the family was united.

"I will not keep you and I certainly do not want to be a nuisance just as you are sitting down to table. No, I came now because I know it's more or less the only time in the day when I am sure to find Charles. I'll be gone in two minutes. Charles, I have a missive for you. Look, here you are, a sealed letter from a certain Mr Verron. He came to the presbytery this afternoon and asked if I could deliver it to you personally."

All three looked up in great surprise. Charles especially was more than flabbergasted. He had expected to hear nothing from that quarter ever again. He took the thickish wad of vellum paper from the priest's hand inspecting the envelope with great curiosity. Only his name, Mr Charles Berger, was inscribed thereon.

CHAPTER 10

Father Farfault left as quickly as he had arrived with profuse apologies for having disturbed the Berger family. As he was shown to the door by Charles he gave him a very cordial and encouraging smile as if to say, "I'm sure it's good news ..." or similar. Charles simply tucked the envelope into his waistcoat and returned to table. His parents looked at him somewhat quizzically but asked no questions. He was, after all, 24 years old and theoretically master of his own destiny. Charles told his father of the work he had done that day and told him to expect much better yields. His father was of course sceptical assuming that farming was an occupation that did not evolve, that one carried on as one's parents and grandparents had always done. Mrs Berger asked her husband to fetch some vegetables that were stored in an outbuilding packed in straw to protect them. The conversations often resumed in such manner. There were no daily papers in their commune and one had to go to the town hall to read the latest news in the weekly rag. When the meal of soup with bread followed by home-made cheese and ham and washed down by a local red wine was over and the dishes cleared, Charles slipped up to his attic room that was far from warm at that time of year, sat on his bed and carefully opened the letter with the knife he always carried in his belt. There were two letters inside one of which was contained in a smaller envelope. The open letter had no sender's address and in red ink was inscribed, 'Please burn after reading'. This inscription intrigued Charles to say the least. He started reading.

'Dear Mr Charles Berger. This note is very difficult for me to write for I have to swallow my pride and you might have noticed that I do not lack any of that quality if one can call it a quality. First of all, I would like to apologize for my behaviour the other day which was entirely against the precepts of behaviour taught me by my mother. I realize now that I have always been pretentious and some might say overbearing. I have presumed in my life that I could always win in any contentious exchange with another man and you were no exception especially as you are, as we say in our circle, of lower social rank which I now realize is a horribly arrogant attitude to take. All men, in the wide sense of the word, are equal and it is not to our merit if some of us are given unfair advantages from birth. You received few advantages at birth and yet you have proved yourself to be more than the equal of persons like myself. Our duel which should have been an easy win for someone with the experience and teachings obtained by merit of their station in life showed me that someone modest, intelligent, generous and in good health, like yourself, could by dint of his innate superiority (and believe me I have no hesitation in calling you superior) and general empathy have the edge on someone like me. I also have something to admit to you and if I do not confide it to you, you will think all the worse of me. Beside my assets, I have set my sights on a political career as a deputy for the administrative department of Puy-de-Dôme. If it got known that I had been defeated in a duel, especially where my opponent did not have a sword, I could say goodbye to that political career as to many of my acquaintances. Perhaps you had also thought of my second and the harm he might have done me by divulging your feat of arms. I have succeeded in persuading him not to relate it. Do not ask me how.

So, this aspect of your greatness (I would call it that) was your refusal to relate the incident of the duel to anyone. At this moment, only my second and I, you yourself, Fr Farfault and Priscilla are aware that it took place and of the outcome. Your generosity in the matter knows no bounds. Thank you.

You have enabled me, for the first time in my life, to see myself as I am and not the image I see of myself. My mother and father, to some extent, have always considered me pompous, disrespectful to others and presumptuous. I would agree with them now. My mother could not understand it yesterday when I presented her with a large bunch of flowers. She in fact said. "That's not at all like you." But I sincerely believe that your enormous courage –how could you think you could win, a stick against a sword? – your generosity and goodness have changed the way I look at people and I will never forget your disdain for inflicting injury on me when you were in a position to do so. I do not hesitate in saying that had it been me I am not at all sure that you would now be alive.

I say once again, I am sincerely sorry for the wrong I have done you and naturally I am now convinced you are more fit to be the husband of Priscilla than I. I have not contacted her for I felt sure you would have done so but imagine my surprise on hearing from the *curé* that you hadn't either.

Which brings me to another matter. As you might or might not know, I own land of considerable acreage by inheritance. I have a proposal to put to you if you would care to read the missive in the other envelope and send me a reply as soon as possible.

Please burn the letter you have just read. I now know you will do so. I trust you like I trust no other person.

Yours Sincerely,

Hugo Verron

It now remained for Charles to carefully open the other wax-sealed envelope which contained a document of two pages, all the words, punctuation and figures written in a very neat and bold hand.

The sender's address at top right of the first sheet gave the name of a domain fairly near Clermont Ferrand.

The document started thus:

Dear Mr Berger.

We, the owners and admministrators of Domaine de Ste Claire, are looking into the possibilities of expanding our production of cereals, especially wheat, and are actively seeking a person highly experienced in the running of an agricultural unit with particular expertise in the area of cereals. The person selected will be expected to have knowledge of the latest developments in agriculture and to ensure that his knowledge is solid and continually renewed we will organize a period of training in England where developments in the area are known to be advanced. All expenses will be covered and the period of training will be of three (3) months.

The person selected will be responsible for the running of the nine agricultural units involved two of which involve winemaking and another two which produce milk and cheese. The manager chosen, for this will be the title of his occupation, will also have a practical working knowledge, let it be clearly understood, of these two honorable occupations.

Mr Berger, we have seen how well you work your family farm and how diligent you are and we have also noted that you are ahead of your time in the use of what are now known as fertilizers to increase your crop yields. On the subject of your family farm, you will have no worries. You yourself will appoint and train a worker to ensure the day-to-day running of your family farm but who will be paid by us directly. Your parents can therefore be reassured that the farm will not suffer from your absence in any way.

You will receive a salary of xxxxx francs paid monthly and a suitable house will be placed at your disposal. There are three houses linked to our farms that are presently unoccupied so you will be able to choose from among them.

Christmastide will be upon us soon and we propose that your appointment will start on March 1st 1818 with a trial period of 3 months.

Dated and signed by:

Mr Hugo Verron on behalf of Domaine Ste Claire

and

Mr Charles Berger

Charles was completely nonplussed on reading this. It was the last thing he would have expected remembering Hugo's face when he had him in his power in the barn. But when he remembered Fr Farfault's wink and smile just 15 minutes before he thought finally that the offer of the very good job must be serious especially when taking into account the other letter of apology.

Charles now lay back on his bed, covered himself with a thick blanket because the cold was penetrating especially as he was close to the roof with little or no draught-proof protection. He had to think the matter through. To accept the offer would be to place himself in the hands of Mr Verron – he could not think of him as Hugo, not for the moment – and he could not be sure that his almost abject apologies were completely sincere and that his so-called new behavior could be sustained over time. On the other hand he himself held a major card in that he had soundly beaten the man under really unequal conditions and that this information could not be divulged to anyone on pain of placing Mr Verron in a humiliating situation. He therefore came to the conclusion that if only for that reason the offer was tempting but if one was to add the attraction of wooing and probably marrying Priscilla then he could not and should not hesitate. There remained the problem of the farm and the introduction into the farm of a newcomer to take his place. He was not sure how his parents would accept the news but he was sure that with time and the realization that their son had obtained a good situation they could be convinced and after all, he was of an age where he could decide for himself! He decided that after his coffee and tending the animals in the morning he would pay a visit to Fr Farfault to seek his advice. With that he fell fast asleep.

CHAPTER 11

After his usual breakfast of coffee and wheat bread Charles sped off on foot to the presbytery where he would be sure to find his benefactor at that time of day. However, when he neared the church he could hear the organ, entered and crept without a sound along a side aisle and sat down on the bench in the front left-hand row. Fr Farfault was playing some music that was certainly not sacred but was lively, bouncy, contrary to much church music and not at all sad. He was having some difficulty feeling his way through the score open before him and there were many hesitations, stops and starts. Something must have made him aware of the presence of someone because without warning he took has hands off the keyboards and suddenly turned facing the aisle of the church where Charles was seated.

With his thick brows raised, a large smile etched itself on his face. "Well now, what unexpected devotion from a lukewarm Christian like you, my dear Charles" and he burst out laughing before turning and bowing humbly before the cross mumbling, "I beg your pardon, My Lord."

On seeing the priest' reaction to his visit Charles was immediately put at ease, stood up, moved promptly forward to shake hands very warmly. He guessed that the priest had more or less expected this to happen. "Sorry to have interrupted your playing, Father. By the way what was that music? It was very cheerful, not at all like the works you usually play in church."

"Well my lad, that was a piece composed by Amadeus Mozart. Have you heard of him, an Austrian composer? He has composed some absolutely fabulous music and started, would you believe it, at the age of five years old. I persuaded the bishop to send me some copies of his scores. But you have not come to discuss music, I imagine."

"No, Fr Farfault, you've guessed as much. You have probably also guessed that I have come in respect of the letter you handed me last night. I would like you to read it and see if you think it is absolutely sincere or something else …? Would you have a little time to read it?"

"Come, my dear boy – young man, I should say but I've known you so long you are still a boy to me –we'll go into the presbytery. I don't think we want to involve the Good Lord in our palavers!" With that, he genuflected before the altar, turned towards the entrance and invited Charles with a welcoming gesture of his arm to follow him.

They entered the presbytery, situated at about 100 meters from the church and always left unlocked.

I expect you can drink another coffee. He did not wait for the reply - "Mrs Robillard, he called out, can you make us some coffee please" and after welcoming the two men his housekeeper sped away to some distant kitchen. "Well, now, Charles, don't just stand there, hand me the letter and I'll tell you what I honestly think." He smiled encouragingly. "Let's see. Now then, please be seated. If you wish to read the weekly paper, a little out of date, I'm afraid, it's there on my desk." He then took the envelope containing the letter and the document and started walking slowly around the room. He naturally started with the letter and once or twice said "Tut, tut!."

Charles guessed that that brief expletive alluded to the 'letter burning' injunction made by Hugo in the latter.

While he was reading, then rereading the very personal letter, the coffee in a large Empire style coffee pot was placed on the table with two matching cups. The housekeeper smiled coyly at Charles and left the room without a word. Charles had never seen such lovely household objects but on a gesture from the *curé* he poured out two generous cupfuls.

There was a wood fire in the grate and after looking intently at Charles and shaking his head he deliberately tore the letter into small pieces and fed it to the fire.

He took a sip of coffee from his cup, looked Charles quite frankly in the face while shaking his head and said. "Two surprises there - one, the content of the letter. I have never seen such an honest appraisal of one's own failings and two, you were wrong in not burning the letter straightaway. For the moment, I have not looked at the second missive but I think you owe it to Mr Verron to explain to me why you did not burn the letter!"

Charles looked not at the priest but at the floor and it was obvious that feelings of guilt were engulfing him. "Well, I ..., hesitation before saying, ...it was so unexpected that I thought it must have been some sort of trap, though what, I couldn't say." Here he gulped with great nervousness before continuing. "I know I should have destroyed it but I could not but remember his face at the end of the duel. I do not wish to criticize him but I just wanted to know if what he had written was genuine and as I trust your judgment I wanted to be sure that it was not double talk, so to speak...?"

"Charles, this is one occasion when I shall not say anything at all. The feud was between you and Mr Verron and I cannot and will not impart my ideas to you on so personal a matter. I trust you to do the right thing and act positively. It's a pity you showed me the letter because I would have liked to make up my own mind with respect to the gentleman but now I am in the same position as you." He then took the pressure out of the conversation by giving Charles the hint of a wink and could that have been a smile? The time taken for those facial expressions was infinitesimal and Charles was not sure he had really seen them but a huge weight was nevertheless removed from his mind. "However, went on Fr Farfault, the second document, for I would call it a document rather than a letter, is absolutely explicit. You have the offer of an occupation only a wealthy person could make. I think it speaks for itself and I don't think you need any advice at all on what to do. There is a third person in this whose very existence ought to remove any scruples you might have as to accepting the offer, or not. I think, therefore you have all the cards, now play them!"

Charles took everything the *curé* said or had not said as corroborating his own view of the situation and decided there and then that he now had to fend for himself and that he had to move decisively but not too fast to take his future and possibly Priscilla's in hand. He also had to advise his parents on his plans but that would be after meeting Priscilla. First of all, he knew he would have to reply to Hugo's offer but he also knew that that would take a little time having had no experience of such letter-writing. All this now raced clearly through his head where hitherto there had been just foggy, unstructured feelings and counter-feelings.

Charles left the priest thanking him for the coffee and for having read and burnt the letter.

"Remember, Charles, I have seen nothing other than the offer of a tremendous job and I have not given you any advice at all. Just one other thing. You probably find the behavior of Mr Verron inexplicable but just remember the story of Saul and St Paul!"

Charles leant forward placed his head very briefly on the priest's shoulder while pressing the latter's lower shoulders with each hand at the same time and departed swiftly and silently. Fr Farfault, with a look almost of happiness on his face, watched Charles disappear up the presbytery path and through the gate.

CHAPTER 12

Charles's parents were anxiously awaiting his return especially as he had naturally enough said nothing of his visit to the priest but he thought as he scanned their rather dejected looking faces that he owed it to them to say something about the amazing project thrust upon him by divine intervention, as it were.

He closed the entrance-cum-kitchen door behind him slowly, silently and attentively which was not his usual way of doing so. He turned to his parents and invited them to sit down at the table which they did without uttering a word but looking a little lost before this hitherto unknown behaviour of their son.

"Maman, Papa, I have something very important to tell you that will be a great opportunity for me and will affect you both but only to a small extent. In the end it will be good for everyone." He then told of the letter he had received the evening before from the hand of the *curé* and explained the nature of the very important offer from Mr Verron whom they knew by sight but had never spoken to.

His parents looked bewildered – "But how can we manage the farm without you?" managed to say his father.

Charles explained that a farm labourer under his orders would be there to take his place and that his work would be paid for directly by the company of which Mr Verron was the director. He said nothing of the duel but stressed the fact that his new employer had been impressed by the way the Bergers ran their farm. He said nothing about Priscilla either. There would be time over the coming weeks to fill in the details of his new life.

His parents hated change and this promised to be a major upheaval in their lives. They were silent but downcast and it was obvious they would need time to absorb the great change that was being thrust upon them by their son upon whom they had counted to spend his life, just like them, to eke out a living on their splendid but small farm.

"Maman and Papa, I will not let you down. You are good parents to me and I will make sure you are not disappointed by my good luck. I must now write my reply to the offer but once that is done I will see to all the jobs to be done today and that will continue every day until my replacement takes on his duties here." His parents said nothing, just nodded but apparently did not share their son's optimism.

There was another ground floor room in the modest farmhouse but a room that was only used for festive occasions. There was a table with eight chairs around it each one leaning at an angle against it in a position of storage. Charles went into the room, opened the shutters and climbed up to his room to fetch a quill pen and ink. While he was gone, his mother swept into the room, dusted the table, placed several chairs upright, dusted them as well and polished the table. She could now feel that life was going to change for her son and she was after reflection, pleased about this. Imagine his surprise when he entered the room armed with the letter, writing paper, quill and ink to find his mother so busy to facilitate the task he now had to perform. It was rare that his mother smiled, her life being the harsh life of a modest farmer's wife, but smile she now did and succeeded in making Charles feel loved and important to her. This had never happened before and gave him the motivation he needed to write a letter that was equal to the situation. He felt strongly he had to write a letter that showed genuine pleasure without either belittling himself or being boastful and that was on a par with the prevailing mood of the offer. It was no small matter to know what to put to paper as he had little experience in writing 'official' letters but after an hour or so he had set out a plan of the reply and opened his writing pad to a clean sheet. The writing of the final letter came reasonably easily but he took his time to write carefully without making spelling mistakes or mistakes of grammar. He was helped psychologically by his mother who brought him coffee and seemed more than happy to do so. The letter in his bold but slightly sloping hand was eventually written as he had planned. He wanted it to look neat but unpretentious with a suggestion of stability, calmness and yet of force. He applied the wax seal and sat back with his cup in his hand smiling at his mother. She in turn smiled at her son but said nothing. It wasn't her way but some positive exchange had certainly taken place between the two. Charles then returned his belongings to his room and set about helping his father with the various jobs to be done on the farm including cleaning out the stable and some fencing. His father, like his mother, said little except to give instructions to his son in relation to the particular job they were engaged in.

As soon as these tasks had been performed Charles took his sealed letter to the local agent who handled the mail for Clermont Ferrand. There would be a departure the following day so in two days Hugo would have received his reply. Charles heaved a sigh of relief but before returning home he knew he would have to procure some sort of dignified clothing in order to be able to visit Priscilla's home. There was a minimum level of decorum to be maintained. One of his friends was the son of a farmer but on a slightly higher social rung than himself. He would try to borrow a frockcoat and perhaps a waistcoat to fit the occasion. He had decent shoes that needed to be polished that would pass muster but he needed a horse to pay a visit to the Graftons, ostensibly to pay a visit to the parents who certainly had no knowledge of the importance Charles had to Priscilla. First things first. He went to his friend's dwelling place on the spur of the moment and finding him available to talk told him about the offer of the post and of his attachment to Priscilla but without, as he had promised, going into the details. His friend, Henri, slightly older than he, ran the family farm with the help of a farmhand as his parents had all but retired from the exacting tasks of farming of that period. Henri quickly realized that Charles, were he to be successful in his bid to be an 'estate'-cum-farm manager, would more than likely have business deals to enact with him, things like the purchase and sale of grain. But he was a real friend so without hesitation lent him the clothes he required (the two men were luckily of more or less the same build) and told him that his horse, a fine black 4-year old stallion, would be his on the Tuesday, two days later.

Thus assured, Charles returned home and told his parents roughly what he would be doing on the day after the morrow. He tried on the clothes lent to him by Henri and found they were almost a perfect fit but for the waistcoat that would have to be taken in with pins temporarily as his friend's waistline was slightly more generous than his own. With the frockcoat, some passable breeches and his shoes he looked good, quite handsome in fact and decided to leave a small patch of unshaven hair around his chin when he shaved on the day of the famous visit. The one remaining problem was to concoct a reason for the visit but decided in the end that it would be impossible to foresee the unfolding of events and that he would just have to let things take their course, so to speak. He felt sure that Priscilla would find a way of talking to him privately.

CHAPTER 13

The day of the visit to the Graftons had arrived. Charles, nicely garbed in the borrowed garments and now mounted on Henri's steed was trotting casually up the lane that ran along the edge of the field where he had first met Priscilla and towards the main entrance with its tree-lined drive. At that precise time in the early afternoon Mrs Grafton was practicing on the piano and she now heard above the ecstatic notes of Mozart in exactly the same way as she had some time before when Hugo had paid Priscilla a visit, the sound of horse's hoofs approaching from the direction of the drive, so she presumed it was a visit by the same gentleman and not too soon, either, to her mind. As before she went into the rarely used salon at right angles to the music room and saw a fine gentleman on a fine steed approaching the house.

"Priscilla!" she nearly shouted. "Who is the man who has now handed his horse to the stable boy? Do you know him? One minute, I believe that Honorine is showing him in. Can you come down and help me with the introductions?"

Honorine the maid duly showed Charles into the salon where Mrs Grafton had been doing her piano practice saying, "Mr Berger, Madame, would like a word with you." She hardly had time to finish when Priscilla floated in silently wearing a long white dress with short sleeves embroidered around the collar and the hemline with motifs of different animals.

"Oh, Hello Mr Berger, how nice to see you. Mother , this is the gentleman I was telling you about who plays the organ and guitar and runs his father's farm just opposite. You can see his fields from here."

"Oh yes indeed, I remember seeing you at the church service some time ago. I'm afraid that I'm a bit of a heathen and I don't go to church very much," with a little laugh. "Well, come in and Honorine will fetch us some tea and cakes. Can you see to that Honorine? Now then, sit down and tell us what we can do for you."

Priscilla's eyes were wide open at seeing Charles dressed quite stylishly for a provincial gentleman far from Paris. Her mother could not but fail to notice it which prompted her remark.

"If I'm not mistaken, Priscilla, you know Mr Berger a little more than you make out which would explain why you are very reticent in respect of Mr Verron!"

Priscilla and Charles looked at each other almost shamefacedly but then smiled broadly and looked at Mrs Grafton with knowing contentment shining from their eyes.

It was now Charles's turn to speak. "In point of fact, Mrs Grafton I have a great favour to ask of you and of course it goes without saying that the service I ask of you would be properly remunerated. I will explain – this to the puzzled glances of both ladies – You know Mr Verron, I believe, both of you, and I have had a contact with the gentleman which at first I thought might be to my great disadvantage but I was very thankfully completely wrong and to come to the point, he has offered me a very fine post which I have accepted – that of managing his estate made up of quite a few farms and vineyards. However, one condition is that to be aware of the latest developments in agriculture I will have to go to your home country for a time to learn the latest techniques and I think you will have guessed, I will need to be fluent in English which I am definitely not …" Here his discourse fell a little flat as he saw that the two ladies were looking at each other, the one slightly disapprovingly and the other quite beseechingly.

There was a long pause during which the three persons looked from one to the other in turn but it was obvious that the atmosphere was gradually changing from one of puzzlement and incertitude to one of benevolent understanding. However, Honorine now came in laden with all the necessities for a typical English tea. Charles was staggered at what he saw – scones with cream and jam, small tarts and a newly baked fruit cake, together, of course with tea and milk – he had never seen such a feast and one to be devoured, to boot, between normal meal times!

Mrs Grafton had poured the tea taking care to ask Charles whether he wanted milk in his tea or not – of this he was not sure as tea to him was an exotic beverage – and had served the delicious scones filled with clotted cream and strawberry jam when she suddenly said looking from Priscilla to Charles and back again. "I think you two know each other well and I would like some explanations."

So the whole story from the beginning to the present unwound slowly between the two young people with the exception of the duel and with Priscilla telling her mother that the offer of the post was unknown to her and that she had not seen Charles for some time. They talked also about the go-between role of Fr Farfault. The mother seemed convinced and said with resignation.

"So, the English lessons have nicely hidden your request for the hand of my daughter in marriage, is that not so, Mr Berger? Priscilla has already told me that Mr Verron will no longer seek her hand and that I found very strange, to say the least. All this seems shrouded in secrecy"

"Speaking of Mr Verron, I have met him and he has requested that I work for him after seeing some of the changes my father and I have introduced on the farm. As for seeking the hand of your daughter I would not have put it so bluntly. I wanted that aspect to become obvious more gradually, but, yes, there is nothing I would like more in this world than to be your daughter's husband! However, Priscilla is aware of my entirely proper intentions but I think it would be appropriate to say that our hopes in that direction have been, until now, completely without hope."

"Perhaps, young man, you ought to consult my daughter first before you broach the subject again. I will say nothing to my husband for the moment. If it happens that my daughter feels the same way for you as you for her we could perhaps move on to more practical matters. I leave it to you,

Mr Berger, to discuss the situation with Priscilla and then to seek an appointment with my husband and I when things can be discussed and decided in detail."

They continued their tea almost in silence except to make comments on the weather, the political situation, Priscilla's love of being outside, Charles's music and so on and so forth. Then Mrs Grafton somewhat surprisingly said with no introduction. "I have things to discuss with Honorine and the stable boy so I will leave you two to get your ideas in place," and with that she whisked out leaving Honorine to clear away the tea things. The latter had the kindness to close the door when leaving as if she knew that important matters were brewing for the household.

Priscilla, her greenish hazelnut eyes flashing with emphasis, moved quickly into Charles's arms and thrust her head hard against his chest. He in turn closed his strong arms around her shoulders and then simultaneously but silently they kissed with great passion and this lasted a full minute. Then gasping slightly, they looked each other in the eye and laughed joyously.

"Well, what do you say, Priscilla?"

"You know what I think. Of course I will marry you but I'm absolutely staggered by what has come to pass. How is it that Mr Verron offered you the job since you really did humiliate him?"

"If you had read the letter he sent me with the contract you would understand but I admit I have completely changed my opinion of him, and him of me, I might add. And that's not all. We will have the choice of a house among three that are available on his properties."

"I am overwhelmed, Charles. I never expected such good news. When do you start your work as estate manager?"

"The date of March 1st 1818 was mentioned in the contract so I start in just a few weeks. I must wait of course for a letter from Mr Verron to confirm his offer."

"I'll call mother and tell her about the house and of course we will be only too pleased to teach you English. I think she will agree. She doesn't say as much but I think she has great admiration for you, Charles!"

She went into the large open hallway and called out to her mother who very quickly came as if she had been waiting just for that.

CHAPTER 14

The wedding in Clermont Ferrand's Our Lady of the Assumption cathedral could only be called splendid. The cathedral was practically full for the occasion and in the front row could be seen all the finery from France and England. Charles's family felt a little small beside the relative wealth of Priscilla's. However, and this was quite extraordinary, Hugo Verron had arranged for new clothes fit for the occasion to be made for Mr and Mrs Berger and he had more or less paid for the wedding reception held on a sunlit day in February in a fine nearby château. Charles's first month's work had been difficult as he tried to grasp the ins and outs of wine-making but nevertheless he enjoyed it enormously.

He and Priscilla had visited the three houses available for occupation and had finally settled for a handsome but relatively modest south-facing abode overlooking a valley. Nonetheless, for Charles this house went way above his dreams and for Priscilla, too, it traced out a new and hopefully wonderful future. She was responsible for the upkeep of the house including managing the work schedules of the stable boy-cum gardener and the maid. They settled into their new home immediately after the wedding for their "honeymoon" which at that time in France signified the first months of marriage. Hugo Verron paid them a visit at their invitation several times. He was completely different and nobody in his circle of friends and family could explain why. Even when alone with Priscilla, a rare event but one which happened on several occasions, he was polite and never attempted any compromising move.

Charles was very often absent for whole days when he was supervising work on the outlying estates but he was beginning to become acquainted with the various crop schedules and most of his workforce were only too pleased to work for someone who did not treat them like slaves.

Having found his feet, so to speak, after a few months, the question of travelling to England for study purposes was once again aired. This would entail all aspects of agriculture including plant breeding and genetics, soil science, entomology and many other subjects, all under the heading of agricultural science. Hugo had contacts in England and Charles would be given thorough training in new systems being tried out on the other side of the Channel and all the teaching and training he would receive would be in the English language. He therefore had to practise written and spoken English for roughly a year before the voyage. Priscilla and her mother, sometimes together or one at a time, spent long hours, practically always in the evening, improving Charles's vocabulary, his writing and above all his accent. In fact the three of them enjoyed the experience and as Charles was a very fast learner at the end of the one-year period, he was reasonably fluent in the language much to the satisfaction of his teachers! He would be able to understand the lectures he was to attend in England as long as he was able to memorize and translate into French the technical topics he would be learning and practising.

One whole year after the wedding sped by very quickly and was spent rigorously and arduously by Charles at his new post. He received at the turn of the year 1819 a note from Hugo asking him to meet him at his business address in Clermont Ferrand. Charles knew quite well that the voyage to England would be the subject of the meeting and would almost certainly be confirmed. He had previously talked about the matter with Priscilla who was of the opinion that he should go alone to be completely free of constraints of any kind. He did not fully agree as he had grown used to his new life with Priscilla at his side. It could be said that their marriage was one of harmony and joy and he found it difficult to realize he would be wrenched from her orbit.

He set out on horseback riding the official steed as manager of the estates. The horse was white with grey patches here and there and was indeed a fine animal. The journey would take some 4 or 5 hours, so after a good breakfast with Priscilla he made off in the direction of the regional capital. The appointment was at 12 noon and would be attended by Hugo Verron, Charles Berger and two gentlemen who were interested in investing in Hugo's estates owing to the improved yields that were promised thanks notably to Hugo's commercial propensity and to Charles who would be doing the footwork.

Charles freshened himself a little and changed into the high buttoned shirt, waistcoat, tailed jacket, and long trousers that Priscilla with the maid's help had prepared for him.

When he arrived in the room he immediately commanded the attention of the three businessmen. His fair hair was now slightly bushy and he had decided that he would no longer wear a beard. His blue green eyes showed a sort of amiable puzzlement but his stance showed he was ready to discuss matters intelligently and benignly.

"How are you, Mr Berger?" asked Hugo in a perfectly friendly tone of voice.

"Very well, thank you."

"And Mrs Berger?"

"She's fine and greatly attached to her new life."

"I'm very glad to hear that. Well, I've been telling my partners here, Mr Subileau and Mr Le Garrec, about your keen interest in improving farming practices, how you greatly increased yields on your family farm and about the journey to England we agreed upon to enable you to be entirely up to date in matters involving agricultural science and agronomy. They would like to ask you some questions on where you think the future lies in farming in France today. Go ahead, gentlemen."

Mr Subileau, a tall angular man then caught Charles's attention. "Good day, Mr Berger. I am a farmer myself but I also collaborate with the Chamber of Agriculture and we have conferences from time to time, so I would be very interested to hear your views. By the way, I hear you are learning English. Are you making progress?"

Charles, much to the astonishment of all present, broke into a very satisfactory rendition of a piece of prose from Shakespeare's Hamlet that Priscilla and her mother had taken much time to teach him by heart. He rendered it with feeling to the very end. The company was truly amazed and although all three had knowledge of English not one of them understood a word after the famous first line had been recited.

"OK, I'm sorry I asked that question, Mr Berger." The three men laughed heartedly and even Charles felt bucked by his demonstration and smiled. "The question on my mind is that of fertilizers. Can you …?" The questions poured out one after the other and Charles answered from his practical knowledge on the family farm and from his readings (in English) that he now received directly from England.

The other gentleman, a small stocky man, more of a scientist than a farmer, asked Charles questions on new crops and soil management. Charles answered as best he could but he made the point that he was going to England for that very reason – to be made aware of new trends so that he could put them into practice on his return and also to understand certain scientific agricultural basics. The man could only agree with Charles's replies and ended his what could only be called an interrogation by smiling and commenting. "Mr Verron has already convinced us of your qualities and I am certain you are the man for the job. Don't you agree gentlemen?" Noddings of heads.

Hugo then brought the meeting to an end by inviting all three to lunch. He handed Charles his ticket for the cross-channel ferry, various letters of introduction to the specialists and experts from whom he would be receiving training and instructions and a large envelope containing English pounds sterling to cover his expenses. The visit he reminded Charles would last three months starting from March of the same year. That gave him just a little more than two months to prepare his voyage, arrange for the supervision of the Verron estates in his absence, spend a little time with his parents who missed him and last but not least ensure that Priscilla was happy and comfortable in her new life. He need not have worried about his wife who had found perfect equilibrium between her tasks in the house, frequent rides on horseback and occasional visits to friends she had made in the regional capital. She also found time to carry out several rock climbing expeditions with some other women she had met and recruited to form a small band of enthusiasts much to the amazement of families and friends. This activity was practically unheard of at that time even for men but was deemed unbecoming and improper for women. It required much courage on the part of Priscilla but owing to her nationality she was partially forgiven, people thinking that it must have been one of those strange wild practices in Albion!

CHAPTER 15

Charles's first trip to England unfolded as planned. The only difficult part of the voyage was the crossing from Calais to Dover because most of the ferries were still driven by wind although there was one steamboat that had recently been put into service. Charles had to wait several hours at Calais before the right winds condescended to blow for his ship. The journey, too, by coach from Ferrand to Paris and then to Calais was very long and tedious. Trains would be introduced on these routes a few decades later.

Charles missed his wife especially during such moments. He frequently wrote letters to Priscilla and received replies two or three weeks later. The learning, training and practical part of his - shall we call it a course – opened his eyes to the possibilities offered on Hugo's estates but he learned quickly and was able to master and remember all the necessary English technical terms without too much difficulty.

He returned home under much the same conditions as for the outward journey although this time he was lucky enough to sail on the steamboat which was much faster and much more reliable than the sailing ships.

So the year 1819 unfolded in all its seasonal phases bringing Priscilla and Charles to a most comfortable and tender union they could only have dreamt of two years previously and all due to Charles's magic oak stick. They often chuckled about that but then immediately afterwards felt ashamed seeing that their lives had been transformed not only by the duel but by Hugo's unexpected display of humanity.

The following year the happy couple would be 24 and 25 years of age, still very young with great hopes for the future.

Towards the middle of the following year Charles received a letter from Hugo telling him of a great discovery. It was the invention of a grain harvesting machine in England he had heard about and he wanted to be one of the first to introduce the machine in France. It was being used in an experimental capacity for the moment. Charles was thus given instructions to once more undertake the difficult journey to England to be in time to see the experimental machine in action in the Summer of that year.

Priscilla was at first slightly put out when Charles announced the news to her thinking there was something odd about the necessity of going to England on two consecutive years. At that time it would have appeared excessive. However, when he asked her if she cared to accompany him she was delighted and immediately answered affirmatively especially as she and Charles would be able to stay with her grandparents who lived in the county of Kent, the very county where the harvesting demonstration would be taking place.

So, once again, meticulous preparations were made for the voyage, this time for the couple, by various stagecoaches to Calais where they would board a ship and have the advantage of a cabin for the crossing.

They set off in the month of July to the cries of *bon voyage* from the parents of both Priscilla and Charles and arrived in Calais on the appointed day some eight days after their departure and a fairly harassing journey. For the night of their arrival at the port they stayed at an inn at about one kilometer from the waterfront and after a good meal fell into each other's arms in their room and realized that their physical attraction one for the other had not in the least diminished. Their love-making was more elaborate and refined than ever before as each of them did their utmost to please the other. They slept their best night in weeks and the following morning felt completely refreshed, full of energy and ready for the crossing.

CHAPTER 16

They were surprised to see that the sky was overcast with a hint of rain in the air. However, they ate their breakfast of baguette and coffee with relish having asked the innkeeper to arrange for a hansom cab to take them and their belongings to the harbor at the appointed time. The cab arrived on time but it started to rain and there was a fairly strong wind blowing. It was high tide and the ship, a sailing vessel, was waiting for them at the quayside. They were out of luck since the steamship was just arriving from Dover and would not set sail until the afternoon. Never mind, it might be a bumpy voyage but the wind-blown ship would get them to Dover just as well as the steam-driven one.

They climbed on board and were welcomed with the other fifty or so passengers by the captain who was waiting for them at the top of the gangplank. A porter was bearing their luggage. He announced the following to groups of five to ten passengers:

"Welcome on board Neptune IV. We are expecting reasonably high winds today luckily enough from the portside which will help reduce the time for the crossing but you must be prepared for the sea to be reasonably rough so I advise you all to stay in your cabins once we are well out of the harbor. We will be setting sail shortly and should arrive at Dover at 4 p.m. at the latest. I hope you enjoy your voyage."

A good half an hour later the ship edged out of the harbor using very little sail but with the now gathering storm making significant headway.

Priscilla and Charles, both of them smiling somewhat woodenly and standing close together on the deck, were taking in the unfolding scene of sky and sea with a little trepidation but nothing more, after all the two of them were together. However, after some thirty minutes of watching the elements below them and above them they decided to follow the captain's advice and climbed down the fairly steep stairs into the body of the ship and retired into their cabin. By now the ship was beginning to toss and pitch and the two travelers were beginning to feel the initial symptoms of seasickness. They lay on their bunks, one opposite the other, holding hands when the spasms were not too uncomfortable and watched the waves crash down on the side of the ship and against their porthole.

"You know, managed to utter Priscilla, I imagine we will get to Dover in reasonable shape, but in case we don't I want you to know that my life has become so fulfilled and rich with deep love for you, my Charles ever since I met you. My love for you is so strong that I am certain our encounter will go down in the annals of history as an example of everlasting passion. That's how I feel." She tossed her long auburn hair which she had previously tied in a bun back over her shoulders and stroked Charles's face smiling at him with candour and conviction. There was then a huge pitching of the vessel and both of them were sent halfway across the cabin as a huge wave broke over the bows. Their queasiness was wearing off but only to be replaced by a veritable fear. They clung together. Charles, gazing into Priscilla's eyes went even further in letting his heart rather than his head speak for him.

"Priscilla, I knew from the start that we were destined to belong to one another but I could not see how that could come to pass. My life became a marvelous tale to tell and in such a strange way. If we get to Dover the story will continue, I think, forever and if we don't get to Dover the forever will take over our story. I would do anything for you, Priscilla but I do not wish you to do anything for me, just be with me for as long as you can. That's all I want." He placed Priscilla's head on his shoulder and his blue green eyes took on a deep sadness as they narrowed and closed.

There was then an almighty crashing sound and they could hear a member of the crew walking heavily and with much splashing down the corridor shouting time and time again, "All passengers to the lifeboats."

CHAPTER 16b

At Dover, the small building used as a terminal for passengers crossing to France was packed with people. It was 6 p.m. and there was no sign of the arrival of Neptune IV from France. An official dressed in naval attire was moving among the people who had arrived to meet their kinsfolk. He was saying but with very little conviction. "As you can hear and see there are gale force winds blowing and as a result there will be a delay but the ship has seen far worse seas than these and so should not be long in berthing."

The following morning, the Kentish Gazette, put out as its front page headline.

'Fifty-five passengers and ten crew missing from cross-channel schooner Neptune IV'.

'Lost, yesterday afternoon when an unexpected and very local hurricane swept up the Channel before dispersing into gale force winds. All our thoughts are with the families of victims. There is some hope that there will be survivors but until now only pieces of wreckage have been found'.

BOOK 2

CHAPTER 1

Margaret Sturge, an English woman of 26 years of age in 1923 was a nurse who had seen terrible wounds at the end of the war when she started her training. This had in no way prevented her from continuing in the same career but it would be true to say that in the year in question, 1923, most of her patients were still war victims and for the most part, men. She now worked on an independent basis with general medical practices in the south of London and in reach of the town where she lived, notably Croydon. Doctors and indeed hospitals would telephone her in the morning and she would travel by tram, train, bus or bicycle to the areas where she was needed. A motor car was out of the question for the time being. She was very interested in recent discoveries in the world of medicine and worked on a one-off basis with several laboratories selling their new products both in London and in Paris. She spoke fluent French as her mother was of that nationality. One such product was the newly discovered Band-Aid, the predecessor of Elastoplast and Margaret was able to receive a comfortable remuneration in the form of commission mostly from her contacts in Paris. For these commercial ventures which were very infrequent she travelled to Paris by train and steamboat but it took a whole day and was tiring. She had latterly envisaged taking advantage of the new air services between the two capitals. It would depend on her earnings.

One day in the early Summer of 1923 she decided to accept the invitation of a dandy-like man whom she had met the previous Saturday at a jazz club who proposed taking her in his sports car to a motor car race for amateurs that would take place on the perimeter track of an aerodrome at Weybridge in Surrey. She accepted because the weather promised to be mild and she had nothing lined up as yet for that day. She liked the man but nothing more. He was witty, had been to a public school, quite good looking, was up-to-date in all things politic and would have seemed a good catch to many a young woman. However, he very much liked the sound of his own voice, was a little conceited and in a way that was what Margaret liked about being with him, that is she could disagree with him up to a point and often succeeded in turning points of view into laughing matters. She too was quite witty. Margaret was not in the least vain but she had to pretend to be his equal in the sphere of boasting. So she adopted a character that she definitely did not possess. She pretended that her job as nurse was just to fill in time and that she had many friends, both male and female, which was certainly not the case. She pretended her parents lived a very comfortable life in the tropics somewhere and that was not the case either. They lived in a small semi-detached house in Carshalton not far from her Croydon flat by trolleybus.

So in his company she was able to become the person of her dreams and forget about her daily worries and problems. One of these problems was the fact that she in fact had no companion probably because she had met so many young men who were to varying degrees in bad shape. There were few young men available, it was as simple as that. But it could not be said that she liked the man, Percival, to a very great extent even though he fancied his chances with her after dancing with her at the jazz club. It could be said that she looked very much the part of the character she had adopted. She was tallish, slim, had firm flesh on account of her frequent exercises and looked, well, very attractive. She would never buy cheap clothes preferring to buy less often but well, so the dresses, skirts, tops, coats and shoes she bought gave her the impression of being someone with pecuniary resources. But it was not out of ordinary vanity that made her dress well. She needed to convey an aura of knowledge when she made her commercial visits especially as in nearly all cases her interlocutors were men.

Here we were then on the day planned for the outing to the amateur "grand prix" at Brooklands. As our young 33 year-old dandy lived well he resided in a luxury flat in the West End inherited from an uncle. It was there that Margaret agreed to meet him at 9 a.m. after more than 45 minutes by tram and bus on that Saturday morning. He opened the door with a huge smile and showed her into a room he had designated as the breakfast room where a large table was garnered with many eatables that looked enticing, especially after a less than calm journey. There was orange and grapefruit juice and ready in the pan were eggs and bacon ready to be cooked and slices of bread ready to be toasted. The marmalade looked great, too.

He gave her an enthusiastic kiss on the cheek saying, "Do come and sit down. We have plenty of time before we have to leave and don't worry about the dishes. I have a woman who comes in twice a week. She will deal with that. Now then, how are you?"

"Very well thank you, Percival, I had a tiring week with a trip to Paris by boat but I think the next time I will fly there, yes, indeed, fly there from Croydon aerodrome. I recently received a nice commission payment for a new medical product I sold in Paris so I feel I can spoil myself next time." She said this on a laughing tone but it could be said that she was genuinely pleased with the way things had turned out. She was nicely dressed in a straight cut dress of the period with a short hemline, hair in a bob and with a cloche hat that she took off on entering the flat. She wore her comfortable nursing shoes rather than the 2-inch heels she wore on her business trips.

"Well, tuck in" said Percival as he served the customary English breakfast accompanied by wonderful coffee that he had himself ground. They chatted about this and that, his job in finance and of course her two connected occupations. They were on good terms, true enough, but for Margaret that was enough. She wanted to meet someone who was modest, active in mind and body, generous and if possible nice looking and with a broad shoulder to lay her head on. Percival was all this except for the first mentioned virtue for he was far from modest – on the contrary he always wanted, or even needed to have, the last say which he often did with the result that anyone in his job, his friends or his family avoided any deep discussion with him. Margaret just wanted company for the weekend and really nothing more so, apart from moments when they joked together, she often preferred to be silent. She notably steered away from any allusions to the war knowing as she did from other sources that he had not personally contributed to the war effort as he had been away on business in remote parts of the world, on government business, he liked to say.

Breakfast over, Margaret accompanied Percival with her arm amicably through his to his garage not far from his flat. He asked her to wait a moment while he unlocked the door and inside she could see some gleaming monster. The car was a 1920 Vauxhall type Velox, very impressive. The car started with a huge vroom and even when just idling one could hear or guess the power it would be able to exert on the open road. Margaret hitched herself in feeling, all the same, quite proud to be a passenger in such a machine. The year was 1923 so one could say there was practically no traffic once outside of London itself and although there were speed limits Percival largely ignored them. There were few policemen anyway to enforce them. So, they left a noisy, roaring trail all the way to Weybridge. Margaret did not know where to look at first and kept her head down. She was somewhat ashamed of the show they were making of themselves but little by little she relaxed and found the speed and noise quite exhilarating by the time they reached their destination.

They arrived approximately at lunchtime so found their way after parking the car amongst all the other sports cars and luxury saloon cars to a large marquee where a good lunch was served. That was one big advantage of being with Percival – one was sure of a good time especially if, like Margaret, you were an attractive young woman. Still, she felt vaguely uncomfortable mostly due to the fact that for Percival it was an investment whereas for her she just wanted to enjoy herself. Once seated, she looked around her. Percival was engaged in various discussions with men he knew professionally or acquaintances he would have met on occasions like the present one. He made a point of introducing all of them to Margaret in much the same way as if he had been showing them his car, with a flourish, as if he were saying "look at my latest acquisition". It must be said that most of them were suitably impressed and even Margaret was not left without a slight tinge of pride. She saw various men and women of various ages who seemed very well heeled, most of them, but there was one young man who must have been of roughly her age and from whom she could not withdraw her gaze. She was sure she had seen him somewhere but could not at all place him. Well, that's life, she thought. He, on the other hand had not particularly noticed her surrounded as she was by Percival's acquaintances. He was holding a helmet and goggles in his hand so was obviously a participant in the race that was to take place at 3 p.m. He left the marquee and she saw him wandering over to the cordoned off area where the cars that would be racing were parked. Then she lost him to view.

When the festivities were over and all those present were slightly tipsy including one must say, Margaret, although to a much lesser extent, it was time to move towards the grandstand where Percival had reserved the best seats. This was only an amateur motor race but the bookies were there to take bets. Percival placed a large bet on the biggest, fastest, most powerful car in the race, a Mercedes Benz. It belonged to, and was driven by, one of his friends or acquaintances and both he and Percival reckoned that nobody was in the running to beat him. It must be said that the race was a free for all with no handicaps on the most powerful vehicles so it was logical that the Mercedes would win. Before finding their seats in the grandstand they had inspected the sports cars that would be racing against each other. Margaret noticed the man she had seen with goggles and helmet looking over the engine of a very small and strange vehicle. It had only 3 wheels, two at the front and the third behind and someone in Percival's little group explained that it was chain driven and that its accelerator was not on the floor but on the steering wheel. It was a Morgan 3-wheeler and had quite a good reputation for acceleration. The vehicle and above all its driver intrigued Margaret and she thought she would place a few shillings on that car.

"Oh, Margaret, don't waste your money on that silly Heath Robinson mechanism. It's like a museum piece and can never win."

"Well, with all due respect, Percival, I am going to persevere and bet on that odd piece of machinery."

"It's your money but you will regret it. Don't tell me I didn't warn you."

The vehicles, some twenty or so of all different shapes, makes and power began to line up. The participants had cast lots for their starting positions. Had the selection system been fair? We would never know but whether by chance or design the Mercedes had been allotted a pole position with a Bugatti Brescia and an Alvis while the Morgan was lined up in the fourth row behind a collection of lesser cars including a Vauxhall Velox (like Percival's but souped up) and A Ballot 2LS. The first 2 or 3 rows were tipped to take second or third place.

The starting pistol rang out and the sports cars leapt into life with the Mercedes already ten or twenty yards ahead of all the others.

"There, what did I tell you, Margaret, he can't fail to win!"

"Not so sure, Dear Percival", said Margaret gaily. Her eyes were glued on the little Morgan which by many intricate movements to the right and to the left, with some quite astounding accelerations, was now in the second row of vehicles and one could see that it was itching to break away from that row to challenge the favourite. They could not really see what was happening on the far side of the track but when the competitors arrived once more under the grandstand the Morgan was now just behind the Mercedes and trying to ease up alongside the monster. The latter would have none of it. When the driver saw with his wing mirrors the Morgan approaching on the left or right he blocked his progress. The Mercedes was a powerful car indeed and in a long straight had no match for top speed but the Morgan being light was excellent at acceleration. The driver, whoever he was, was looking for such an opportunity and after two more laps and near the end of the race it suddenly accelerated at a terrific rate on the last bend and zipped past its competitor, the driver of which had thought he had the race in the bag who then very aggressively accelerated and was about to overtake the Morgan when the finishing line beat him to it. The game little Morgan had won by a matter of feet.

"Well, Percival, what do you say?" rang out Margaret joyfully. It must be said that she was as astounded as he.

"I just cannot explain that", he blustered foolishly, "but what on earth gave you the idea to bet on that little rat of a car?"

"Aha, wouldn't you like to know! No be reassured, I have no clairvoyance powers, it was just intuition", she declared somewhat untruthfully."

"You'd better collect your winnings then. That should be a little packet. Well done", he said hiding his former dissatisfaction with a big effort at being generous in his deception, not at all like his normal behavior making Margaret see him in a different light. Perhaps he was not so ill-suited to her as she had previously thought. However, Percival was a calculating person and if he had sounded generous it was because he played a role that was not his own and was determined, even to the extent of demeaning himself, to use everything in his arsenal of conduct to win over Margaret. She took him at face value in that particular incident and then thought nothing more of it.

She descended into the rather cramped hall where the few bookmakers were paying out winnings. "Well, my fine lady, you did rather well out of that," muttered the bookie as he handed over the handful of one-pound notes. "Yes didn't I? I would never have …" Here her voice trailed off as the driver of the Morgan, beaming broadly and shaking hands here and there with competitors who good-naturedly were congratulating him, strode slowly the length of the hall. She moved towards him saying joyfully. "Excuse me, Sir, but can I thank you for allowing me to win a small fortune for myself this afternoon? … but don't I know you. I'm sure we have met somewhere before but I can't remember where or when. That's strange …"

"That is strange, he said in a heavily French-accented but pleasant voice. Now I look at you, yes, you're right, we have met somewhere but the details have slipped my memory as well. Here, here's my telephone number until tomorrow afternoon. I'm staying in a company-owned flat in Croydon. As you can hear, I'm French but I love most things English. That's why I'm here. Perhaps I will hear from you," he said as he moved away not without keeping his eyes on hers for several seconds. She took the slip of paper on which was scrawled Croydon 5405.

Just at that moment Percival appeared looking for her and had viewed the strange scene that had unfolded before his eyes. He now looked livid. "Oh, so that's why you betted on that nasty little car. You knew the driver all along and he gave you an insight." He was red in the face.

"No, I can assure you, my dear Percival that I have no idea who he is but I just took the opportunity of thanking him for allowing me to win this …" and she held the wad of banknotes under his gaze. "I don't suppose I shall ever see him again." Again she had uttered an untruth since she knew in her inner self that she would have to telephone the man who had not even given her his name. Still, there were lists of the cars and their drivers littered about everywhere and without Percival noticing she stooped down to pick up a leaflet. She stuffed it into her handbag. "Well, perhaps we should be going. I've had a brilliant day, thanks to you," and she gave Percival a kindly hug. He was still peevish and grumpy but the hug and her smile softened his mood.

"Right, let's go. I'll drop you off in Croydon. It's only a short detour for me. I agree, the day was good, we had some fun and even if I won nothing, you did!" You could see he said this with quite an effort to please. He obviously wished to remain on good terms with Margaret. She was no fool and was easily able to read his motivations. She was now convinced she would have to go carefully with him and press down on the brake pedal a little.

CHAPTER 2

Percival dropped her off at Moreton Rd without entering her flat at her invitation. She was secretly relieved as the day had been psychologically tiring coping at the same time with her jubilance at winning and at meeting the driver of the car who had led to her good fortune but also with Percival's changing moods. She needed to be alone. So what do English persons (or half English) do to relax? Yes, she put a kettle on the hob and settled down with a cup of tea, some biscuits and a newspaper, albeit a day old. Then she remembered that she had kept the list of competitors and cars on a tatty brochure in her handbag and reached down to retrieve it. So, the young unknown (or known?) driver's first name was Alexandre and his family name Boyer. That was something to go on. Now, where had she put his telephone number? Oh no, she had lost it! Then groping among all the things a lady carries in her handbag she found the number screwed up in her handkerchief. Wow, that was a close thing! She scribbled the number more legibly in her address book with his name set proudly above it. She was about to unhook the telephone when she thought that it was perhaps a little premature to ring him now. She would wait until the following evening. You can't just do what you want in life without giving things a little thought and without looking at possible or probable consequences to your actions. Even though she had seen the results of the most uncivilized actions ever unleashed on mankind she always stuck to firm principles and acted in a civilized manner. Still, she was longing to know where she had seen the man before because he seemed familiar to her. She must have seen him at one of her appointments, perhaps in Paris. Yes, it was certainly that. He also had seemed to recognize her. She could not wait until the morrow when she would try to telephone. Then she remembered her medical visits booked for the next day and her first aerial trip booked to Paris in three days time. She would probably have to tidy Alexandre away into a darkish cupboard in her mind for the time being. Oh well, that was life!

However, she thought she might start a journal to try to get things a bit more shipshape in her head. Percival, although quite a diversion at times, might prove to be a difficulty at some point in the near future if she did not make it clear to him that she had no intention of making a long-term commitment to him in the form of, shall we say, marriage. She knew perfectly well that that was his goal and that he was making a super human effort, for him, to appear relaxed and nonchalant to reassure her. But she also knew that his behavior with her was out of character. She had seen his bombastic and pretentious ways of treating his friends and knew only too well that once hooked she would be submitted to the same treatment. She would continue to see him, to lunch with him, accompany him to the theatre and so on but diminuendo. It's true that he did afford her quite a bit of entertainment but it would be unfair of her to continue as in the recent past. She now realized that her reasoning had completely changed since her chance encounter with

Alexandre. This was incredible, abnormal and not at all like her customary behavior.

She had to get all this down on paper to see in which direction she was going. She was 26, an age at which most young women had already settled down and had already given birth to one or more children. She fetched a pad, that would do for now, her fountain pen and settled down in her one good comfortable armchair to write. She had only written one line when her lovely hazelnut eyes became heavy and started closing and before she knew where she was, she was dozing and images of strange persons and places flashed across her mind in her sleep.

CHAPTER 3

Alexandre Boyer enjoyed his short stays in England very much. He found life freer and more relaxed in England than in France though he would once again do anything to defend his country as he had done during that terrible conflict of the 1914-1918 World War. It was a miracle that he was still alive and he put it down simply to luck but there was no doubt he enjoyed moments of life very much like that amateur grand prix he had just won. One could say that he had almost fallen in love with his little Morgan 3-wheeler and knew its character better than his own. When he saw the huge powerful Mercedes listed as a competitor he knew that that was the vehicle which would be his only real rival. He had played with death so many times during the war that this formula motor race was just like going for a bike ride for him – a little more adrenalin, it's true, but no real excitement until the moment when he would have his opponent face to face, so to speak, at the end of the race. That was certainly the case. Nearly everyone connected with motor racing had almost laughed in his face when they saw the little, almost fragile 2-seater and with only 3 wheels. It was so light you could lift the back end single handed but that in fact was its strength. It was so light that its small 8 hp V-twin Jap engine gave it superb acceleration although its power could not be sustained and was not to be raced on circuits with very long straight stretches but rather on tight-cornered circuits where it could overtake in short bursts of power. That had been the case at Weybridge.

He had bought the car just a month or so previously on a whim on seeing an advert in an English sports paper and had since spent all his spare time in England tuning up the engine, changing brake pads, renewing wiring and of course polishing the little beast so that it shone. He had already raced once but that was just a trial and he had made no effort to win coming in almost last. Of course many people connected with amateur motor racing prior to the Weybridge race knew about him and the Morgan but had not taken him seriously. That was why all the odds were against him for the race at which Margaret and Percival were spectators.

The race was now over and he had to now take the car to its garage in Croydon for the days of his absence from England. He had been highly intrigued to see that dashing young woman at the race since he knew he had seen her somewhere before but he could not at all place her. When he closed his eyes sometimes he could roughly remember the shape of her face, the colour of her eyes, hair, her slim build and the clothing she was wearing that Saturday. That was rather strange because he had met quite a few lovely young women but none could he remember in such detail, but there was one important detail lacking – her Christian name and surname. He had been really stupid not to, at least, have asked her for her name. Well, it was up to her now. If she had any of the feelings he thought she had for him she could easily phone him. He did not feel very hopeful. "Still, you never know," he said to himself.

It was getting late and he had to get some sleep after quite an exhausting day and to be in readiness for his return trip to Paris the next day. Perhaps the lady would phone him tonight but he had seen from her way of talking, her general behavior during those few minutes of the encounter that she would not. She was well brought up, that was obvious and would not ignore social conventions even if she had wanted to.

CHAPTER 4

Margaret had spent three busy days since the motor race and had agreed to see Percival two evenings later for a restaurant meal in London. She had duly, as was her wont, travelled by tram and tube before walking to the restaurant in the West End. They chatted amiably together about his occupation of estate agent and his interests in banking and other domains which rolled off his tongue in such a way that Margaret was unable to register them in her mind. In any case she did not really care in the least about them. She talked about her mostly male patients some with terrible war wounds that would not enable them to walk again. She noticed that Percival did not take too great an interest in her accounts of these victims. He preferred to talk about medical cures and about her job of selling precisely those medical products that were a breakthrough for their time. She talked excitedly about a tuberculosis vaccine that had just started being used and one that for once, originated in France and not England or the US. She was spending much time at present attending lectures in Paris and then visiting hospitals in the London area to convince the medical profession of the efficacy and safety of the discovery. She hoped to help humanity by so doing and if she gained a little financially she was not against it!

However, all the time they were chatting, she could not keep Alexandre from her mind. She had tried to call him a couple of times the day before but to no avail. She wondered what he did for a living to be absent such a lot but then she remembered that he was wholly French so obviously lived mostly in France. She now realized that her penchant for him was a little exaggerated and wondered if she should consult someone about it. Psychotherapy was becoming a branch of medicine in the early 20s with particular importance for those suffering from significant mental problems like depression, mood swings and others but it was well known that a good therapist could help people with mild disorders. However, on further reflection she told herself that it was just normal attraction of one person for another and to just await developments if there were to be any. Perhaps her preoccupation with Alexandre would just disappear naturally. That was to be hoped for. Anyway the conversation with Percival continued but she realized that she was not paying the least attention to what he was saying but was simply playing a role with her "yes's", her "no's" and her "Oh, really?" quite often. Percival being a highly egoistical character did not seem to notice her inattention and seemed quite pleased with himself, with what he was saying, all to the relief of Margaret. She knew now, though, that her relationship with Percival had got to slow down as she could see much more clearly since the Saturday of the motor race that he was a pretentious bore and that never could she spend more than a short time with him. So it was only fair to let him become aware of this and the only way she could think of doing so was to space out the meetings. She knew that if she told him that she did not want to see him again frankly and with no warning he could become a danger to her. She had seen some of his irrational behaviour with other people. No, the only way was to reduce the voltage, so to speak, and let him realize after a certain time that he was wasting his time with her. It was the least bad option to her mind. Back in her flat she knew she had a concrete task to carry out the next morning and that was to go to Croydon Airport to collect her ticket for Le Bourget from Daimler Airways.

The new impressive building housing the two or three airlines operating out of the airport and the control tower that would stand out high and firm in the middle of the building had not yet been completed but all the same the part including the new control tower was already in place and gave her a reassuring feeling. It was at the forefront of innovation for the period. It was the first air traffic control unit in the world and although the resources were very basic the crew of the few aircraft engaged in commercial flights did have radio contact with the Croydon controllers and were given permission to land and take off as is still the case today. Air traffic control was in its infancy but was effective.

So she cycled to the airport and entered the main building. The weighing-in counter and offices of Daimler Airway were to be found immediately on the left on entering the building. She duly paid for her ticket for the flight the next day aboard a De Havilland 34 biplane for a flight due to take off at 10.15 a.m. She then sped home. She was quite excited about her flight as this will have been her first experience of flying. She knew she would have to try to keep calm in order to sleep that night but she was determined all the same to try Alexandre's Croydon number once again. Here again she drew a blank and had to be thankful she had a good book to read.

The following morning, after a night of broken sleep, she gathered up her suitcase for two nights' stay in Paris together with her briefcase containing all that was necessary for note-taking and a dossier setting out the conclusions of the first studies on the new tuberculosis vaccine. She was going to Paris to attend a 2-day conference on this very subject, to meet the revered researcher surgeons and to collect enough verbal and written ammunition to be able to persuade English surgeons to carry out trials. She already knew many medical names in Paris due to her commercial ventures in the opposite direction. Most inventions and discoveries emanated from the Anglo-Saxon world and found their target buyers elsewhere in the world, including France and Europe. Finding a reliable and safe vaccine would be a breakthrough in the domain and Margaret was eager to be part of the adventure, albeit simply a communicative role but one that was crucial to the establishment of Anglo-French relations in this area of medicine.

She arrived at Croydon aerodrome at 9.30 a.m. but was told that there was a technical hitch on the DH 34 aircraft she was due to board but that the delay would only be about 30 minutes. She would be kept up to date and when all was ready she would be able to check in and have her baggage stowed on the aircraft. So she settled down in the café restaurant with her book, ordered a coffee and started to wait patiently. After waiting for news of her flight for some 45 minutes she started getting restless and wandered up onto the roof of the building under the control tower to see what was going on. She could see no sign of her Daimler Airways flight so assumed the repair, whatever it was, was taking place inside a hangar. On the other hand she could hear the deep roar of an aeroplane and could see a passenger biplane flying around the airfield. Three or four minutes later it passed close to the tower on landing on the SW / NE runway. It was marked Union Air so was French and had necessarily flown in from Paris. Having watched that still uncommon event for the period – the landing or takeoff of a passenger plane – she descended once more to the lounge where she found a hostess looking for her to give her the news. The flight with Daimler was cancelled and instead she would be flying to Paris with Union Air. All the airlines operating out of Croydon had an agreement by which they would accept the passengers of the other lines if there was any technical hitch and if they had room. So the aeroplane she had seen landing would be taking her to Le Bourget. So be it. She hoped it would not be too late in getting airborne.

Finally, Margaret and the other eleven passengers (quite wealthy looking as far as she could see) were ushered through the customs area then onto the tarmac to board the aircraft, a Farman Goliath. They were met at the top of a short stairway by the air stewardess who welcomed them one by one and showed them to their seats which were wide and comfortable. The aircrew of two were already in the open cockpit and with the help of ground staff who swung the propellers the engines sprung into life with a roar. There were no other aircraft in the circuit or even manoeuvring on the ground so they taxied into takeoff position at the end of the same runway where they had landed an hour before. With a brief "all clear for takeoff" from the tower the aircraft lumbered forward a little awkwardly, gathered speed and was airborne in no time. It climbed and when it had gained 3,000 ft it turned to portside and got on a direct compass bearing for Paris. The weather was reasonably good, a slight south-westerly wind and sunshine from time to time. They made good time to the coast and then the aircraft took a heading towards Dieppe. Margaret was delighted to see the vessels from above, it was a sheer joy. The French coast came into view and now she was able to see across the huge expanse of forest and farmland people going about their daily business. Each time she saw a carthorse working in a field her heart leapt but she had no idea why. They sped across small towns and villages and there were horses and carts everywhere and the occasional motor but neither of these had the same effect as to see a horse working in a field. Why, she wondered? Two hours after takeoff they landed at Le Bourget and as she was gathering her suitcase and briefcase she had stacked next to her she had bent downwards and had not noticed the two pilots who had descended from their cockpit and had made for the door where they were wishing their passengers good day before they descended the steps and hoping they had had a good flight.

The pilot and co-pilot had removed their flying gear to reveal their uniforms. As Margaret passed before them to walk down the short mobile stairway she glanced at each pilot and would have fallen down the stairway if one of them had not very rapidly grasped her arm. It was her glance towards the taller of the young pilots that was the cause of her surprise, or was it a shock? The man was none other than Alexandre whom she had tried to telephone in Croydon several times.

"Gosh, I had no idea that your job was pilot. I'm speechless. And to think that if my booked flight had not been cancelled ..." She did not finish what she was saying for there were other passengers behind her anxious to leave the aircraft. "I will see you in the lounge" he had time to say before she clambered down the steps and made for the buildings to go through customs and immigration formalities. Margaret's head was in a whirl. She did not believe in providential intervention but here was a pure example of just that. She had tried to contact Alexandre by telephone several times and although her head had a clear vision of his face and physique she had become more or less convinced that the man would just disappear from her life and that she would never see him again and worse still that perhaps she would end up becoming a partner for life with Percival ...and she shivered. Oh no, not that!

She went through immigration and then customs very quickly then she was a little lost. She decided to wait in the small bar/restaurant at the airport so she ordered an espresso coffee and settled in an armchair with her eyes glued to the doors that gave onto the tarmac where she could see the Goliath and two other aircraft parked. There was a mechanic inspecting the engines of the aircraft she had flown in while another was refueling it. There was no sign of the aircrew but she supposed they also had to go through the same formalities as the passengers and would have to report to their company about the trip, debriefing was the technical term though she would not have heard of it. However, some thirty minutes later, Alexandre in his uniform but holding his cap under his arm came into the space where she was seated searching in all directions, presumably looking for her. When he saw her in the corner he gave a visible sigh of relief and she rose from her armchair to exchange French *bisous* – that is two kisses on both cheeks – a nice custom that most foreigners in France take to with much pleasure!

"What a surprise to see you on my flight. I had no idea you were a hardened air traveler! Here he laughed and continued, but how did that come about? I always glance at the list of passengers but of course, how stupid of me, I don't even know your name. I don't think I gave you my name either. I'm Alexandre Boyer."

"How nice to meet you and so unexpectedly. I'm Margaret Sturge and I am half French, on my mother's side. I'm in France for business reasons. My real job is nursing but I also do another job for pharmaceutical laboratories presenting their various inventions and discoveries on both sides of the Channel and promoting new products to medical organizations, surgeons and the like. At the moment I'm involved with a discovery, a vaccine called BCG to treat tuberculosis. It was discovered before the war but is now gathering speed around the world. I have got appointments with tuberculosis specialists, doctors and the laboratory that is producing it. I will be taking a few samples to England afterwards to persuade scientists there to try it out. We'll see, but I am staying here two nights so back to Croydon in two days but by Daimler Airways unfortunately!"

"Well, that is highly interesting. How do you manage to do nursing in the meanwhile? You can't have much time."

"That's true but tell me about yourself. How come you are a pilot in one of these new aeroplanes?" She looked really earnest when she posed this question, her nice hazelnut eyes narrowing to slits.

"I was always fascinated by aviation ever since Blériot and when as a conscripted serviceman I learnt they were looking for recruits to fly fighter planes and bombers I jumped at the chance. I spent the most frenetic four years you can imagine, was shot down twice and crash landed for mechanical reasons several times. It's a wonder I survived because I lost quite a few of my comrades. But, Margaret, can I call you that? (nods from her direction). Good, but I cannot get over the fact that I know you from somewhere although I cannot fit you into any décor or location whatsoever. Isn't that strange? You said at the race track you had the same impression, that you knew me, if I remember rightly. Odd, isn't it but I daresay it will come back to us?

"Since I saw you at Weybridge, Alexandre - I suppose I can address you by your Christian name? – things that I never usually think of cross my mind. I expect there's a very obvious explanation to that."

"I'm sure there is! Well, I'm willing to know you a little better if you yourself are willing. Unfortunately I have to leave you now as I am taking the same aircraft back to Croydon again in one hour's time but you say you are travelling with Daimler. That's a shame because I am spending two nights in England before returning to Paris so we will miss each other again."

"You are a bit difficult to contact, it's true, Alexandre. I have tried to call you at least three or four times. Here, let me give you my telephone number and we will keep trying, both of us, until one of us succeeds! Is that alright?"

"Fine, must go now." They kissed each other again, French style, and Alexandre marched off turning round to give Margaret a huge smile which naturally enough was returned as he left the bar/restaurant.

CHAPTER 5

Four or five days later Alexandre had a 3-day break from his piloting job and as it was still early evening when he arrived in his flat which he shared with another pilot from the same company, he poured himself a glass of wine, put his feet up and started reading a copy of Le Figaro. After becoming slightly depressed at the international and above all European news he got to his feet and went to the telephone holding Margaret's number in his hand. He had little hope of finding her at home but to his amazement he heard, "Croydon 6901, Margaret Sturge speaking."

"Hello, Margaret, it's Alexandre, he said in as unaccented a voice as he could muster, It's a bit of a miracle that we're both at home. First time, eh?"

"Well, Hello, Alexandre, how nice to hear from you." The tone of her voice had of course changed from neutral to a nice, warm and friendly one putting Alexandre immediately at ease. "I don't really know how to start a conversation like that with someone I hardly know and it's not customary for a woman to invite a man but to break the ice, so to speak, how about having a meal together? You would be my guest. However, I must admit, the only really good restaurant I know is at the airport. Could you make it this evening? I'm free. What about you? Would eating at the airport put you off?" All of that came out in a rush making the two of them laugh.

"Don't worry about that, Margaret, he replied with a chuckle, I will eat anywhere you like but the meal will be on me, and as for the airport, what does it matter? It's a nice atmosphere there."

"Alright then, can you make it for 9 p.m. say?" she ended up by talking in a more relaxed way and with a joyous tone in her voice. Anyone near her would have seen her standing upright, running the fingers of her right hand through her hair, her hazelnut eyes now laughing quite merrily.

"Superb, see you at 9 at the airport hotel," he also said gaily shaking his head with sheer joy. They both rang off.

Both entered the vestibule at the same moment, at precisely 9.10 p.m. and they both smiled broadly as they met, each one knowing the reason for their arrival at that exact time – not really too difficult to guess. They gave each other the French style *bisous,* two kisses on each cheek and made their way into the restaurant where they were met by the *maître d'hôtel* who escorted them to a convenient table to the side of the dining space where they would not be disturbed. A waiter took the light coats they were wearing on that Spring evening and hung them on a clothes stand nearby, held Margaret's chair while she sat down and handed each a menu card. He then asked them if they wanted an aperitif. They decided on a Pastis, the aniseed alcoholic drink, as both of them were fond of the South of France. That loosened their tongues straightaway.

"It's really strange, isn't it? almost whispered Alexandre, we hardly know each other yet here we are dining together like a couple who have been together for years."

"I know, she replied, screwing up her eyes with more than a hint of a smile about her lips, but what you just said is very much to the point, I feel I do know you but it's impossible to identify either the time or the place we met."

"Well, that is extraordinary. He now looked a little stern but very quickly broke into a smile and ran his hands through his hair and continued. There is a huge mystery surrounding all that but what if we pretended we did know each other very well and forgot the whys and wherefores …? I suggest we raise our glasses to our newfound friendship!"

"Here, here!" broke in Margaret, raising her glass in unison with Alexandre and the two of them laughed and laughed until the tears streamed down their faces.

The few diners in the room looked across at them most of them pleased to see such good humour pervading the atmosphere.

Margaret continued after the joy of laughing together had subsided. "I should imagine that the first thing to do would be to set out a sort of programme of when and where we can meet together. That might not be all that easy as we both travel between England and France a lot, but not impossible."

"OK, then, Margaret, I have my work agenda with me. Let's set out the days, evenings, possible weekends when we can be together. That's what we both want, is it not?"

"It is, indeed. I have a small pad in my handbag. Let's start."

So a good 20 minutes or half-an-hour elapsed fairly rapidly as they managed to arrange their meetings which as the minutes passed they perceived as amorous rendezvous! At the end of the session they looked each other in the eye for a few seconds, burst out laughing and, as one, held each other's hands and real desire could almost be seen flowing one from the other.

Margaret now sat up straight, unclasped her hand from Alexandre's and changing expression completely said with a perceptible tinge of concern in her voice which she considerably lowered in tone."Alexandre, I have something to tell you. It's important. Do you remember seeing me with anyone when you raced your Morris, was it, the other day …?

"Morgan, actually …"

"Oh yes, Sorry, to insult you." Slight chuckles ensued from both of them.

"Well, actually, I did notice you for the reasons we have already stated, before the race but I was quite occupied by preparations so I didn't see you with anyone at that time. However, yes, I saw you in the company of a well-dressed man who seemed very upset about something, I seem to remember …"

"He was upset because you won! Margaret almost shrieked with laughter and made heads turn in the restaurant. He had betted several pounds on that big racer, a Mercedes wasn't it? And said it could not but fail to win. He was really angry that you managed to beat him. Even more annoyed when he saw me talking, all but briefly, with you. Well, this man whose name is Percival is a person who believes that one day I will cave in to his demands and marry him. I accompany him from time to time to various events, concerts, exhibitions and the like and I even stay the night at his place occasionally but never in the same bed! I have tried in vain, it would seem, to convince him that I only ever intend to be his friend and nothing more but he will not budge in his belief that it's just a matter of time. I have seen him time and time again with his friends and business partners. He always has the last word in any conversation and he can be quite odious at times. He simply tramples on people. His behavior with me at the moment, on the other hand, is quite reasonable but I know quite well that if ever I chose to be his wife - which God forbid I would ever do – he would adopt the same tactics on me. Now, you know. But he will, sooner or later, become aware of our relationship – if it continues, of course (muffled chuckle). So what do you think?"

"Let's take the last observation first, can we? Our relationship. I think we can safely say that we have now established a relationship. How it will develop we just don't know. The main thing is, I think, that we feel at ease in each other's company (nods from Margaret) and perhaps this might be related to the fact that we have the impression of already knowing each other. That really is strange and it leaves me feeling completely nonplussed but it also means that we should be able to build on that. Now, for the question of, of ...yes, Percival, you must not force him to take any rash action. Continue to see him – (hesitation) preferably not at his home – but try to see him less and try also to make it obvious that the friendship can go no further – but you've already said you are working on that. We'll just have to deal with any awkward situation when it arises."

All this time they were being served and were eating a typical meal of the period including delicately sliced beef with potatoes and peas but all nicely served and accompanied by a red wine chosen by Margaret, followed by a selection of British cheeses, then very tasty slices of fruit pie with vanilla ice cream. Coffee rounded off the meal.

They were now silent, holding each other's hands across the table, their eyes focused intently at the others'. Suddenly they both coughed slightly as one, laughed and both seemed to ask the question, what now? without actually uttering it. They got up from their seats somewhat awkwardly and while Alexandre paid the bill at the reception desk Margaret waited next to the coat stand for the *maître d'hôtel* to hand the two of them their coats.

Of one accord they went to the hotel part of the establishment and asked for a double room in the name of Mr and Mrs Boyer.

They eventually got off to sleep at some time between 3 a.m. and 4 a.m. after a night of wonderful lovemaking but here again, in spite of preliminary forebodings they made delightful, sensual but delicate love together as if it was not the first time. They were, once again, highly intrigued by this perplexing situation but could as usual offer no explanation.

CHAPTER 6

They each of them then took up their usual occupations after a quite heart-rending parting. Margaret had several patients to visit and Alexandre was due to leave for Le Bourget again that evening. However, when Margaret arrived at her flat lacking energy after her day's work, which because of its very nature was very tiring she found a note from Percival thrust halfway under the door. She knew it was Percival due to the writing. She frowned, cursed fairly loudly to such an extent that she glanced around to see if anyone had heard her. Nobody had, so extracting her door key from her handbag she entered knowing only too well that the note would be a pain. And so it was. Scrawled across the notepaper was the following.

"Have tried to get in touch with you without success. What are you up to? Please phone as soon as possible."

Well, that seemed like an order but she decided she would not ring for a while. Anyway she had to concoct a kind of alibi to allay His Highness's suspicions. She would think of something - probably it would be an emergency call that required her to be up all night and at a person's abode where there was no telephone. She later phoned his home number but as it was mid-morning Percival's housekeeper answered and told her he had left for his office not long before and, she added as an afterthought in a strange hushed voice (she had recognized Margaret's voice) that he had been in a very bad mood when he left. Well, she would sort that problem out in due time. How, she did not know but she would find a way. She felt quite hot in the face and was beginning to have antipathetic feelings towards Percival. She was determined not to let it ruin her nascent relationship with Alexandre. She set her head high, shook it vigorously so that her hair flew in all directions and looked determinedly out of the window to show anyone who might be passing that she meant business. However, she knew that the situation would not be resolved as easily as that and tried to fathom out how she could one day be rid of Percival. She had to find a way of becoming less pleasing to him – let herself go a little, perhaps? Wear no makeup and old, worn out clothes? Perhaps look bored and converse in a humdrum, common sort of way or perhaps not answer his queries? She suddenly laughed out loud because her examination of her own potential future behavior in respect of her suitor made her forget his daily proven inalterable behavior. She had forgotten that he was so taken up by himself, so narcissistic, that whatever she might do would never change the way he had always reacted to anything she did or said. He very rarely listened to what she said anyway except when she told a very good joke that in no way impinged on him and hardly noticed what she was wearing unless the garment revealed an expanse of skin he had not seen before. She had therefore to rule out that approach. Well, what else then?

With that she lay her head back in the armchair she had settled into and fell fast asleep.

She awoke some forty-five minutes later from a strange dream. In it there were fields and sunshine and glimpses of horses bearing what must have been crusaders for they were wielding swords. Funny dream but then they often are she told herself.

After shaking herself out of her dream-penetrated sleepiness she decided that she would not contact Percival at all and just wait for his what she would expect to be a stormy call. Ringing him would only cause him to think she had something to hide. So she collected her wits, consulted her agenda and saw she had a couple of visits to make. All this time she was thinking of Alexandre and of their next meeting. When did he say he was flying into Croydon – that very day or the morrow? She could not recall what he had said. How very silly of her!

The call from Percival was not long in coming. The tone of his voice, seemingly calm and kindly but with a hint of annoyance, revealed the hidden anger. He wanted to know what she had been doing the night before and she very convincingly narrated a fictitious visit to a patient battling against the final days of a life-condemning cancer. She thought herself how real her account had seemed – just the right emphasis in the right place – perhaps a shade too convincing because contrary to his normal practice he was listening and posed her questions, what type of cancer, man or woman, etc, etc? This took her off guard and made her bluster a little, excusing herself by saying that she was very, very tired. He finally accepted her account and insisted on seeing her that evening as he said he had something important to show her and say.

This made her sit up straight, fiddle with a pen lying near the telephone and wonder just what that could be. Oh no, he was not going to propose to her with a ring and all the farcical declarations of undying love? Christ, it was worse than she thought. She told him that she might not be back at the time he suggested so he said he would come anyway and take her out somewhere to dine. This was not going to be easy.

He arrived at 8 p.m. looking bright and cheerful and dressed in a very expensive grey suit with a bluish silk tie. His black shoes, immaculately polished, shouted out their quality and his perfect taste. When Margaret saw him arrive through her lounge window in his gleaming Velox her heart sank into her shoes. Oh no! What had she let herself in for? Luckily, because he was so pleased with himself, with the outward shine of his wealth in his clothes and his car, he did not stop his monologue on politics, about his job – apparently a high-flying financier of some sort – and one could almost say that he had forgotten the neat, attractive young woman at his side and did not even mention her absence the previous night just asking her if she was feeling festive for it was an evening, it would appear, to celebrate something or other but he would not say what. This did not augur well or so Margaret thought. The evening could only finish badly. The Criterion restaurant facing Piccadilly Circus was their destination.

As soon as the swish Velox poked its nose in front of the Criterion a parking valet appeared from nowhere and took the keys from Percival. Margaret and Percival were ushered through the swing door across a vast vestibule and into the restaurant where they were shown to their table that Percival had taken pains to reserve. It would appear that he knew the restaurant well and even addressed the maître d'hôtel by his first name and family name at which the latter replied, "Good evening, Madam / Sir", a shade obsequiously to Margaret's mind but she knew Percival would lap that up as servitude due to someone of higher rank!

"Well, what do you think of the establishment?" he asked with a glimmer of knowing what her answer would be.

"Very impressive," she said slowly but with no exuberance. In her inner self she found the place a shade too showy and garish. She preferred smaller more intimate environments but, she mused, it was all one to her as there was apparently a great revelation to be made and this made her uneasy. She hid her feelings offering Percival a weak smile.

However, he did not seem to be aware of anything different in Margaret's demeanor so full was he of the great surprise (revelation?) he intended to announce. He did not even notice that Margaret was wearing her ordinary daytime all-purpose clothing. She was wearing a day dress and blouse set and a pair of mid-heel Oxfords – she hardly needed any makeup as her face was classical with a well shaped nose, slightly elongated, hazelnut eyes and a mouth that you could imagine only kindly words would flow from. Her makeup consisted of a touch of eye shadow that made her eyes stand out sharply and pale pink lipstick to downplay her sensuality. Her haircut was of the latest bobbed style and overall she looked good. She wore practically no jewellery, just a beaded necklace – nice but simple.

She had in fact gone out of her way to look as ordinary as possible but as her body was nicely proportioned – slim but muscular – it would have been difficult for her to look anything but attractive. So Percival noticed nothing that he might have thought to be unfitting or inapt for the occasion. He was full of himself and very exuberant talking without stopping about nothing of any importance to Margaret. He talked of share prices, motor cars, the wealth of his family and the mansion or two they owned in the West Country or Scotland. So boring, thought Margaret.

However he did have the presence of mind to summon a waiter and order starters. Without even asking for Margaret's advice he ordered a bottle of the best champagne and her heart now started to thump with apprehension. When the shallow champagne glasses had been filled and the glistening liquid had revealed its enticement, the butler handed each of them a menu card to enable them to choose a starter. Percival asked her briefly if a salmon dish would suit her but said it in such a way that she could hardly refuse.

"Well, he said, this is the moment I have been waiting for since we met." His eyes were gleaming with the self-induced assurance that Margaret would be overjoyed by the great announcement he was about to make. His right hand was now reaching down very slowly into his trouser pocket to dramatic effect …

At that very moment, two men, one stout and slightly red-faced, the other tall and disdainful accompanied by a young woman who could have been the daughter of one of them but seeing her extravagant outfit and jewellery was obviously there for show, strode up to Margaret's and Percival's table from behind Percival and the stout one thumped him on the back reasonably vigorously making the recipient start.

"What the …?" but turning round his very puzzled but annoyed expression changed instantaneously to one of kindness tempered with a good dose of ingratiation."Oh Charles, what a pleasure seeing you. May I introduce you to Margaret?"

Margaret stood up to shake the man's hand but he simply nodded to her, took Percival by the arm and led him to a table at some distance from Margaret. She heard the start of the phrase, "Henry and I were just discussing your fabulous investment plan and we think that …" and here it became garbled.

So Percival was just one of a crowd of high flying businessmen who had no room for ordinary human relations and effectively were very good at treating ordinary people like dirt. So Margaret was left high and dry. The waiter who had witnessed the scene came up to her and kindly asked her if he could help. "Can I pour you another glass of champagne …?"

All this time Percival had not even turned his head in her direction and seemed to be as engrossed as the other two men in the highly important proceedings. She looked across at the young woman and turning in her direction the latter just shrugged her shoulders as if what was happening was to her just the way things were. But not to Margaret. Oh no! Without hesitation she asked the waiter if he could arrange a taxi for her and five minutes later at his behest she made her way to the vestibule where she was met by the taxi driver. Following her mood of sheer anger and shock at Percival's behaviour as she now saw that she hardly existed for him except in the same way as the young lady who accompanied the two rude businessmen, she now burst out laughing and realized that she had escaped, at least temporarily, from a very embarrassing situation. When she reached home the telephone was already ringing. She ignored it. She let it ring yet another time but the third time she picked up the receiver and feigning to yawn, but only slightly of course, she said faintly but with a note of boredom hardly concealed. "Margaret Sturge here, can I help you?"

There was no real reply, just a sort of sound that could have been an "er…er…er" but from a male throat. "Sorry, this is a very bad line. Could you call me back tomorrow? Thank you." She rubbed her hands gleefully knowing however that she was not going to escape so easily.

Effectively, five minutes later Percival had pulled himself together and was able to bluster. "Margaret, I really am terribly sorry about this evening but I could not get out of the discussion with Neville Van der Wiel. It is of the utmost importance for our future finances."

"How dare he say 'our' finances?" thought Margaret. "Listen Percival, I do not want to hear that now. I'm tired and need to sleep. I am free tomorrow morning until 11, so come here before or telephone again. Goodnight." With that she slammed down the receiver then took it off its hook. She felt quite flushed and knew she would have to calm down to enable her to sleep. It was now close on 11 p.m. She suddenly now remembered that Alexandre would be flying into Croydon the next morning and that she had been looking forward to their meeting, even more than she would admit to herself. He would probably expect her to be at the airport to meet her. What should she do?

She knew in her innermost being that she had to tell Percival that their friendship was at an end. She could not continue telling mistruths to him and even half truths to herself for she realized now that for want of anyone better she had tolerated his misogyny to a much greater extent than she should have. In fact, she was now quite ready to be honest with herself. She had quite simply made use of him to keep loneliness at bay but then she convinced herself that he also was making use of her as a sort of status symbol. She was nice to have at his side especially in the company of colleagues and partners. Well, how could she resolve the issue?

She closed her eyes and without any warning whatsoever the image of a person holding a sword flashed across her line of vision, which in her childhood she would have called a dreaming picture. She opened her eyes wondering whether she had been asleep or not and what could have explained such a dream which she was unable to associate with any event in her life. She briefly noted from the clock on the wall that it was 11.15 p.m. She decided she would tell Alexandre about the dreaming picture. He would certainly not laugh at her. Margaret then did her evening ablutions, made herself a herbal tea, read a few articles in the Times while propped up against her pillows in her bed sipping her drink and trying to allow her limbs to go limp to enable her to sleep.

CHAPTER 7

It was now 7.30 on Monday morning. Margaret knew that Alexandre would be arriving at Croydon in the Farmann sometime between 11 a.m. and 11.30. Aeroplane flying times were not precise at that time and an adverse wind could make quite a difference even over a distance of a little more that 250 miles. However, she wanted to be at the airport no later than 12 midday as the pilot's debriefing process would take nearly an hour even in the most optimistic of circumstances.

She quickly washed and ate some cornflakes with fresh milk to be followed by egg and bacon but was unable to eat much of the latter. She felt quite on tenterhooks and was not looking forward at all, no, not at all, to Percival's visit or call. She was more or less certain he would come in person as she knew how his mind functioned. He presumed that by his very presence he could resolve any situation so Margaret with much difficulty tried to put herself in his place. He would certainly apologize for his evening's disastrous performance but would just as certainly find it of little importance and would want to behave as if nothing had happened. She knew that it was now or never that she had to cut the Gordian Knot of their relationship. No sooner had she reached this stage in her train of thought than she heard the powerful vroom vroom of Percival's car outside. He could not but emphasize his arrival to all and sundry but especially to Margaret and as of late her heart fell into her boots.

She greeted him with a half smile, but he, as she might have expected had a beaming, self-satisfied expression – a wide smile, eyes shining with anticipation. "Oh my God, thought she, I've got to get through this as if it's a piece of theatre." She gritted her teeth while turning her head and decided - damn it – that she would try to play a part, to be another person, not herself. She momentarily thought of Alexandre and suddenly got her inspiration from some fleeting notion that passed through her head like a strike of lightning. In this, once more, a dreaming picture, she was riding a horse and rushing towards a person who was in difficulty of some sort and a vision of Alexandre flashed across her mind, all of this simultaneously. How could that be?

When she turned round again to face Percival she was almost literally a different person. She faced him and from her dull half smile there now emanated an expression of complete confidence and candour. Percival, who had arrived full of himself was now faced with a being that, apart from her outward appearance, he was unable to place. He gazed at her and his jaw dropped. There was something he could not understand. She held his gaze with absolute mastery.

"Percival, as I said on the phone I have very little time. I have two visits to make this morning." She was giving nothing away whatsoever. "Just forget the minor incident last night. I have already forgotten about it. Now then, what is the urgency?" She raised a brow and looked at him steadily, smiling a sort of smile that an employer might deign to offer a new employee to show that the latter could have trust in him as long as he or she kept to the rules …

He was completely thrown off guard. Things had been so easy for him until now. He was, or had been, the boss and he had imagined that he could, within certain limits, do and say what he wanted. She would always be there to look up to him and to more or less keep her opinions to herself. What was happening? He now opened his mouth but nothing would escape his lips. He was in fact speechless.

"I'll make you a coffee, Percival. But how nice of you to come here!" This was not Margaret talking at all but how jubilant she felt in reciting what one could take to be the simple lines of some play. She then outlined what nursing tasks she had to fulfill that very morning. The tasks she mentioned were real but were not on her agenda until later in the afternoon. She uttered her words with such studied sincerity that Percival could only listen. It was as if their roles had been exchanged which was now exactly what Margaret was seeking. It was true, she no longer considered him with discouragement but with a sort of disdain that frankly, she decided, he certainly deserved. Strange, how that mysterious flash had given her instantaneous confidence in herself.

Percival was gathering himself together. He said somewhat hesitatingly. "We-ell, I was wondering whether we could dine again sometime soon, say, tomorrow …?" He had found his words, just, but could not bring himself to talk about the ring.

"Sorry, Percival, not tomorrow but I'm sure you can manage Friday. Come and fetch me at about 8 p.m. That would be splendid. Now if you've finished your coffee, I must be off." Her hazelnut eyes were gleaming with a new-found expression, one could say, almost of joy.

Percival could say nothing but, "yes, certainly at 8." He put his coffee cup down on the table and grasping his coat he shuffled more than walked to the door.

Margaret heard the Velox start up and sputter away but without the familiar vroom. "Aha" she thought.

However she had no way of knowing that Percival had simply hidden his car further up the street down a turning and was now watching the entrance to her flat in Moreton Road from behind a heavy goods vehicle.

He saw her descend the steps of the former Victorian semi-detached house, now divided into flats, saunter apparently happily down the sloping road and off left to the station where he imagined she would catch the bus to wherever. He started up his car and eased it down the road until he came to the more important thoroughfare where he had seen Margaret turn. Ah, there she was now walking jauntily under the bridge of South Croydon station and towards the bus stop a little further away. As it happened a bus came to a halt at the stop just a couple of minutes after she arrived there. She jumped on board and he saw her climb to the upper deck. The bus headed west. Where was she going?

"That's strange, he thought, the bus seems to be going in the direction of Croydon Airport. She didn't say she was going to Paris. I'm sure she said she had some nursing visits to make." His eyes narrowed and had anyone seen him they would have seen the anger that was starting to appear on his face. His expression hardened as he saw Margaret descend from the bus and start to walk crisply in the direction indeed of the airport. He kept well out of sight and of earshot knowing too well she would recognize the sound of the engine. He parked the car in front of a pub very nearby and set off on foot in the direction she had taken.

He was not mistaken. The airport with its still unimpressive silhouette (not to be mistaken for the lovely building that was to be completed in a few years' time) came into view as he saw his would-be wife disappear into the edifice. "Odd, could she have a patient at that place? – seems doubtful."

The inside of the building had many nooks and crannies as it had been built fairly hurriedly after WW1 to cope with the new era of air travel so Percival was able to keep out of sight while pretending to look at the advertisements for travel by air to Paris and Brussels. There was nobody about. Suddenly he heard voices coming from behind a closed door quite near. He moved closer and leaning on the counter of some company or other was able to identify the tone of voice of Margaret though not what she said and also a man's voice and he distinctly heard the voice say "Margaret" several times. His blood was beginning to boil when suddenly the door opened and out stepped Margaret beaming with apparent happiness followed by a man in the uniform of a pilot. He shifted his position so as to be out of sight and then suddenly he remembered where he had already seen the man – it was at Weybridge for the amateur motor racing championship and he was the man who had won the competition with that devilish little Morgan –Uh! He then noticed on the counter that the room was occupied by that aeroplane company or airline, yes, that was it, airline, called Daimler Airways and he remembered that Margaret had flown to Paris in a biplane from the same airline. So that was what it was all about. She had a lover. Well, neither he nor she would get away with it like that.

Percival saw that they were now making for the Aerodrome Hotel that was also a restaurant, just a few paces away. He followed them and when they had been led into the restaurant itself he asked at the reception desk if he could use the phone and left some change for the call. If anyone had seen him making the call they would have noticed that he was extremely agitated with his eyes blazing a sort of hatred. He apparently barked a few orders into the mouthpiece and then banged down the receiver before slouching into the bar from where he could keep an eye on the couple through a wide curtained glass-paned separator section. He saw they were sitting face to face with eyes for no-one else. He could now see the very great difference between Margaret's way of looking at that man she was with and the way she looked at him. He could not countenance it.

30 minutes later a taxi drove up to the entrance of the restaurant and two burly men got out. Percival went to meet them and asked them to walk through the restaurant and take a good look at Margaret and the man she was with. They could pretend they were lost so they could walk past the couple twice. This they did and hardly aroused the attention of Margaret and Alexandre, deep in conversation.

"Now what boss?" said the taller, darker, more villainous-looking of the two.

"I want you, George, to follow the woman and tell me when she is alone in her flat. There's a phone booth not far from where she lives. You, Charlie, can follow the man. See where he lives." If I tell you she's the woman I mean to marry, you will understand, I think. But on the other hand, don't think, just do as I say. Is that clear?"

"Yes, Boss," they said in unison.

CHAPTER 8

Margaret and Alexandre, seated comfortably in the large dining room and seemingly to any beholder very happy to be with each other, had hardly noticed the two men walking one way and then the other although Alexandre had effectively for a fleeting moment found their behavior odd. That impression had very quickly disappeared however as their conversation had not been interrupted in any way. They continued eating their roast meat contentedly while sipping a pleasant burgundy.

Margaret suddenly remembered her 'dreaming picture' of the night before and also remembered that she had noted the time, 11.15 p.m. "Alexandre, her tone of voice had changed as her forehead creased, something very strange happened to me last night." She looked up into his eyes seeking either incredulity or mystification in his look but he concentrated his gaze on her eyes and showed nothing out of the ordinary in his expression, just an invitation by his smile for her to continue. "I was relaxing in my armchair last night after an awful evening with Percival when a horseman with a sword passed before my eyes. He seemed real and I can't get the image out of my head."

"What time did you say, Margaret?"

"At a quarter past eleven exactly. I noted it."

"Well, as you say, extraordinary, because I had just settled into my bed in the hotel near Le Bourget, must have been around that time, when a very indistinct woman wearing a long garment stood with her back to me looking at something that seemed to be clinking. Above all, I remember the clinking noise. I assumed I had fallen asleep without knowing it and that it was some sort of instantaneous bad dream. What does it mean? We must have something in common, one with the other, to have had the same or similar dream, or dreaming picture as you put it, at the same time."

"Yes, and the fact that we both have the impression of knowing one another. It is very peculiar."

"Yes, I agree, nodded Alexandre, very odd, but I think we must keep our feet well on the ground and not get carried away. There is certainly a logical explanation. If we're not careful we'll start believing that we knew each other in another life …"

"I suppose you're right, but it's strange how I feel so calm, reassured and confident when I'm with you and yet we have only seen each other a handful of times. I feel as if I have known you a long time."

Alexandre reached out and gently took Margaret's hand in his own and declared while gazing into her eyes. "I'm the same. I feel, to go one step further, that we belong to each other. That cannot be so - because, even though we spent a night together –and that was, well, really great – you could say that that night was the normal sensual beginning of any affair. I'm sorry, I'm not putting it very delicately. What I'm trying to say is that we did not say that we would love each other for always, but now, well now, I feel without even saying it that I would be lost without you. Oh my God, what am I saying?" He was visibly flustered.

Margaret squeezed his hand while reaching out and taking his other hand in hers. "That's lovely what you are saying. I feel exactly the same. I feel quite strongly that we are really attached to each other. So what's the next move? – and of course there is one big problem and that's Percival. He will do everything he can to keep me in his orbit, so to speak."

"Now then, is there anything you want to do this afternoon? I'm not due to fly back to Paris until tomorrow so I have time."

"Well actually, I have a few visits to make, so could we see each other tonight? Do you know what I'd love to do? I haven't got one of these new-fangled radios –they're very expensive – but I was in a department store the other day and there is a special department for these things and I heard some absolutely incredible modern music, called jazz. They were playing gramophone records, I think they call them, and some music from a band called the Red Hot Peppers of all things was being played and I would just love to hear it again. I see in the paper that there's a dance hall in London where you hear this sort of music. Could we go there this evening? We could take a taxi. What do you think."

"Sounds a great idea. Yes, I too like this modern music and would love to hear it. Can you dance there? That would be good if we could practice a little dancing – not that I'm a good dancer but I would like to try."

"Right, Alexandre, I'll get the details and we could meet at say, 8 this evening. A good central place in Croydon to meet would be East Croydon station. We could meet at the ticket office …. Would 8.30 be OK?"

He nodded. "That's settled then. I'll pay and we'll be off. I haven't got the car here today – I really must find a garage somewhere to keep it. At the moment it's still at Weybridge where I like to do a little racing as you well know."

They left the restaurant not quite holding hands but at least rubbing shoulders. They did not of course notice the shadows following them.

CHAPTER 9

Each of them was followed by Percival's henchmen, Margaret to her first nursing call and Alexandre to his flat. When they phoned their boss he told them to take it in turns to follow Margaret and to leave the man. When she would eventually reach her own flat he was determined to knock on her door a few minutes afterwards. His mood had changed. He was now once again the single-minded man that would not take "No" for an answer. He had a rather nasty, cruel expression on his face which went white with anger and he was clenching his fists.

At around 4 p.m. the taller but shadier-looking bootlicker got in touch with his "employer" with the news that Margaret had indeed entered her flat in Moreton Rd. He was told to leave it at that and contact him the next day. Percival then mounted into his powerful machine and drew up in front of the flat some 15 minutes later. He had waited in one of the offices he owned dotted about the London area, this one in Croydon, from where he carried out his, what could only be called, dubious transactions. Each office was registered under a different name, each one had a secretary who had no idea of the nature of his doings and who simply typed his letters and answered the telephone. He had sent the Croydon secretary home early to be alone in the office when either George or Charlie phoned him. He had been perusing some financial documents while waiting, making calls to various collaborators in whatever line of business he was engaged – one could only guess – and had eventually taken a bottle of scotch from inside a locked drawer and had been about to pour himself a glass when he thought better of it and replaced the bottle and glass in the drawer. It would not do for Margaret to smell his breath.

So, 15 minutes later he climbed the ten or so steps to the entrance of the house which had been divided into 3 flats and rang the doorbell marked Miss Sturge. There was no intercom system available to ordinary people at that time so Margaret on hearing the bell looked down from her bedroom window and was horrified to see Percival there. What should she do? He was the last person she wished to see at that moment. "Keep calm, put on your most relaxed expression and look pleased to see him. Luckily, I haven't started making up yet." She went slowly down the stairs and opened the door. "Oh, how nice to see you, Percival. I didn't expect to see you before Friday."

She could see he was in a villainous mood. His mouth was tight and his eyes glowering but even so, he did not really know or had forgotten what he had to say. "Margaret, I feel very strongly about you, you must know that, and I will do all in my power to persuade you to be my wife …"

"Wow, Percival, you have taken my breath away. I know you like me, as I like you, but to me we are friends and we spend some pleasurable times together but from there to becoming your wife, I would never have imagined that." She emphasized the last phrase with the word "that" especially accentuated. "Won't you come in for a moment? I have an important meeting to attend concerning my medical laboratory work tomorrow morning in Reading so I musn't be late for my train from London a little later on," she lied through her teeth but all the time managing an engaging smile. She gave a very convincing performance and Percival, had he not been witness to the late morning's events at the aerodrome, would have been taken in.

However, he acquiesced saying, "no, if you are in a hurry we will see each other on Friday as arranged." In fact his former self-assurance in her company had evaporated and he felt on the back foot but this in no way put paid to his determination to take his revenge on that pilot. Malicious plans were now forming in his head.

"So you will come and pick me up on Friday? Have you anything planned? Personally, I shan't want to eat a heavy meal and I fancy hearing some good music or maybe watching a ballet or going to the opera or something similar. Could that be arranged? I will leave the choice to you." All this she said on a playful tone. She did not want to give him the opportunity of placing that terrible jewel case in front of her again. But she was now feeling that things were getting a bit out of hand and at this moment she would have liked to have been one of those persons who could speak their minds without fearing the consequences. He also played the game and gave the impression of being empathetic when in fact he was in a state of what could only be described as hate towards that pilot man and now even towards Margaret.

He moved slowly in the direction of the door giving Margaret a wan smile although he could not hide a momentary grimace which did not escape her. She vaguely wondered why. He slipped out leaving Margaret breathing heavily and leaning against the door post. She knew that Percival would have to exit her life. But how?

She now had an hour to get herself ready and walk to East Croydon station. A good walk even in town often did a great deal to evacuate stress and anxiety and she knew that once she was with Alexandre she would once again feel relaxed and ready to tackle any situation. Half an hour later she closed the door behind her. Her makeup was basic- hardly any lipstick and only a slight touch of mascara. She wore very little perfume, just a little eau-de-cologne behind the ears. She hardly even needed that - she practically never perspired - and anyone in close proximity to her would just sense an agreeable sort of garden fragrance. Alexandre had of course noticed the refined, deliciously natural odour that emanated from her being from their very first real meeting which dated from her flight in the Farmann piloted by him.

Alexandre was there at the station as arranged and in next to no time had hailed a taxi and they were on their way to the capital. They had not of course noticed the Velox belonging to Percival cruising almost out of sight behind them. The venue that Alexandre had discovered was in Archer Street in South West London where several theatres and night clubs were situated. It was a jazz club, the Memphis, that had opened just a few weeks before and organized the visits of American jazz bands and a few British ones.

"Sorry, Margaret, but we will not be hearing Jelly Roll Morton. From what I have heard he has never played in London but we will be hearing Sidney Bechet who is nearly as good. However let's get seated, have a bite to eat while waiting for the musicians. Look, there's a good dance floor here." Well-dressed people were beginning to arrive and waiters were buzzing about doing what waiters do. They ordered a fish dish and sipped white wine and chatted about this and that while waiting for the musicians to take their places. After some thirty minutes or so Sidney Bechet and his band found their places behind their instruments and started tuning up before Sidney Bechet himself stood up in front of the microphone and in his wonderful southern American drawl announced the names of the musicians who accordingly rose and bowed in turn and then the titles of the first two pieces that they intended to play. The first was Summertime that many people in the room had already heard one way or another and there was an instant hush as the band got underway.

All this time Percival, who had seen from his car where the two had entered, had come into the restaurant-cum-dance hall and after identifying his preys found a seat hidden somewhat in the shadows and ordered a drink. He watched them with great attention. They were holding hands across the table and gazing into each other's eyes or so it seemed. His blood started to boil and his eyes blazed with anger. She had no business to be with that – what ? driver of a flying paper-like contraption? That was no job. It was just a way of passing the time, that's right , a pastime. Could be dangerous, it's true but just a way of attracting attention and especially female attention and apparently it had worked very well because there he was stealing his wife-to-be. He could stand it no more. He went to reception, asked to use the phone and ordered George and Charlie to come to the jazz club and follow the couple when they eventually left after their evening's entertainment. He was now in a terrible state and vowed to make them pay for it – well, not so much Margaret but that pilot fellow.

CHAPTER 10

Margaret and Alexandre had never in their lives felt so close to a member of the opposite sex. They chatted, listened intently to the music and when a Blues was played they danced slowly and in perfect unison together. They even managed to dance what they discovered to be swing and also boogie-woogie. They soon got the hang of it by watching other people and thanks to the helping hand of a nice, well-dressed man for Margaret and his partner for Alexandre. Towards 1 a.m. they decided to return to Croydon so arranged for a taxi. On the way back Alexandre asked Margaret if she would care to spend the night at his place but after she explained that she would prefer to return to her own flat for strictly feminine reasons they broke up, the taxi dropping Alexandre off first, then Margaret. They kissed each other very passionately on the way so Alexandre was in no way put out by her explanation.

Of course they had not noticed – and why should they? – the Ford model T following the taxi at a certain distance. However, Percival's two henchmen could not understand why the man was being dropped off unaccompanied. They began to think that their boss had made a miscalculation in relation to the couple but they noted the address and then followed the taxi to Margaret's place. Percival was woken from his booze-laden sleep at about 2 a.m.by George's call.

"What do you want us to do now Boss?" asked George when he had recounted the evening's proceedings.

"Nothing for the moment. I will call you tomorrow morning. I've got to think." He came to the conclusion that the only thing he could do to prevent that man from taking her from him was to separate them, but how? But it was strange that that pilot man had not stayed the night at Margaret's place. Maybe he was reading too much into it. But, no, seeing them gazing at each other and dancing together made him absolutely certain that there was something between them. He would work something out.

The next morning, in spite of a restless night, he got up early and made for Alexandre's flat as indicated by his virtual servants. He rang the bell and after several minutes a sleepy looking Alexandre raised the sash window giving onto the entrance and asked who it was. "Sorry, do I know you?"

"Yes, you certainly do. Please can I come in?" asked Percival on a tone that expected no refusal.

"Well, I suppose you can. Let me put on my dressing gown first and I'll open the door."

Two minutes later he was face to face with a suit and tie clad man of average build, good looking in a conventional way but with a terrible scowl on his face. "Come in, let me see, I believe I have seen you somewhere but I do not recall where …?

"Well, I'll tell you. You made me lose my bet at Weybridge a little while ago with your tinpot Morgan. That's where you saw me – and more to the point, I was with my wife-to-be Margaret who it seems has been taken in by your heroic wartime stories."

"Hey, wait a minute, you burst in here and I don't even know who you are. You wouldn't be a man called Percival by any chance (he pronounced Percival by heavily emphasizing the "al" which did not appear to please him)?

"I certainly am. You have been trying to steal Margaret, my wife-to-be from me, and I do not take kindly to that in the slightest degree. It was only going to be a matter of time before we got married until you came along." His eyes were blazing with anger although he stopped himself from shouting but only just."She has practically promised to marry me." A perfect lie but one that was meant to throw the doubt in Alexandre's mind. It did to some extent but when he remembered her encouraging, consoling words and her hands in his all doubt flew out of the window.

"Well listen dear Mr, I'm sorry I didn't catch your surname …"

"Phelps is my name."

"Right, Mr Phelps, I think you ought to have it out with Margaret as to what the two of you want. If she really wants to espouse you it's not for me to interfere but I really had no idea things were so advanced between you."

Alexandre closed his eyes briefly, clenching his teeth in sheer consternation. He did indeed feel uneasy and unhappy as if there was now a huge question mark placed behind their wonderfully lived encounters, hidden from view for the moment but ready to slide out and make itself visible. "A question, Mr Phelps, he said slowly with his voice descending in pitch on the word 'question' but ascending on the word 'Phelps', to mark his outright dubiousness in respect of Percival's behavior, how did you know I lived just here in Firtree Lane?"

"Well … I… happened to be just passing when I saw you enter this building. You may not know it but I was at Croydon Aerodrome yesterday to get information on a flight to Germany when I saw you in the company of Margaret. I assumed, naturally enough, he lied through his teeth, that you had met by accident but when I saw you both in the restaurant I was left in little doubt. You are trying to wrest her from the love, care and attention I bestow on her."

"What a liar," thought Alexandre but instead of saying exactly what he thought he exclaimed slowly and with much emphasis. "But why were you driving up Firtree Lane as it is plainly marked as being a cul-de-sac? The railway cuts it in two …"

"I was, well … yes, I was deep in thought at that moment and didn't notice the sign." Even a child could have seen it was a blatant untruth he had spoken especially as his face reddened and had twisted itself into a grotesque smile.

"As I said, I do not want to get in the way of any legitimate (he almost spat out the latter word to Percival) relationship between two people but as I said, I think you ought to get things straight with Miss Sturge before we do anything rash. She has never spoken ill of you, he half lied, so maybe you are speaking the truth. I will await news from her. In the meantime, I have to get ready for work. I have a flight this afternoon, so I will await a word from Miss Sturge. Good day, Mr Phelps" and ushering Percival to the door he closed it firmly but not noisily behind him.

Alexandre rightly thought that it would not get him (and Margaret) anywhere by phoning her and kicking up a huge row. He had been used to conflictual relationships during his service in the *armée de l'air* (French air force) during the war. He had always found that although he often wished to speak his mind it was always best to let the opponent say what he had to say and then when he (always "he") had quietened down he would invariably come back to him and a civilized discussion would take place leading the way to a solution acceptable to both. This very often happened after raids on enemy positions when one or other of the pilots would accuse his comrade(s) of carrying out unduly risky operations or on the contrary of not having the guts to strike in such or such a way.

This was not the present position and in fact even though he found Percival obnoxious he could not but feel that Margaret must have let him feel the benefit of the doubt in some way and had been, well not exactly dishonest with him but had let him swim in a sort of positive torpor that had made the man feel he would win her hand in the end. This made Alexandre reflect quite deeply and automatically took on Margaret's possible arguments. She was lonely, had little contact with her family or at least never talked of them and Percival was her chance of seeing Life a little more and his lifestyle offered something out of the ordinary – his fast, luxurious car, his lavish way of dining. As long as he left her in peace as much as possible she did not object too much to being with him.

"Hey, wait a minute, *mon ami*, you have your own point of view. Think about it without coming to any hasty conclusion and wait until you see Margaret again when you can discuss it." "OK chief", he uttered to himself and then started laughing out loud. Anyone listening would have thought him completely crazy!

CHAPTER 11

Margaret, of course, had no idea what Percival had been up to. Had she known she would have been completely at a loss to know what to do. She realized that although she had tried to explain to Alexandre the relationship she had with Percival she saw now that he would see her position as being ambivalent. She was starting to feel desperate but saw no easy way out.

It was just then as these uneasy thoughts were flowing through her mind or rather dwelling therein that she heard a fairly powerful car drawing up outside. She pulled the curtain back and saw a vehicle that she thought she might have already seen somewhere. She saw that there were two swarthy individuals inside one of whom was climbing out of his vehicle.

She broke out into a sweat, drew her brows together and squeezed her eyes shut for a brief moment. She knew inside of her that this was not a moment that was going to be easy and also guessed rather than knew that it was to do with Alexandre. During this short but almost agonizing interlude she could hear the footsteps approaching the door and then the clang of the bell which was not electric but mechanically wound so fairly noisy. This was designed to be heard even when the occupant of the flat was at the southern side overlooking the railway.

However, she took her courage in both hands and went downstairs to open the door. Opening the door she saw before her an almost expressionless individual – black hair, sturdily built, of medium height, dark coat, roundish but hard face and unsmiling.

"Mrs Sturge, I believe?"

"Yes, what can I do for you?"

"Mr Phelps would like a word with you, if you have half an hour or so. We will take you there."

"Hey, but wait a moment, I am about to visit an elderly patient who needs her daily care. I'm afraid I cannot come for the moment. Tell Per…, Mr Phelp that I will go to see him later. I'm sorry."

"Well we are even more sorry, came the reply in a dead pan voice, he said you were to come at any price. So follow me, please."

She made to close the door but his foot was already in place and in spite of her struggling the man had little trouble entering the hallway shared by the three occupants of the building. "Just get your coat and handbag please.

She saw she had no option and did not want to cause a huge scandal in that tightly-knit community of lodgers. She obediently climbed the stairs and fetched her belongings, a light spring coat and her handbag, and descended again. Her heart was pounding and she was, let's face it, a little apprehensive seeing the aspect of the man. Many thoughts were racing through her head – her patient, how would she let them know she would be late, she, who was never late and also questions focused on Percival. What on earth was his work if he had two great louts as employees? She was now starting, frankly, to feel decidedly scared.

The man kept close to her to make sure, she presumed, that she would not dart away or call for help from someone. She climbed into the back of a large Vauxhall 30-98, similar to Percival's Velox but larger and more plush. She could not help but wonder again. "What on earth does Percival do for a living?" She started to have doubts. They eventually arrived in the West End where Percival had his luxury flat. The two men now got out of the car and accompanied her to the door of the flat.

It was not Percival himself who opened the door but a maid servant, very pretty but with a docile expression – probably chosen by Percival for her submissiveness, thought Margaret. Her panic was over but she was now feeling distinctly angry. How dare he kidnap her like that without even a 'by your leave'. She was ushered into the vestibule and she could see at a glance that the flat was vast. It was in fact what would later be called an apartment suite – luxury everywhere – but to Margaret and her modest tastes it was almost obscene. One of the men, apparently called Charlie, stayed by her side while the other strode off, chest held high and almost arrogantly, to God knows where, thought

Margaret. She was kept waiting some two or three minutes and she was quite surprised to see that the other man, George, had disappeared and she could see why. The door through which she had just come looked impregnable so she just had to wait.

So now the great Percival came in looking at one and the same time falsely apologetic and very pleased with himself.

"Now, my dear Margaret won't you come in and have something to drink, a martini, vodka orange ..., anything you wish,"

"Look, Percival, I'm not too pleased at what has happened. I have, or had, an appointment with an elderly patient and I was forcibly accompanied here by two very suspicious characters. Are they your employees ...?"

"I'm sorry, Margaret, he said sheepishly but not very convincingly, but you know what I feel for you. I want you to be my wife and you have more or less agreed to that seeing the way we have been together these last few weeks. I have the impression you were happy in my company. Is that not so?"

"I have not been unhappy in your company, Percival, but that's a long way from saying that I was ready to marry you. In any case there is no question of marrying anyone for the moment. I wish to be freed and allowed to carry out my profession."

"Listen Margaret, I'm a man of principle (yes, but what principles? thought Margaret) and as a man also of determination and of getting things done, I want this sorted out rather quickly. I know about this pilot fellow, you know, and you ought to know you cannot have it both ways."Margaret was more than surprised at this revelation and it came to her as a shock. She now understood the presence of the two doubtful-looking individuals. They were mercenaries in the pay of Percival. He was now looking rather grim and almost aggressive but he changed his posture almost instantaneously to one of supplication and mock benevolence. "In fact, he said on a tone of triumphalism, I will have to have it out with him one way or another, like having a duel as in former centuries." The last phrase caught Margaret off guard as suddenly inexplicable images flashed across her mind and she had to sit down and hold her forehead as though she had a terrible headache.

"This won't do, she thought, stood up again and felt strangely enough, somehow invigorated by the strange sensation she had just experienced. She now felt perfectly equal to this abject person before her and declared defiantly and persuasively. Well why not do as they did in years gone by. You both have sports cars. Why not have a race and the winner will have the option of asking for my hand. But I am not obliged to accept the winner's proposal. The loser, on the other hand, will have to withdraw and I will part company with them. This will have to be set out in writing and signed by both competitors." As the last exclamation poured from her lips her eyes blazed with fury and she stood up tall to face Percival and stared him straight in the eye.

He looked flabbergasted for a few seconds having never seen her like that but soon recovered his composure. There was a short silence in which presumably he was going through the pros and cons of the suggestion. "I agree to your proposal but this 'duel', he said flippantly, will be of my choosing. That is to say, it will be me who decides the course and distance."

It was obvious that he thought the pilot man had not a chance on a course that was a relatively straight road from say Purley in Surrey to Brighton which was the itinerary he had in mind. His own vehicle was far more powerful and with great acceleration compared to other cars of the day and especially compared to the little Morgan. Margaret, on the other hand thought that Alexandre had a very good chance of beating him and had proved his superior handling of a racing car at Weybridge. She was confident in his ability but unfortunately she had not taken into account the two criteria of engine power and the lack of tight bends along the route. If she had known a little more about these basic points she would never have suggested the contest but there was in fact more to it than that. She had an intuitive feeling that it was somehow ordained that Alexandre would be the winner. She had no idea why she thought along those lines but that strange, almost divine sensation she had experienced a few minutes before had inculcated in her mind the absolute certainty of the outcome.

"In the meantime, Margaret, he continued, you will have to stay here under the eyes of Charlie and George and you will be well looked after by Charlotte, the French maid. She cooks well. You will phone that pilot fellow as soon as possible. He said he was flying to Paris this afternoon – yes, I saw him earlier today – (Margaret started when she heard this latter statement) so you will be able to do that tomorrow morning. I allow you to phone your employers, the hospital and patients to tell them you are momentarily ill. But do not be tempted to phone the police or friends. My employees will be keeping an eye on you. You will tell your friend that he is to stay at his home to wait for one of my men to hand him details of the course. He will have a few hours to study it and get his pathetic automobile ready for the race. He spat out the last few words with such utter contempt. I will of course draw up two copies of the racing agreement with its terms and conditions which we will both sign before you at the start of the race. You will be able to observe the event from the 30-98." With that he left the room without a further word but looking thoroughly disgruntled.

Margaret had nothing more to do now than just wait and hope that things would pan out positively. She asked the less intimidating of the two so-called employees the whereabouts of the bathroom to tidy up a little and the library because time was necessarily going to drag.

CHAPTER 12

The morning arrived at last. Margaret had been left entirely alone in the guest room all night after the very tasty meal, it should be admitted, prepared by Charlotte.

A breakfast was given to her in her bed but she ate very little as she was now on edge with the prospect of having to tell Alexandre very shortly what was in store for him. It was frankly a very distressing situation and one that was criminal in the eyes of the law but she knew she had no hope of redressing the present state of affairs, for Percival, in spite of all this heavy-handed treatment would almost certainly have the last say and she was now almost certain that he had two activities – one above board (finance?) and the other, probably more lucrative, hiding behind this smokescreen of professional propriety (arms dealer or something of the sort?). In any case he would be able to prove that she was fully consenting. Remember, there were two witnesses, Charlie and George, who would have no scruples about committing perjury. She knew that she had to stay quiet and pretend to go along with it.

She spent the 2 or 3 hours she had to wait before phoning Alexandre as best she could pacing around the large living room, sometimes endeavouring to read a newspaper that had been placed on a table but all the time deep in thought trying not to imagine what would happen if Percival happened to win the race. She still did not realize that if the race were to have been a properly organized event the bookies would have set the odds heavily against Alexandre.

It was now coming up to 1 p.m. and she guessed that Alexandre would have arrived at his flat feeling quite exhausted after his flight with the responsibility it involved of ensuring the safety of twelve passengers and the onboard stewardess. A few years later he would have piloted an aircraft that was better equipped and more comfortable for the pilots than the Goliath he captained – above all the cockpit would have been sealed in and perhaps even heated by the engines – there would be no wind rushing through his hair!

She called the switchboard and asked for his number; Croydon 5405, was put through and heard the ring tone of Alexandre's phone. It kept ringing and she was about to abandon the attempt when he unhooked his phone.

"Hello, Croydon 5405, who's calling?"

"It's me, Margaret. I can't say much as I'm at Percival's home and there are people listening to what I say. I am not free. I cannot leave until you agree to a plan of Percival's that more or less decides who is to marry me – him or you. I really am sorry, Alexandre, I have really made a terrible mess-up of the whole thing …"

Alexandre was silent although she could hear his heavy breathing through the wire. He said but not unkindly. "Well perhaps you had better tell me what this great plan is so that I can see whether it's feasible or not. I'm not blaming you Margaret. I hope you're alright and not under any threat or anything."

"I'm alright, Alexandre, but I am housebound here. I cannot move until you agree to this plan of his which is a race between you and him, between your Morgan and his Velox from Purley near Croydon, I believe, to Brighton. What is more, he has planned it for tomorrow. Even if you agree, can you possibly take part in such a venture? I'm so sorry for all this but I think it's the only way I can escape from his clutches." She whispered the last words as one of the men moved menacingly nearer.

"Margaret, you have got embroiled in all this through no fault of your own. He's a real tyrant and he is committing a criminal offence keeping you there under duress. I do not want to exacerbate the problem by bringing in the police at this point because I know the sort of person he is. He will be able to pull strings in the right places and you will suffer from it. I will take up his challenge although you surely know that his vehicle is so much more powerful than mine so my chances of winning on straight stretches like the Brighton road cannot be more that 25% but I will do all I can. We'll see what happens afterwards. I'm afraid we'll just have to play his game for the moment. I will see what I can do to get the Morgan in fighting shape. I'll fiddle with the carburetor, get the tyres as hard as possible, oil the chain and then I'll have a good look at large scale road maps of the route where I might possibly have the edge on him. I'm not too optimistic but you never know … What time did you say the so-called race will begin?"

"Actually I didn't say but you will be receiving instructions from one of his men in an envelope this evening. He will be coming to your place. He seems to know everything about you."

Alexandre seemed to hear or see a question mark in her observation and replied, "I had a visit from your Percival character. I think he's got very big personal problems. He winced as he said this and added. I would not like to think of you trapped in his impregnable castle. He almost snapped out this last phrase. We'll find a way out of it but first just give him the impression you agree that whoever wins the race wins your hand. Try to be convincing. Say you've thought it over and make him think it's a reasonable proposition. Don't forget he's looking at it like a sort of business affair. He's attracted to you – that's true – but you can tell by the way he's dealing with it, in a Mafioso way, that he will do all in his power, even by force, to have his own way. He seems convinced that he cannot fail to win. Try to make him feel relaxed about it and he'll make some sort of mistake. I have some ideas already for the driving part of it."He suddenly made a movement as if of surprise and his voice changed from a matter of fact tone to one of extreme tension and incomprehension.

Margaret noticed the change in his voice saying, "What's happened Alexandre? You sound strange."

"Difficult to explain but some sort of weird vision crossed before my eyes. I don't know what it was. It wasn't the white lady but it almost blinded me even though it lasted a microsecond only. What can it mean? I had a similar experience a while ago and you had the same sort of ...illusion? could it be? at precisely the same moment. This is strange and I have the impression that it is linked in some way with our present predicament but of course I could be wrong."

"I think you're right Alexandre but unfortunately I cannot talk about it now. One of Percival's men is telling me to hang up. Do your best. I will see you tomorrow from the back of the Velox!"

CHAPTER 13

The scene is Purley, a mid-upper class suburb of London not far from Croydon and the terminus of the tram network in South London. There is a crossroads where the two major destinations are London and Brighton on the North-South axis and Woodmansterne and Caterham in the West-East direction. The weather for a day in June was fairly typical – mild in the morning but very warm in the afternoon.

He had seen Margaret briefly but instead of doing a French style *bise* (mouth to cheek on both cheeks) as was their custom they simply nodded somewhat unconvincingly to one another. There was no need to stoke Percival's ire at this stage. He had a brief, very brief, encounter with the owner of the Velox who simply said magnanimously, to impress Margaret presumably. "I will give you 30 seconds' start. I can guarantee that you will be behind me at the next crossroads." This with an added touch of condescension, provocation and derision." He was obviously perfectly convinced that he could not but win the race and Alexandre was not perfectly convinced that he would be proved wrong.

The meeting had been designated for 7.45 a.m. by Percival, neatly hand-written and signed by the latter himself on good quality vellum paper and delivered the evening before by one of Percival's henchmen. He had been told to counter-sign the said document. Alexandre had spent an hour before the meeting at Purley servicing his Morgan, pumping up the tyres slightly harder than usual, greasing the drive chain, cleaning the tiny two-section windscreen and generally polishing the little ruby-red gem of a racer. He was proud of his car but knew that it was more adapted to winding circuits than to long straight stretches of road. Being low on the ground it was able to hug the macadam and negotiate tight bends with precision. Unfortunately there were very few such stretches on the London to Brighton road. He had studied the map carefully and saw that it would only be in or near the towns of Redhill, Crawley or Burgess Hill that he might have a small chance of catching up the Velox but he knew he would have an even smaller chance of overtaking it. However, he was not one to give up before at least trying.

He was parked in front of the Velox with Percival standing ostentatiously beside his car which also, it must be said, looked gleaming, powerful and impressive. He held a whistle and stopwatch in his hands. "What a conceited ass," thought Alexandre.

There was a fairly longish pause while Percival said something to his men and also to Margaret, then he came back to his original position beside the Velox, the engine of which was running, exuding a powerful, confident purring sound, to the image of its master. He suddenly blew the whistle and Alexandre had no option but to release his handbrake and pull down the accelerator lever positioned on the steering wheel (no accelerator pedal) to maximum and roar away as best he could. He could almost feel Percival and his men chuckling but also Margaret crying. He tried to shake away that image from his head. He kept his eyes glued as much as possible to the wing mirrors and eventually saw (after exactly 30 seconds) the Velox thrust itself forward with a large puff of smoke trailing from it. Alexandre kept his machine at a speed that was fast but not dangerous either for himself or for pedestrians who might have wanted to cross the road at any time. He could see that Percival was gaining on him but knew that he had to relax as much as possible and used some of the techniques he had taught himself when piloting at the end of the war –breathing in deeply, concentrating his mind on something pleasant (Margaret laughing?) while his brain sought solutions to practical matters and the practical matter now was that the Velox was just behind. Suddenly without any warning two carts, each pulled by a large walking horse, suddenly came out of a shaded side road just 100 yards in front and started clattering along slowly without a care in the world. Charles and Percival just behind had to brake sharply. At the same time a truck-type vehicle heaved into view in the opposite direction meaning that it was impossible for the Vauxhall to overtake him and what was more they were now at the entry to Coulsdon. Alexandre, despite the extreme tension of the whole situation, managed a crisp smile as he imagined Percival cursing behind his wheel. Could this possibly be a sign of things to come? Was there such a phenomenon as divine intervention? And just as this thought echoed in some inaccessible corner of his mind a bright image again raced through his head but this time there was a change. The bright thing whatever it was came into view as before but just as suddenly doubled back the way it had come, the two motions just as instantaneous as one sole movement. He shook his head in disbelief and concentrated once more on his driving.

The road going through the small town of Coulsdon was not at all regular in width but none of the wide parts were long enough to allow the Velox to overtake the little Morgan as there were quite a number of trucks, a few private cars and many horse-drawn vehicles like the milk float that forced Alexandre to brake sharply once again as the milkman crossed the road with nonchalance and a crate of milk bottles. There was a loud braking sound from behind and the tearing noise of tyres scraping the road surface. Percival only just managed to avoid hitting the fragile tail part of the Morgan with its one, indispensable drive wheel. Goodness knows what the mood must have been within the confines of the vociferous machine. As a result, Percival kept his distance which put him immediately at a very slight disadvantage.

When Alexandre eventually came to the sign marking the exit from the town he found a clear, straight road ahead and gave the little Morgan all the power he could. The Velox was not immediately behind at first because it was wedged between two fairly wide horse-drawn wagons carrying hay and it was difficult for him to overtake the wagon in front because the projecting loose hay blocked his view of the road. However, this did not last long and in next to no time Alexandre could see the familiar shape of the rival car in his wing mirrors getting bigger and bigger and then it was gone, it had overtaken him with much symbolic honking of its horn and at an almost dangerous speed. A symbol of power and domination. However, Alexandre found himself once more just behind the Velox as they crossed a hamlet where there were the usual horse-drawn wagons to be seen almost constantly as it was an early haymaking season. Alexandre wondered if the possibility of getting jammed by such vehicles had crossed the mind of Percival. The convoy of carts and cars went slowly along the narrow road but as soon as the open stretch of road at the exit from the hamlet heaved into view the Velox rocketed off at great speed once more leaving the Morgan desperately trying to reduce the distance between them.

This was the same story going through Redhill and at one time just in front of the Ship and Anchor Alexandre almost had a unique occasion of creeping past Percival as he was once more stuck between carts. This was not to be, however, and the same story unfolded on many occasions going through Horley, Crawley and Burgess Hill. Alexandre was greatly amazed that the Velox was still in view and he now knew that he had a small chance of getting past the monster if he kept his eyes skinned and treated the affair as an aerial combat and not as a mere motor race. In an aerial combat you have to know intuitively what the opponent plans to do, you have to put yourself in their place which is difficult in that extreme, highly charged state of nervousness of battle which sitting in a cockpit and trying to hold the stick with precision and knowing that its you or the other who will be saved or not. The endgame was life or death. Here, in the current state of 'combat' the nerves were not strung to the same extent but the evolution of what might come to pass kept the mind turning over at the same rate and with the same intensity as in the air. He was accustomed to that and that might just prove to be the aspect that could put the two drivers on an equal footing. Who knows? Whatever the outcome, Alexandre was sure that the situation would be sorted out one way or another. This was more of a reasoned hope than certitude – just like aerial combat, he thought. But while these thoughts were being processed in his head, he was aware that behind it all, as a sort of pinnacle of the pyramid of his reflection lay his now deep affection for Margaret and that what he was doing and what he aspired to most was to give her the chance of a full life, hopefully with him. As this thought traversed his mind the image that until now he had been unable to identify suddenly took on the shape of a sword and came into view for perhaps a hundredth of a second. It was upright and pointing down to something lifelike below it. The image was so brief that he was unable to see what the moving object was. What if Margaret had seen the same vision as himself, thought he?

The Velox suddenly pulled out on the right to overtake a couple of vehicles and Alexandre, luckily, was able to do the same so he was now just behind Percival. Suddenly a hay cart came onto the road from the right some 200 yards or more ahead clattering and clunking followed by a small procession of other such carts and the Velox was forced to stop to avoid them. The men accompanying the wagons got their horses and vehicles to cross the road without so much as a 'by your leave' and as if the road belonged to just them. The arrival of the hay carts was very fortuitous for Alexandre because the loads of loose hay, especially the one just in front of Percival was rather badly laid on the wagon and projected out on both sides but especially on the right-hand side and suddenly Percival's field of vision was very much reduced. However as the cart had large wheels and as its loading surface was quite high off the ground, Alexandre, his car being very close to the ground, was able to see what Percival could not and at this very moment what came to the pilot's view was a long widish stretch of road peeling off to the right. Without a second's hesitation he veered very quickly to the right and overtook the Velox and then the line of wagons with a great chattering of its rather small engine. He could imagine Percival's expression but did not dwell on it as the latter, realizing that he had been 'had' was very quickly behind him. Alexandre had instinctively calculated that he had the time before any vehicle would come into sight in the opposite direction and this was indeed the case for him but not for his pursuer ...

Indeed, Percival must have subconsciously decided that as Alexandre had been able to whip past him and the row of carts then he too could do so with impunity. Unfortunately for him that was not to be the case because just at that moment a large car loomed into view. Alexandre had taken that possibility into account and was safely tucked back into the line of vehicles but now at the front of the convoy. He looked into his right-hand wing mirror and was horrified to see that the Velox was about to strike the oncoming vehicle. The driver of the other car fortunately for everyone took evasive action and Alexandre saw some metal objects flying into the air and immediately afterwards the vehicle dived into the roadside ditch. Percival was still behind but he could, even above the sound of his own engine, hear a strange rather unhealthy noise emitting from the Velox. Some part of the front right wheel or tyre must now be scraping against the mudguard –Alexandre could not see due to his angle of view but guessed that the damage must be significant. Anyway he felt half safe now and could only guess in what state of mind might be Percival and above all Margaret. Notwithstanding what could have been a horrific and fatal incident, Alexandre knew he now had to concentrate more than ever on the task in hand which was to reach Brighton Pier before Percival. He went as fast as he possibly could, exceeding the speed limit by only some 10 mph so as not to be too conspicuous and was waiting for the Velox, in spite of the unknown damage to the vehicle, to at least try to overtake him but it made no attempt to do so presumably waiting for a location near the destination where the driver would have nothing to lose, despite the handicap of a damaged vehicle, by making an attempt at overtaking him. Alexandre's eyes were fastened on his right wing mirror just waiting for that attempt to manifest itself.

It was not long in coming. Alexandre had just managed to see a sign notifying that Brighton centre was now only 10 miles distant and almost immediately the Velox swung over to its right to overtake the Morgan. Alexandre had no option but to let it pass. Overtaking was now a very dangerous operation as the outskirts of Brighton with posh houses, the occasional pub and garage zipped past. Percival was about to discover for the second time that he was driving dangerously, for once more some sort of goods truck came into view and the Velox's front wing (once again) glanced off the passing vehicle's hub caps or whatever with a terrible screeching noise. The vehicle honked its horn in anger, not surprisingly, but Percival typically disregarded any "inconvenience" he had caused and carried on with Alexandre close behind. The mileage to the pier at Brighton was now very quickly being reduced from ten to eight to five and now just three miles and Alexandre could not imagine how he was going to get past the monster which was now not only emitting a highly unsynchronized noise from its engine but there were sparks flying off into the air at regular intervals. Even so, the Morgan's driver was now convinced he could not win the race due to The Velox's driver's practically suicidal manner of driving.

Suddenly the Velox screeched to a halt in the middle of the road and Alexandre, but for his extremely brisk reaction, would have crashed into its rear. He just managed to avoid the large car by a hair's breadth and found himself coasting along a shop-lined avenue leading to the area around the pier. When he had stopped just in front of the pier he looked back to see the Velox chugging along noisily and emitting vast volumes of exhaust smoke. It came to a halt a hundred yards or so to the rear of the Morgan.

The rear door opened and who did he see clamber down from the now half-wrecked Velox (the right-hand side of the vehicle could now be seen to be somewhat flattened and in a piteous state) but Margaret who now walked very shakily towards Alexandre.

Just as they were about to throw their arms one about the other the Velox, still in a state as if it had been crossing a war zone limped away followed now by a police vehicle. The police must have been informed of the behaviour of a mad, dangerous driver on the road to Brighton and were now seeking the culprit. Alexandre had no doubt that Percival would be able to talk his way out of any difficulty. Now back to Margaret.

"Oh, Alexandre, thank goodness you are in one piece. I have just gone through one of the worst experiences of my life. I now know Percival that much better and I can tell you that it's not the best side of him that I have seen. His driving was completely reckless – he had thought at the start that you hadn't a chance. But as the race progressed he came to realize that power is not the sole ingredient of any venture even one such as a motor race. He did not say so, of course, but I saw that he admired your absolute control of any situation and when you overtook him the first time I could see he was sweating and there was a real desire in him to outwit you. But he was unable to." She had her head on his shoulder all this time and now and again looked up into his eyes, her own eyes wet with emotion and happiness.

Alexandre, for his part held her head firmly but gently, stroking her hair from time to time. "I admit the race was not easy but it was thanks to those hay carts and to Percival's impatience that I was able to win but frankly I shouldn't have. The dice was weighed against me. But I was so worried about you especially when the Velox scraped against the passing car. I thought you were going to be injured, if not worse. Gosh, I'm really relieved to see you well and I'm so happy to be with you again." Indeed, his eyes had lit up with sheer contentment and his whole face was engulfed by a huge smile that was now joined by Margaret's. Then on a sudden coordinated impulse they kissed, gently at first then with passion. This had never happened before and they were, each of them, as surprised, one as the other, at the intensity of their emotions. Margaret suddenly had another of her visions but this time it took on a recognizable shape, that of a sword, and sped off from her view but there was a flash of light as it disappeared. Margaret started in surprise and Alexandre felt her body shudder. She described to him what she had just experienced.

"Strange, but I also have just experienced a manifestation of the same sort of image that I can now definitely identify as a sword but I also saw the flash of light in my head and perhaps that means the end of the vision. It's extraordinary but we are definitely associated in what can only be described as a surreal but repetitive phenomenon."

"Alexandre, what on earth can it all mean? All I now know is that I am so happy to be with you and to see the back of Percival. You know, he is not entirely bad but he's so vain and eaten up by his own importance. But there is a good side, too. He gave me a certain form of happiness when I felt so lonely so I'm not going to condemn him out of hand and I know I didn't do enough to put him off." She scrunched up her face as she said this.

"Margaret, I do not condemn him, either. You are such a nice, intelligent and generous woman that I'm surprised he didn't make the effort to become important to you. However, there's one thing which intrigues me. What does he do for a living? It doesn't look very legitimate to me. What do you know about his business?"

"I don't really know what his exact business is. He seems to be involved in some sort of financial matters - money is very important to him – but what it is precisely, I wouldn't know. If he's one thing though, he's a man of his word and will not disturb either you or me again. I somehow don't think we'll see any more of him. That's a positive point."

"Absolutely, my dear Margaret, I must admit I was getting very worried and I was more than convinced that he had to win the race and he thought before we started off that he had it in the bag but the fact that he has now vanished without saying anything is proof enough that he is, as you say, a man of his word. I think he must have been half ashamed of his behaviour. What do you think, you know him better than I do?"

"Yes, I think you are right because he would never have behaved like that before and I believe sincerely that he was amazed at how you outwitted him."

"Actually, I didn't outwit him; he was at a disadvantage because of the height of the car and that his view was obstructed by the hay on the wagons. Obviously, he couldn't have foreseen that and it just shows how small things are important in life."

"Small things like small cars ...?" Her mouth creased into a huge smile and they could not help but laugh out loud before holding each other tightly again and stealing a very passionate kiss.

"We'll have a bite to eat before venturing back to Croydon. I expect you'd prefer returning by train ...?"

"No, not at all, I shall enjoy sitting next to you and a ride in your car. I saw at first hand how you drive and I know we'll get there safe and sound." Here again, Margaret burst out laughing and the relief she felt was almost palpable.

"OK then, a beer and a mince pie in the pub over there?"

"Yes, wonderful."

CHAPTER 13

Alexandre returned to Le Bourget early the next morning and Margaret had to visit her missed appointments and apologise. She made some excuse about temporarily losing her voice and coughed appropriately from time to time with the patients she had missed and with the doctors at the hospital where she had been due to talk about a new drug. She managed to convince everyone that she could not have done otherwise. The day went by as in the days before the "race" but there was now a fundamental difference. Percival had somehow been whisked out of her life like an actor exiting the scene of a play and his place taken by someone whose overflowing love, goodness and Yes, beauty (in the philosophical sense), was hard to imagine for Margaret who had always been used to second-best. She was not the only woman in this situation because so many young men had been sacrificed on the crude altar of national pride. The day went by but it was long and she had difficulty concentrating on her two jobs, caring and selling, especially her pharmaceutical endeavour.

However, the day done, she eventually went to bed and slept deeply for six or seven hours without the slightest dream. On getting up the next morning, she shook herself briskly, had a shower, changing temperature gradually from hot to cold to give herself energy and dynamism, dried herself and daubed her thick, towelled dressing gown before making herself a leisurely breakfast. Her first appointment was not before 11 a.m.

She was about to don her simple body-clinging dress with matching cape and felt hat when she was very surprised to hear the phone ring and Alexandre, although he would have returned to Croydon from Le Bourget, knew that she had work to catch up on. So, imagine her surprise when she did indeed hear the voice of Alexandre.

"What's happened Alexandre? Are you alright? You sound out of breath, excited .....?"

"Well, Margaret, something strange has just happened. I didn't want to dither at the airport so I took a taxi back to my flat as soon as possible and whom did I see as I was about to alight from the taxi – I asked the driver to wait a few seconds so that I could step down unnoticed – but one of Percival's henchman but the strange thing was he didn't look at all gangsterish but a quietly dressed young man who looked quite pleasant. I was amazed. Even more amazed when I found a letter from Percival on the doormat inside."

"That certainly is strange. Gosh, I hope he's not going to go back on his word and bother us after all ...,"

"No wait, not at all like that. He wants to see us both as soon as possible – he suggests tonight, latish – as he has, he says, an attractive offer to make. I really don't think it's a trap and the fact that his man looked sort of very ordinary might mean that up until now he has been playing a game, albeit very unnerving and quite dangerous ..."

"That is incredible, said Margaret dazedly, what can it mean?"

"No idea, but he wants to see us at the Great Gatsby at 9 p.m. Can you make it? I will pick you up anywhere you like in a taxi. As it's Saturday, my next flight is not until Monday, so I'm free. What about you?"

"Yes, I'm game, said Margaret without hesitation, I must admit I am more than surprised."

"Right, I'll come and pick you up at your place in the taxi at about 8.15 if that suits you."

"That's fine, I'll try and dress up a bit so that I harmonize with the decor" she said laughingly but her voice was tinged with apprehension.

Margaret almost rushed her round of duties to get back to her flat in time to be picked up by Alexandre at the agreed time. It's true, she was very tired especially as she had had trouble explaining her absence to one or two irritable patients. However, as soon as she had donned her tailored dress made of a silk blend crepe with a natural waist sash, put on her Mary Jane heeled shoes with their single strap across the front and her cloche hat she felt much better. She looked at herself in the body height mirror and thought she would pass muster. All she had to do now was put on a touch of makeup. This was normally a hint of mascara and some light-coloured lipstick. As a rule she made up only very slightly as she had always been a natural sort of outdoor girl and contrary to the customs of that period often went for a run in the nearby park much to the astonishment of passers-by. That done, she sat back in one of her armchairs, took in deep breaths and awaited the arrival of Alexandre's taxi. She did not have long to wait because in next to no time she heard the squeak of the taxi's brakes and she went straight to the door holding her neat little handbag. The motor of the vehicle kept running as she descended the exterior stairway and headed towards the rear door of the taxi which was now opened in style by the driver. In she went and was soon in her love one's arms. What a delicious feeling for both of them. She now had no sensation of fatigue. She was now thoroughly in tune with the changed circumstances but like Alexandre was somewhat on tenterhooks not knowing what to expect from the evening.

They arrived at the Great Gatsby at the appointed time, gave their names to the host who immediately ushered them to a secluded, dim-lighted, chic part of the restaurant to be welcomed by Percival who was dressed to a tee – in black with a perfect bowtie in the latest fashion. Even if he was probably in a conciliatory mood he obviously had to outdo Alexandre in terms of dress. Alexandre did not care in the slightest and was dressed in a good suit but with a discreet, blue coloured tie. It was in fact a company tie with the outline of an aircraft sewn into its lower half but as he wore a V-necked, light pullover the embroidered image could not be seen.

"Well, sit down my friends, he said giving Margaret a very quick hug and shaking Alexandre's hand very cordially indeed. Now then what are we going to drink as apéritif? Waiter, can we have the wine list please?" he said even though the waiter was already hovering over the trio with the requested list. They all decided on a choice sherry for apéritifs which was not long in being served. Until that was achieved they smiled at each other (beamed would be the word for Percival's expression) but stayed silent. When finally each one held their drink in their hand and had clinked glasses Percival started his what must have been a prepared speech. "I have some important things to say to you but first of all I would like to congratulate you, Alexandre, on the extraordinary way you handled our so-called race. I must admit that I would never have expected it and I would also admit that I carried out some very silly manoeuvres and frankly put our lives in danger. I apologise sincerely to you, Margaret. The only good thing about it all was that for once I was able to reflect on things in general and on that episode in particular late last night after I had very callously stolen away from the scene at Brighton yesterday. But in fact, although I had no right to do what I did from a moral point of view I had very little choice in the matter" There was a silence of some ten seconds while the three of them sipped their sherry and nibbled titbits laid out on pretty dishes on the table.

" I will try to explain but first of all I'm going to ask you to be as discreet as possible as I have never given anyone, not even you Margaret, any indication of what I do for a living. This is top secret and must be divulged to nobody." Both the volume and tone of his voice diminished as he said this as if he was afraid there might be eavesdroppers "though where they could have hid themselves goodness only knows," thought Margaret. Percival's forehead creased as he said this and he brought his head towards the middle of the table so that he was as close to them as possible.

"I work for the government, Customs in fact, and my job is to infiltrate large scale Mafioso arms-smuggling operations. That is why you probably had the impression that what I was doing was something shady. The two men who work with me are accountable to me but do not work for me. Like me, they work for the government. We are obliged to give the impression of being unscrupulous and there again, Margaret, I am very sorry for the way you were treated at my flat. Unfortunately I had to give the Mafia the impression, had to give them proof that I am unscrupulous before they would agree to my being an intrinsic part of a huge arms deal which was planned for the benefit of the military in the Weimar Republic. That was why I was forced to kidnap you, Margaret. They were watching all the time. They thought you were a rich heiress. I convinced them on that score as I told them you often flew to Paris, unlike almost anyone else today so that implies means and money. They duly checked on it and were satisfied on that score, and they were also convinced I was not lying because one of their members was in my flat all the time you were confined there and saw all the moves I was making. However, the race to Brighton was not part of the deal in any way and I have to admit that I took advantage of my position to try to win your hand, Margaret, by means of my powerful car. I thought I could convince you of my worth by beating you, Alexandre. I must also admit, Alexandre that I really did want to teach you a lesson, you and your "tin can" against me with my omnipotent steed." Here he almost suppressed a laugh but his guests could see the laugh was against himself by the way he pursed his lips and held his head down. "Obviously, I no longer think like that and I can now say quite honestly that I am glad that you won because I really don't know what I would be doing now otherwise. I therefore had two aims both connected with pride and self importance and both connected with winning – your hand Margaret and the race, the satisfaction of beating you, Alexandre. So I have to crawl under the carpet and make an abject apology to you both. I am now very bitterly ashamed. I was using my government mission to take advantage of you, Margaret. Knowing you both a little better I can see now that it would never have succeeded. You have both done me a great favour – you could say it was shock treatment – and I now realize what a conceited, egoistical ass I was. I have now come to agree with my parents. They always said I trod on everyone, that I listened to no-one but myself and that frankly they were disappointed by me in view of the good upbringing and education I had received. Obviously you can never change your character – that is the result of genes and upbringing but you can come to realize who you are and change your behaviour. This is what I hope to do in future. Both of you submitted me to that shock treatment and I am very grateful to you. Do you realize that a few days ago I could never have spoken like this. It seems absurd, doesn't it? Frankly, what I did I now realize was inadmissible. So back to my mea culpa. Margaret, can you forgive me?"

"Listen Percival, almost whispered Margaret and she paled as she spoke, I did think you were overstepping the mark, to say the least, for the race, but I will say that apart from that incident, although you have sometimes been inaccessible to what I have had to say – in short you often didn't listen to me, there I've said it (this with a shrug) – you have always treated me well. I'm ready to listen to you now. What do you think Alexandre?"

"I think I'll keep out of this for a while. Like Margaret, I will listen to what you have to say and your explanations as to why you, can I say 'convened' us here this evening?"

"Riiight, continued Percival hesitatingly, I will continue. You might have guessed that I do not lack resources. My job is well paid but I have considerable shares in various companies including shares in an aeroplane manufacturing concern. I bought them years ago when my father left me a fortune and that was even before the war when I could see there was a future for what we now classify as aviation. They have grown in value and I am now in a position, with the help of a bank loan, to launch an airline, say with 3 or 4 machines to start with. I wouldn't know which aircraft are the most reliable and the most profitable but you can help me there, Alexandre – allow me to call you by your Christian name?"

"Yes, I have seen them but I have never flown them, but where do I come into the picture, Percival? –there I've used your first name, too!" The three chuckled at this not because it was particularly funny but as a way of loosening the tension that had gripped Margaret and Alexandre.

"Well, said Percival, we'll see about that all in good time. For the moment my proposal is for you to set up an airline with the aircraft of your choice, become the managing director and at the same time chief pilot. You can do a short training course on economics, if you wish, but after seeing how you manage the most difficult and hazardous situations I know you will bring in results pretty quickly. I trust you entirely. I have not forgotten you, either, Margaret. It's not for me to say but if you have plans to marry Alexandre I will arrange a very good wedding reception. You can also help him with his new job – if you Alexandre – accept or continue as now in your present job. I will buy you a car if that will help you. If, as is usually the case, but it's not for me to say, you plan to have a family I intend to buy a property for you both but for which you can repay me back like a mortgage, from your salaries. I know all that is quite a mouthful but what do you say?"

Margaret and Alexandre looked at each other. Alexandre's eyebrows rose as he closed his mouth tightly and he squinted slightly. Margaret looked intensely at him while turning her head into what could have been interpreted as a negative sign or even a positive one and ran her hand through her hair slowly but deliberately. It was obvious that they were at a loss to know what to say and it was, in fact, Percival who broke the brief stalemate.

"You must talk it over together this weekend and let me know on Monday evening. Will you be in England in the evening, Alexandre?"

"Yes, I will be back in time but I would like to stress, Percival and I'm sure Margaret would agree that I do not want any charity. If, as you say I will enjoy a reasonable salary, there will be no need to buy a house on our behalf. I think we would be able to look after that. Do you not agree, Margaret?"

"Oh, absolutely."

"But Percival we have made no decision as yet. We will talk about it and let you know on Monday. It's very tempting but there must be disadvantages, I'm sure."

"Well, my dear friends the only disadvantage that I can see is that you will have some decisions to make and hard work to do. All I can say is that I am going ahead with the small fleet of aircraft come what may. I see now what a cool-headed and determined organizer and action-taking party can deal with. I am not trying to blackmail you, just trying to convince you of your advantages. And of course I wish the two of you much happiness. I have been very silly in my behaviour towards you, Margaret, and to a lesser extent towards you, Alexandre, but I want you to think of all that as definitively over and start a new life. Waiter, can we have the menu?"

CHAPTER 14

Margaret and Alexandre spent the night together after their fairly long drawn-out conversation with Percival but just before they settled into the put-you-up that was part of the furnishings in Alexandre's flat, Margaret said something that almost startled her partner; "Alex, I'm going to call you Alex from now on (he nodded in agreement), just when we were leaving the restaurant last night I had an extremely rapid but intense vision once more. I was suddenly in an old house in an almost heavenly country setting and I had an ultra brief feeling in my belly as if I was extremely content. I think it must have meant that in this flash of unconsciousness I was pregnant. But I repeat, like the sword visions, this lasted much less that a second – instantaneous, you could say."

"Well, that is strange. I had a similar feeling of contentment but I was outdoors and gazing across lines of shrubs but which could have been rows of vines. Like yours it lasted less that a second." "I know it's ridiculous to say so but it's almost like some sort of destiny that we have already encountered and that continues to trace out our lives. I know it sounds stupid but it seems to be larger than our minds and hearts can envisage. It really is extraordinary."

"No, it's not stupid at all and I would go one step further. The fact that these visions are common to both of us, and I think it would be true to say at the same instant, means we have something more in common than we can imagine. I would go even further in bringing back to mind the fact that we somehow knew each other the first time we met but were unable to place when and where we had met and I think that still holds, does it not?"

"I'll say it does. I think we must assume that we do know each other somehow or other and that all these strange events are linked to what I would call predestination. Frankly, I think we have to accept Percival's proposal but shape it, could I say, to our advantage. There, I've said it!"

"Well, my dear Margaret, as always, I was thinking along the same lines at the same time. It's almost as if we were identical twins though I know it's impossible to have identical twins of different sexes. So, alright, we accept but there are a lot of 'buts'!"

"My mother as you know is French and lives to the south-east of Paris in a place called Angers, a nice quiet little cathedral town, so I would like to live, say, in the countryside but within an hour by train from your place of work and accessible to Angers. I seem to remember that Chartres could be a possibility from that point of view but you would have to work from Le Bourget, I suppose, even supposing that Percival would agree to base his new airline or whatever you call it near Paris.

"Well, if he won't accept France as the base for his new outfit I will not accept his offer!"

"Great Alexandre. I agree wholeheartedly!" and she flung her arms around him, smiling hugely and they embraced and kissed with such joy. Margaret then danced around with happiness while Alexandre went to his icebox to get the bottle of champagne he had bought in Paris the Friday before just in case he turned out to be the winner. He uncorked and they drank unrestrainedly until the bottle was empty an hour or so later. All this time they danced together to gramophone records of jazz from Alexandre's collection of jazz records – one was a piece by French jazzman Django Reinhardt – and many American jazz musicians including Jelly Roll Morton, of course.

They ended up by going to bed early and seldom have a couple been so wonderfully satisfied with their lot and so marvellously happy – due also, it should be said, to what was inevitable – some very passionate love-making. Whatever the outcome of the palavers of Monday with Percival might be, all that mattered for the moment was that they were together and so united that one could say they were really as one.

CHAPTER 15

Their appointment with Percival was at 10 a.m. in a pub in Central Croydon. Percival arrived almost at the same moment as Margaret and Alexandre whom we will now refer to as the couple. There were not many patrons or customers in the establishment at that time on a Monday so they chose a table close to a window where they would be able to clearly see any documents that the couple assumed Percival would bring with him.

"Good morning, Margaret and Alexandre – I'm glad we can address each other by our Christian names, he said with a beaming and which must now be assumed to be an authentic smile, what shall we drink, I'll fetch it? " Alexandre opted for a pint while Margaret wanted just a coffee. Percival asked the barman for two pints and a coffee which were very quickly poured and served on a tray that Percival carried back to the table. "Now, where were we, oh yes, the first and biggest question is do you agree to my proposal – wait a minute, I know there will be buts and I'm quite prepared to take them into consideration." Both nodded.

"Well, I'm waiting to hear the buts ...!"

So Alexandre and Margaret between them explained their conditions to Percival and his response was quite unexpected.

"Do you know that I was half hoping for and almost expecting such an idea as, although neither of you will know, I can speak a little French and would like to live in the world's capital of good taste. *C'est une très bonne idée, n'est-ce pas* ? However, I have had a big rethink of the situation and most of all I have had a chat with a fellow from another ministry who I know pretty well and I must admit it throws our plans to the wind for a while but only for a while."

"Well, go on" said Alexandre dubiously

"Yes, do" echoed Margaret, now frowning very obviously.

"Please do not think that I have changed my mind. On the contrary. Well, here goes. I have learnt, Alexandre, that your airline Daimler Airways with one or two other small companies are going to be the object of a takeover bid by a new airline which goes by the name of Emporium or something like that. Did you know that Alexandre?"

"I have heard rumours but I took them to be unreliable and possible malicious so I took no notice. Oh my God and it's you of all people Percival who is confirming it." Alexandre suddenly shrunk in size and he covered his face with his arm.

"Listen, you future candidates for marriage, it could turn out to be a good thing. The new airline will undoubtedly acquire and use the latest aircraft on the market and you, Alexandre, will get the training you need on these aircraft automatically because presumably you will be hired by the new airline, seeing your experience. I would imagine it would take a couple of years for everything to get organized and then we will be able to put our plans into action. But I must insist that you have no obligation to join my airline. I intend to set it up in any case. You will have time to think about it and if you wish to continue as now - that is your choice. I will not try to influence you. You will naturally agree together, as one. In the meantime you can get married and buy a house of your choice in England, for the moment. If you want funding for that I can help you out but I know you will refuse because it would seem to you like blackmail. So no, on second thoughts I withdraw my offer ..." and with that he laughed which made the couple laugh in turn.

CHAPTER 16

Margaret and Alexandre now lived a life that neither could have imagined before. They took out a mortgage for a lovely cottage in Surrey not far from Croydon Airport and a train station to London. They were only too happy to be together every two or so days when their work schedules so allowed. Percival had arranged a wonderful wedding reception with several guests from fairly important government posts and of course their families attended and close friends of both Margaret and Alexandre.

This was now a memory but the end of the two-year period was drawing near and the couple decided that they would indeed now like to live in France so on the condition of setting up the airline in France (which he unexpectedly accepted) they agreed to Percival's renewed offer of an executive / flying post in the new airline for Alexandre while Margaret decided to devote herself to more home-oriented occupations although she continued working part-time at the nearest hospital which was located at Compiegne. Their home was quite near in a small village where they very soon knew all the inhabitants and lived a life of harmony.

The new airline was soon an up-and-going concern once the choice of aircraft was made, the orders placed and delivered, premises in the terminal building at Le Bourget acquired and staff hired to do all the jobs required by an airline. At their board meeting, Alexandre, Percival and the other members had decided that they would concentrate on weekly services at first to Italy and Spain. This meant that Alexandre was very often absent on his trips to one or other of the above nations and frankly, although he enjoyed his new, well-paid job very much, he missed his wife considerably. One evening when at home with Margaret he asked her if she would like to accompany him on a new trip to the Balearic Islands and of course she agreed. They both had a smattering of Spanish so it offered the opportunity of trying out their linguistic abilities. Alexandre would not be flying the aircraft which was one of their new Fokker tri-motors and he would be sitting next to his wife in the cabin to enjoy her company and the view passing over France and a part of the Mediterranean Sea. The crew of two plus a stewardess, for the requirements of training, were duly waiting for them at Le Bourget when they went through customs at 1.30 p.m. for the flight scheduled at 2 p.m.

The engine start-up procedure went smoothly and they were soon given permission to line up on the runway and take off. Percival had come especially to see the departure and as the aircraft left the ground and gained height he waved his hat to wish them good luck.

The flight was scheduled to last 6 hours.

At 8 p.m. the staff at the Balearic Islands branch of the new company were awaiting the arrival of the Fokker. At 9 p.m. they decided to enquire whether the aircraft had stopped off somewhere and managed to get through to the airport at Marseille who had been in contact with the aircraft by radio at about 6.30 p.m.

At 10 p.m. the staff contacted the Spanish National Police and the Civil Guard.

No news was forthcoming of the aircraft or its occupants, either that evening or on any of the following days and weeks.

BOOK 3

CHAPTER 1

Marc Leboucher had always been keen on fiction, either in books, on the stage, on the big screen and even on the little screen. He had tried writing stories at school but had never got past the first two or three chapters which annoyed his parents especially his father. They lived in Anjou in France and because of the links of that ancient province with England Marc soon became interested in history and decided, after succeeding his baccalaureate, to study English and History at one of the famous universities. Unfortunately for him his level was not to the likings of any of the selection boards of the prestigious universities and he was obliged, in the end, to apply for a place at University College London (UCL) which turned out to be a very good thing. His studies went well and being quite bright he obtained the Masters his parents were keen on him to have. They presumed he would return to France to continue his studies to become a teacher and Hey Presto for a quiet life.

This young man of average height, striking green grey eyes and fair hair but now very slightly overweight due to his good appetite and liking for an English pint had met several students like himself, young women and young men, who had discovered the UCL Drama Society. It was relatively easy to apply and be accepted.

Although he was passionate about history and in particular the post-Napoleonic wars period he discovered he had a real talent for acting and was given and enjoyed fairly good parts for several years. What was more he was allowed to improvise which gave him the idea of writing his own scripts.

The first one was a complete disaster and no-one at the drama school would read more than a dozen pages exclaiming that he had to do better than that. When he received rebuffs like that which frankly he came to realize were sometimes deserved, he would put on his track suit and do some jogging. While doing this, for him, quite strenuous exercise he was able to reflect and erase from his mind the pitfalls of boring scripts and was able to put his errors down to a lack of experience and build on them. During this period which was a sort of cultural desert for him he managed to pay his rent and buy the basics of life by working in a pub. This went on for several years until 2010 when at the age of 32 he found the story and wrote the script of a film he thought could be a box office success. Not surprisingly, it was set against an historical backdrop. Now the problem was to cast actors and especially an actress who had to be convincing but not too well-known to be out of his price range, always supposing he found the funding. He decided he would himself play the male part as he had time and again proven his talent. There were other members of the final cast list to be found but they could wait for the moment.

He remembered meeting a young woman at the drama society two or three years before whom he had seen acting for an end of year production and found her excellent. He recalled that she was a woman not to be trodden on and that that had pleased him a lot. He couldn't remember her name but he decided then and there – his script was nearly finished – that he would enquire at the school. When he explained who he was to the drama school secretary and she had looked at his files she agreed to give him her name – a certain Emma Jameson. He thanked her profusely and suddenly remembered that he had seen her name on the cast list of a play at the Gate Theatre at Notting Hill Gate. He was able to find a stand-in for his pub job and decided to see the play, a humoristic piece about a very expensive but uninteresting painting.

After the play which was quite enjoyable but mostly in his opinion due to the performance of Emma who almost carried the other actors along with her, he went down to her lodge and knocked on the door.

"Yes, who is it?" He heard a rather bored sounding woman's voice through the door panelling.

"Emma Jameson, I was at the UCL drama society with you a few years back. My name is Marc Leboucher but you probably won't remember me because we weren't in the same group."

"Oh yes? Well just one moment and I'll open the door."

Marc heard a drawer being shut with a clacking sound, a rustle of clothes (dressing gown?) and there she was in a track suit mostly worn to look inconspicuous, he learned later.

"Hang on, Mark, did you say? I can't honestly remember you from the drama school but y-e-e-e-s... your face rings a bell somewhere."

"Marc, yes but with a 'c'"

"Oh you're French then. You have very little accent. Come in and tell me what you want exactly. Sit down, sorry it's not very comfortable. Will that linen basket do?" and she laughed profusely, probably not due to what she had said but more probably as a sort of acting post-stress phenomenon. But anyway, her dark eyes shone with delight and she shook out her black hair which had been tied in a pony tail. This was so unexpected that Marc himself started to chuckle.

"I have a script to show you and wondered whether you would be interested ..." He saw her eyes light up again and almost change colour or was it the angle of light on them? "Would it be possible to talk over a drink, perhaps even here at the theatre bar?"

"Well, I'll listen to what you have to say, I can't say better than that, but not here. There's a pub just a hundred yards away. I would prefer to see you there, if you don't mind."

"Fine, Emma, can I call you by your first name?"

"Oh yes, I'm not one for useless etiquette ...I'll just put on this top and I'm ready. She ruffled her hair and slung a light scarf loosely around her face which was her way of trying to look incognito. By the way, what did you think of the play?"

"I found it entertaining but the director was lucky to have you – you kept the tempo going. You're a good actress and when I think of "Canvassing" it will be you who springs to mind more than the plot!" Laughter, once more.

They shuffled out into the corridor while Emma closed the door firmly with her key and they made their way upstairs, through the auditorium to the exit. Marc noticed that the few people present in the theatre foyer followed the young actress with their gaze, in spite of her efforts to look one of a crowd, as she left with Marc close behind.

They found a corner table that a couple had just conveniently left vacant – that was fortunate because there were many people inside and they would otherwise have been hard put to have a discussion. Emma decided on a half pint while Marc chose a pint of bitter – he loved English draught beer. He brought back the drinks to find Emma staring at him in a strange way.

"Christ, do I look that weird?" he managed to say.

"No, not in the least, but I *know* you (voice up one octave on the word 'know') and I have the impression that I know you quite well. I mean, I can only remember you vaguely at drama school. Could we have been neighbours at any time? I just cannot understand it."

"You're the same Emma. It's just beginning to sink in that we know each other. I only started to realize it in your lodge. I mean it's quite ludicrous. We are here as complete strangers one to the other but it's as if we are very well acquainted. What I suggest is that we leave that quandary for the moment and behave as if we do not know each other. I'll start. After drama school, I started acting and was told I had a certain talent but I very soon wanted to invent stories, to write my own scripts and eventually produce a film. What I would like you to do is to read the script I have in this envelope – don't worry, it's on my computer so if you tear it up there's no problem, he said shaking his head with a half smile and squinting –and just see if the story and the role of the heroine interest you. If they do, just contact me on my email or send me an SMS. I've marked my details at the top of the script. This is only the first act – there will eventually be three in all but I haven't worked out the details yet."

"It's very strange our seeming to know each other but OK Marc, I'll just take a peak now. I don't want you to have false hopes – not because what I say or feel is gospel but because we can gain a lot of time if it awakens something in me. Just give me 10 minutes to read a few pages and I will be able to tell you straight out what I feel. Relax, Marc, you look tense. Enjoy your drink. Here goes ..." and she extracted the pages carefully from the envelope, sat back as comfortably as possible and it was obvious that she was able to cut herself off from the ambience of the pub chatter. She must have taught herself that art – for art it surely was.

Marc sipped his beer while watching her face changing from a slight frown to the hint of a smile, a pause while she turned her eyes from the script towards the ceiling then back again to quickly changing expressions. Was this a good sign or not, he wondered?

"Marc, did this character Corinne really exist at the time of Napoleon?"

"Oh yes, and she was the subject of a book by a certain Germaine de Staël back in the 19th century but my play is, you will have gathered, about Corinne's housemaid of and her incredible ways of maintaining an appearance of great respect for the notions of good citizenship and decorum while living another life of great independence in secret. As you might have gathered she was hired as a simple, uneducated and submissive maid and always gave that impression to the whole household and guests of her mistress but for two days of every week wrote poems, played the violin and had a clandestine relationship with a young man who was entranced by her genius."

"Well, Marc, I do indeed like what I have read this evening especially as I am very keen on history and especially that period of European history but I will have to study it in slightly more detail to see if it tallies with my acting abilities, to see whether I am capable of putting myself in her skin. But tell me, why do you portray a female character in your play? Why not a man?"

"You're probably going to laugh at me but never mind. I feel that women are completely underrated in our society and indeed almost worldwide and the more I study female characters in history or even in contemporary lives, the more I want to write about them – and well, I love women ...!" This little revelation came out in an outburst completely foreign to Marc's nature of discretion and introversion.

It also surprised Emma whose mouth opened wide at first to reveal her slightly uneven teeth but which then transformed itself into a loud and noticeable laugh making many drinkers' heads turn in her direction. Marc himself laughed with her and could not explain to himself why he had said such a thing to someone he hardly knew – or someone he thought he hardly knew. Emma suddenly looked at him with such tenderness that he was almost overcome with emotion but this he did manage to conceal to some extent. He thought it time to bring the conversation to an end because he was somewhat wary as to how he would be able to chart a course through what might follow. Back to practical matters.

"Em-m-ma, he said stuttering slightly, can you email me or send an SMS and if you feel you are interested at all we'll take it from there? I would add, though, to be honest, that although one or two people I know in the film business did not dismiss my story out of hand, I have no funding at the moment. I thought it was important right from the start to have actors lined up for the main roles. I hope you agree ...?"

"Listen, Marc, as I said before I cannot tell you in advance what I will decide but I will look at the script very closely, read out loud the passages attributed to the housemaid –

Hortense, is it? and I promise I will contact you as soon as possible."

They parted giving each other the French style *bise* on each cheek.

CHAPTER 2

Marc was surprised to receive an SMS early next morning from Emma with a request for him to telephone her. He waited a discreet hour then made the call.

"Hi Marc. I have just finished reading the first act and I must say it suits me very well. It's almost as if you had written it especially for me so I would like to read the rest. Can we meet somewhere?"

"Yes, sure, I live in Notting Hill. Is that too far from you?"

"No, not at all. I live at Holland Park. Easy on the Underground."

"That's fine then. Can we eat together at lunch time? I'll book a table at the Maid's Farm if that's alright with you. 1 p.m., OK?"

They found themselves together again and what struck each of them and almost instantaneously was the ease with which they sat facing one another and it was as much as either of them could do to prevent themselves leaning over and holding the other's hand. They sort of instinctively drew back as if they knew what the other was thinking and by figuratively shaking themselves inside, so to speak, tried to look professional and disinterested waiting for the other to speak. But neither could dissimulate the slight blush to their cheeks!

The waiter arrived and another interesting feature of the encounter was that they discovered that they were both vegetarian. It made their choice of omelettes cooked with cheese, cherry tomatoes and other vegetables and herbs from the menu very easy and the plates placed before them looked absolutely delicious, or so each of them said, there again almost as one voice. They decided on a white wine agreeing to the waiter's suggestion of a classic Sauvignon Blanc.

Marc started the discussion by asking Emma if from her point of view there could be changes made to dialogues that might make them more fitting for the personality of Hortense, the maid.

"Well, as a matter of fact there are – but they're of very little importance. Hortense is a maid and at the time of the story was considered of little importance so would have been expected to adhere to all the etiquette of a nobleman's or rich person's household and I think she speaks her mind just a little bit too much. No problem today but the period of the story is the late 18th century. Look, I've underlined in felt pen the passages I believe could be improved in the light of that. I hope you're not hurt but unfortunately for you, I always say what I mean."

"No, Emma, that's a good point. It is always valid to have the point of view of an actor. You're right. I will try to transform her phrases where appropriate into ironic terms because it is a sort of tragicomedy."

"That's absolutely right, Marc, looked at from that perspective it would make the character much more interesting."

"I have the next act here in this envelope. Did I tell you that I would be taking the part of the nobleman who falls for Hortense? Can I take it that if I can find the financial backing for the film you are willing to lend your expertise and dare I say it – your charm to my endeavour?"

"Thank you, Marc, for saying that, but let's not get carried away. Yes, I'm game to take a chance on this film but remember I shall be just one component in a series of components that will make or break your film – but I have something rather important to tell you." She gave an awkward smile.

Marc looked at her with a trace of trepidation in his face and then sat back to listen trying to look relaxed.

"You look pained, Marc. Why is that? – No forget it! There is a fairly big Hollywood director – I'll tell you his name later – for whom I have already worked in a pretty dreary second role but who has another part, more important, lined up for me. I think he's interested in me for more than one reason, you can guess what - but all film directors are the same, are they not?"

"Emma, do you really think that I am seeking your help to play the part of Hortense simply for your looks and whatever ...? My one aim was and is to produce and direct a play I have written myself and when I saw you in "Canvassing" I knew you would fit the part perfectly although it is true that the sensation of somehow having already met you did enter my thoughts but was nothing more than that, I can assure you."

"Marc, I had no suspicions as to your intentions. I'm quite a good judge of character, especially men's (chuckle), and I knew at a glance that what you were saying was the truth. No, you are not part of my problem. My problem is that I know he could come back at any time to offer me the job and as he is very well connected and has almost unlimited funding, I am placed in a dilemma. Frankly, although I do not detest the man – he's quite generous, nice looking and intelligent – I am not at all interested in any way in any sort of intimate relationship with him but I instinctively know that if I agree to work for him, he will put pressure on me especially as he will probably offer me a big salary. I know that's called blackmail but for film actresses that's the way it often works."

During the conversation they had both ate slowly, enjoying the food and the wine as a pleasant backdrop to the conversation but Marc suddenly put down his knife and fork, sat on the edge of his chair and his eyes narrowed showing a mixture of incomprehension and disbelief at what he was hearing. He looked so miserable and shot an accusing sort of glance at Emma.

"Hey, Marc, I haven't said I prefer to work for Hayward – there I've said his name! – I hadn't finished what I wanted to say. What I wanted to say was that he will almost certainly try to contact me quite soon with a new proposal, I just know he will. I want to work with you – I feel at ease with you and I like the part of Hortense – but how soon can you get the project moving?"

Marc sat back again in his chair and seemed reassured to some extent although not completely. "Are you saying that you want to work with me but if there is no funding very soon, you will be obliged to work for this Hayward director?"

"No Marc, I'm just saying what comes into my head. I don't go in for strategic thinking for my own profit. I just come straight out with it. I wish I didn't sometimes," and she bowed her head in mock shame which made Marc laugh and then they laughed together.

"Listen Emma, this afternoon I intend to make an appointment with the UK Film Council and a couple of producers to see where we can get some financing. I have almost finished the 3rd act so as soon as that is done we will have to shoot some video extracts of the story to show to potential financiers. I have also got to approach the other actors I hope to hire for the second roles. It's going to be difficult but not impossible, especially with you in the role of Hortense."

They agreed to meet two days later – a Friday - to discuss what progress might have been made and the follow-up to be envisaged

CHAPTER 3

Two months later in mid-October, the two fellow actors who were now friends as well, had achieved a great deal. The financing although not yet a palpable element was in the pipeline and this was in part Emma's doing because she accompanied Marc whenever he had an important appointment. Not only did they now have a video of interesting parts of the film to show financiers and sponsors but Emma's natural brio danced like sunbeams during any discussion and this when added to Marc's convincing arguments made all the difference in the otherwise functional but pedestrian discussions. It made a real difference. After each appointment they discovered they were inexplicably content to be in each other's company.

"It's very strange, Marc, but we only met two months ago and yet I feel as if we've known each other for years. Very weird!"

"I'm the same but what is more I have peculiar, incoherent images that pass through my head that only last a fraction of a second – like then, just a moment ago I saw a figure wearing helmet and goggles, really old style. I must be going crazy. It's probably the film taking over my psyche." He laughed as he said this.

"Well, Marc , you probably will not believe me if I tell you that I experience the same type of phenomena – not helmeted people but a strange car whizzes past me - it goes so fast I can't make it out at all. What's happening to us?"

"I daresay the explanation could be classed as psychedelic – we're having hallucinations, probably from overwork. Look, we've worked hard again today. Let's take a break, have a meal somewhere cosy and then listen to some jazz somewhere. I think you told me you liked jazz, didn't you?"

"Yes I love jazz. Shall we call it a day now?"

During a meal in a cosy little restaurant near Ronnie Scott's they discussed this and that and found that many distractions the world and its masters had to offer pleased them both and for many of those distractions one could say that that was an understatement. They both more than appreciated great classical music including opera and ballet. They also liked watching tennis and the fact that Emma enjoyed rugby on the TV surprised Marc greatly. Their appreciation of literature was obvious and Emma was able, there again to Marc's surprise, to quote passages from Voltaire's poems and also Shakespeare. He in his turn surprised her by his love of philosophy and he also was able to quote choice phrases from a philosopher he had just discovered called François Cheng and he found great comfort from such quotes as "Death is the destiny of Life". This conversation between them in some way brought their relationship even closer.

Ronnie Scott's liberated their slightly pent-up spirits and they danced together quite wildly at appropriate musical moments while at other times they simply sat back with a glass in hand sometimes smiling at each other but mostly just listening to and watching the musicians.

It was 1 a.m. when they left the club Emma walking to the left of Marc and holding his arm.

"As it's late, you might just as well stay with me tonight. I have a put-u-up in the living room and clean linen, so no problem."

What was amazing in the circumstances was that neither of them made the slightest move to show their strong attraction one for the other. This was strange because it would have been perfectly natural for the two of them to have nestled into each others' arms and more ..., but it was as if they had verbally agreed not to sleep together although not a word had been uttered. Their agreement had apparently been conveyed gazing at each other by means of a sort of mutual hypnosis. Both were amazed at this turn of events for they had more or less expected the inevitable to happen, but no –something was preventing this ultimate consecration of their relationship. Both pretended that everything was completely natural and although longing to be close one to the other they settled into their respective beds with just a "Good Night. Sleep well." Their night was not particularly calm or restful and each heard the other either going to the WC or bathroom during the night or heard them moving restlessly or even groaning from time to time.

It was Saturday morning so they decided to separate for the weekend as they both agreed that they needed to think very deeply at what was happening because, apart from the need to get the film under way, they could not understand certain phenomena that they were both experiencing. They breakfasted rapidly on toasted bread and marmalade but accompanied by some very nice coffee of Emma's making.

Marc sped off towards his flat after they had performed the sacred *bise* so important to Europeans and with which they had both been brought up from the cradle.

There was an important meeting with a possible financier on the following Monday. However Marc had decided with Emma's prior permission to see a friend from the drama school who now earned a very good living from advertising and most of his work was done in a fairly large lofthouse-type studio in Camden Town that had previously been part of a warehouse. The aim of the visit was to find a location for shooting the long behind-closed-doors sequences of the film. He knew he would be able to obtain reasonable rates from the friend and another advantage was that it could easily be split up into several entities. He had phoned his friend Malcolm beforehand and was met with open arms (they had been quite close friends and had been known as the M&Ms). He explained the situation to Malcolm who told him that as there were three possible sections of the studio that could be used for his film he could start when he liked even if it was in two months' time. They talked together for a while and it turned out that Malcolm had known Emma to a greater extent than had Marc and he was overjoyed that he would be seeing her for the time of the shooting of the film. They also discussed the best ways of finding an outside location in Italy for the scenes which had to be shot in the open, for instance with horses, market scenes and the like. Malcolm had contacts and promised to do what he could to find an appropriate location and all the necessary frills on site or very near. By frills he meant the clothes of the main characters and their means of transport. Apparently some scenes without dialog could be rented from some large film and TV companies that specialized in such services. This was comforting for Marc.

Malcolm had given Marc a key, so on the Sunday, the next day, Emma and Marc decided to make a preliminary attack on the first sequence of the film which was set very briefly in the open before the two main characters entered a large Italian house. As Marc was the director he moved himself and Emma about on the set as he thought fit and each holding their script their voices echoed strangely around the almost empty studio. Emma also had her word to say and some utterances of phrases were the result of consultations between them and often quite a bit of laughter. The start was thought to be very encouraging. They videoed the scene and realized that certain parts of the dialogues had to be altered – not necessarily the words but above all the tones of voice. Emma was very good at discerning what she considered to be shortfalls in this important aspect of the rendition of a conversation and even more so of the several monologues that Marc had written into the scripts. They stopped work at or about 1 p.m. and returned to their respective lodgings for lunch. They decided to resume "rehearsals" the following day. There was no hint of either of them spending the night at the other's. Neither of them in their inner self knew why.

CHAPTER 4

The financing of the film was now arranged – signed and sealed –with very little gain for the subsidy winners even supposing the film was accepted by the critics and the public. The grantee, Marc Leboucher, would take some 15% only of box office takings. Marc was not at all worried about this because he knew that it was just a first step in a promising career if indeed the promise was to be fulfilled.

Three months later, in mid-January, most of the behind-closed-doors scenes had been filmed and approved by Marc and Emma and the acting and technical teams were ready to move to Italy for the outdoor scenes. Marc was disappointed that the season was badly chosen, though it was hardly a question of choice, rather of bad luck since the economics of the future film had to be put in place before anything else.

Marc had of course finished writing his script not without some difficulty and it was Emma who more or less kept the ball rolling with her very appropriate suggestions.

One of the indoor scenes, suitably fitted out with real or false furniture and furnishings of the period, was being filmed when Emma's mobile telephone rang very loudly and made it imperative to stop filming.

"Yes? Hello, who is that?" The sound of a male voice with an American accent could be heard wafting from the handheld telephone but the gist of the conversation could not be followed especially as Emma moved out of the "room" and into the adjoining sector of Malcolm's lofthouse studio.

The whole team waited and waited but Emma did not come back from the other room and as the late afternoon was fast approaching Marc decided to postpone the follow-up scene until the morrow. The technical crew and the two other actors who were necessary for the scene slipped away leaving Marc alone awaiting the return of Emma. She came back looking pale and drawn after what had apparently been an ordeal.

Marc put his arm around Emma, said nothing and waited for her to speak.

"Look Marc, I didn't tell you everything about Hayward. I was just an actress for one of his movies from my point of view and nothing more. As I told you he would have slept with me if he had had half a chance but I never let him come nearer than the distance of a handshake. That's the truth (Marc nodded). He married a beautiful and rather simple woman after his former wife had left him. This new wife was indeed lovely and she did all that was required of her – just like a 19th century French or Italian bourgeois woman – but she had great difficulty doing her duty by her10 year-old autistic daughter. Remember this was two years ago,. This child, very troubled by her mother's apparent lack of concern for her well-being, would often shout at her and the latter, with no real sense of love or even duty towards her daughter often left her to her own devices. There were staff to look after her but nobody had taken the trouble to get her problem diagnosed and a long-term treatment organized. That's where I came in.

One day I happened to be passing her bedroom when I heard suppressed sobbing of a sort that was heart rending. I paused by her door and knocked discreetly. As nobody came I opened the door a crack and saw the child lying on the floor on her back and in a terrible state. I silently knelt down beside her, put my arm under her head and sort of hoisted her up onto my breast and shoulder. She looked at me in wonder and gave me a smile that I can't describe because it was like the expression of someone who was miraculously snatched from the jaws of some horrible fate. From that time some sort of relationship was built up between us. We played games together and I discovered that she was incredibly clever, often beat me at games and especially at chess which I taught her and she learned in one short session. She came to be very dependent on me and to some extent I felt the same because underneath the unhappiness of the abandonment by her mother I found a loving, intelligent and devoted child. I enjoyed being with her. Now then, Hayward was not entirely lacking in compassion and when the new wife in her turn, in the trappings of a sort of cougar, decided to leave him for a younger man and she refused to take her own daughter with her, he decided that the daughter – Esther is her name – would stay with him and especially with me, for a time at least. I encouraged her to be friendly with Hayward and when he took me out to dinner we often let her come with us and she turned out to be charming company, perhaps not in spite of her disability but because of it. She looked at you sort of askance and for anyone who did not know her this was unsettling but for me and to a lesser extent for Hayward this look of hers and the way she held her head to one side and her forever moving fingers that clutched objects to be studied by those penetrating dark eyes while she turned the objects delicately over was captivating.

"Look, Esther apparently needs me and although Hayward, as I said, has become almost attached to this now pre-teenager, he could not contemplate the role of foster father. That's why he phoned. He wants me to accept her, here in the UK, for the time being. I explained I was doing a film that would take another two months but he said she would have to be handed over to the authorities if she could not be with me. What can I do?"

"Listen, Emma, this is astounding news but does not surprise me about you. Let the child come for the time of the film and we might even be able to fit her into the film. I'll think of something. But what happens afterwards?"

"I don't know but he will expect me to go back to the States with the child. That is obvious." Emma started looking very upset and she paced the room with an expression of misery, holding her face in her hands. Sadness clouded her features and her expression closed up. She then sat down in a decor chair and cried and cried until Marc took her in his arms and stroked her hair gently.

"Dear Emma, he was surprised to hear himself using the adjective "dear" which by mutual but unsaid consent the two of them had always avoided, do not get yourself into a state of panic. Let the girl come. Can she stay with you? (emphatic nods from Emma) She can watch the film being made and as I said I'll write a small role into the script for her. We'll see how things go after that. I must admit that I distrust the motives of Hayward but there will be time to sort that out later. What do you think?"

"Oh, would you do that, Marc. Oh, I'm overjoyed because I have worried about her a lot and I certainly did not want to get you involved."

"Listen, Emma, we are not children. We are grown adults and we have feelings one for the other (Emma looked at him in astonishment as if he had said something prohibited) – there, I've dropped another clanger – so I think we can come to one another's aid. Let's clear up a bit, have an early meal somewhere and try to organize our lives on a more positive basis. I think it's time for change ..."

Emma could hardly believe her ears but it must be said that she had been waiting for a disclosure of this type for some time. She stood still, clam-like and expressionless for a full two seconds before breaking into a huge smile and throwing her arms around Marc's neck. He, for his part, was somewhat surprised at such a colourful response but not entirely and they naturally kissed and kissed ...

CHAPTER 5

The pub meal was appreciated but eaten rather hastily as both Emma and Marc were aching to be in each other's arms after such a long period of mutually consented abstinence. When eventually they arrived at Marc's flat, had stripped naked and dived under the duvet, they took their time and enjoyed the thrill of each touch and kiss everywhere on their bodies and faces. This was not an occasion to be wasted in over-hurried love making. The reader can decide how each of them gave pleasure to the other but we can assume that it was shared equally and that they were equally satisfied. They took their shower together afterwards and by virtue of this sanitary activity extended their time of happiness together so rare in the lives of any couple.

They returned to their "work" of being filmed in the indoor setting of the decor of the period and country. It was now difficult for both of them to keep to their roles of wooer and wooed since in the context of their real lives their relationship was now consummated. Still, it was only a play and to some extent they found it amusing.

The next big hurdle was the trip to Italy and the choice of a town whose architecture had to be no later than the late 18th century. Finally they decided to seek a town a short distance from Rome and Marc spent much time in the latter part of the afternoon rummaging in the local library or in the evening on Google. He came up with the town of Orvieto in Umbria, some twenty minutes from Rome, deciding it was just right for the story and for even more precision found that Via del Duomo looked the type of street where the family served by Hortense might easily have lived.

Their source of funding was still intact so the work now involved hiring the costumes of the period but on or near the site of shooting and very probably in Rome itself. Emma decided to devote herself to that side of the organization and together they would have to find extras near or on the site of the shooting. This then required a quick trip to Rome and they decided to arrange the departure in the next two or three weeks after all the indoor scenes had been satisfactorily shot. There was the problem of introducing Esther, the American 12 year-old, into certain scenes but that could be arranged with the technical team. They would however take her with them to Italy for the relatively few outdoor scenes. Emma said she would contact Hayward and take advantage of the call to talk to Esther to explain the situation and persuade her that she would enjoy a trip to Europe and especially to Italy. She knew in any case that young Esther would be overjoyed to see her but it should be said that the pleasure would be mutual.

CHAPTER 6

Shooting in Orvieto in February went as planned with the enthusiastic assistance of the municipality. They cordoned off a wide part of the Via del Duomo (Cathedral Street) where a bourgeois style house of the late 18th century was being reburbished. Its front entrance with a very wide door looked just right for the period – slightly tarnished but expensive all the same. Emma arranged with an events company in Rome the hire of costumes and above all the light horse drawn carriage essential for the comings and goings of Count Bencivenni with his daughter Claudia (Esther). Two or three very short scenes consisted of the carriage passing through a forest. These also were arranged with the municipality in a nearby park. The camera and lighting team carted all the necessary equipment for outdoor shooting to Italy in a break hired in London. Shooting went well and took less than one week. It must be said that the outdoor scenes took up only a small part of the scenario of the film time-wise.

So now everyone is back at Camden Town to carry out post-production tasks like fine-tuning some of the sets, reciting tiny parts of the script once more for the sake of perfection and of course integrating the Italy-shot footage at strategic points in the film. The endeavour as a whole was quite exhausting for all the actors and especially for young Esther who was of course quite fragile but who rose to the occasion and sometimes even gave the impression that she had, at least temporarily, vanquished her condition of autism so immersed was she in her small role in the film but also in the unfolding of the story of the film from start to finish.

The end of February came all too quickly but Marc and Emma were reasonably pleased because they had more or less kept to schedule. They now had to integrate the opening title of the film at the very beginning with the name of the sponsoring company or organization followed by the names of the actors. Their names against their roles would be presented at the end of the film.

Everyone was now demobilised so Emma and Marc thought they would now be able to enjoy the company of Esther together during the day before it was time for her to go to bed. She was a lovely child but because of her autistic state she was often somewhat panicky and had to be reassured and calmed. During the shooting of the film her behaviour had been practically like that of any other child of her age, preteens, perhaps because it gave her a sense of importance.

Marc now of course had to find a distributor for the film, no easy task - and that he knew was an understatement. The big companies would be out of the question but he was keen to have a try at film festivals. He learned that film makers did not on the whole have direct contact with festival organizers but with programmers whose job it was to propose films to the festival organizers. This occurred mostly along non-official circuitry lines so the first task was to find out who these people were exactly. This he did by meeting film festival personnel, explaining the film and generally persuading them that his film would be worth watching for its cultural background and setting. They would then, if convinced by Marc's arguments, propose such or such a programmer. This mission was fairly time consuming what with the telephone calls and appointments it entailed often involving travel both in the UK and in Europe.

One non-working day he and Emma were together in the company of Esther with whom they were playing Scrabble. She turned out to be a first class player and sometimes beat both of them. On this late afternoon after a stroll around the park in the town of of Holland Park they had just started a game of Scrabble when the fixed line telephone started to ring. Emma took her time to unhook as she was still thinking of the word she wanted to play and was in fact holding her letter holder and gazing at it intently not at all bothered about the phone.

However, when she looked at the instrument she instantly knew who it was by the longish number that contained both "44" preceded by the digit "1". "Oh no! she exclaimed visibly deranged, it's Hayward. I'll have to speak to him alone."

"OK Emma, we'll make a cup of tea. Come on Esther, we'll go in the kitchen." Esther of course wanted to know what was going on and tried to catch the tone of Emma's voice and occasionally her words.

"He wants me to go back," she whispered to Marc.

"Of course he wants you to go back, replied Marc, managing a genuine smile, holding Esther against him, who wouldn't want you back? You are so talented and such good company."

"I'm not, she cried, I'm autistic and very difficult to be with."

"Hey, not so fast, Esther. You did a grand job in the film and you keep Emma very pleasantly busy. I know she's only too happy to be with you and it's the same for me when I'm here."

The telephone conversation with Hayward continued for another fifteen minutes or so but eventually Emma hung up and came into the kitchen looking a little haggard and weary.

"He's got a leading role for me in what he thinks will be a blockbuster thriller. I've got to go unfortunately and he wants Esther back."

"Well, it's only natural that Esther returns to her foster father, isn't it Esther, turning to the girl with a kind smile, we were just discussing that and I suppose that you have to accept the role in his film as you will be well paid. My film cannot guarantee any real financial reward, not in the short-term at any rate ..." He looked at Emma with real sadness in his eyes which started to gleam from the tears he was trying to hold back.

"Marc, she said hesitatingly, there's something you ought to know and that is that Hayward more or less forced me to sign an agreement by which I undertook to be available for a part in his next film. It's probably not legally enforceable but I feel morally bound to comply."

During these short exchanges they had looked at one another and then at Esther as if they wondered whether she should hear the conversation. In the end they both shrugged as if to say that she would eventually be obliged to be informed so why not straightaway. Esther of course was gazing at them all this time in some consternation and starting to move her hands about restlessly. Emma took her in her arms cradling her head on her shoulder.

"My dear Esther you can be sure that I will not let you down. I will take you back to California and I will never be far away. I expect Marc will be able to come when he has sorted out the distribution side of his film, won't you Marc?" turning to him with an agree-won't-you smile. Of course he did and not even reluctantly.

Later, when Esther had been tucked in and kissed by the two of them the matter that was absorbing them was broached by Marc.

"Emma, to practical matters. How long does your Hayward millionaire fellow reckon he will be shooting his feature length film?"

"It's going to take at least a couple of months I should think. I know it's a good opportunity for me but I just don't want to leave you Marc. It makes me very unhappy." It's true her eyes were glistening

"Listen, my darling Emma, I think our relationship is very strong and can withstand a parting of several months. We'll find a way through this. When you're working you'll forget everything and then there will be Esther to offer lots of love and distraction. You know what? I shall miss little Esther as well. You're lucky to have her."

"Marc, there is one thing that's worrying me and that's the agreement I signed with Hayward. I just trusted him but I did not look at the small print. I hope there is no catch in it."

"Why should there be? It just ensures you will be available to play the part of the heroine in the film. I imagine the role was made for you. It's a guarantee for him – nothing else."

"Well Marc, the only problem is that he's keen on me. I know how to deal with him but it's almost certain that he will try it on again."

"Sorry I can't be there to kick him up the backside if he tries anything but you have a strong character and I trust you absolutely, so no problem! Let's leave it at that for now, shall we?"

"Oh yes" and the kiss she gave Marc was more than just affectionate – it was frankly sensual.

That evening in bed they were wrapped in each other's arms as usual and their pleasure was still just as intense yet at the same time soothing, both to the mind and body. One or other of them would quite often remind the other of how she or he was experiencing a happiness that was at the same time unbelievably rare but a pleasure, strangely enough, vaguely familiar between them.

"It's very odd", Emma started to say but Marc broke in.

"Very odd that we seem to know not only our faces and voices but also the way we think together. By the way, I haven't told you but from time to time when I have been with you a while strange images flash across my eyes-closed field of vision if I can call it that. I have just had one of what seemed to be a red flag being jerked downwards. I admit it was vague, extremely rapid - far less than a second – and to me, senseless."

Emma sat up in bed abruptly and in the dim light of the bedside lamp Marc could see she was flustered. "That's incredible, Marc. I just saw the same sort of image and although to me it might have been anything, not necessarily a flag, it was definitely red. What does it mean? We can't have super- sensory powers, can we? We are just ordinary people leading quite difficult but ordinary lives."

"It's probably because we are getting to know each other but if I was a fortune teller I would probably say that we are both racing against something, he laughingly declared. Could it be time? I suggest we forget all that. It's a lot of nonsense. "

"Right, let's do that," said Emma and the relief she felt was palpable. They did not make love, so content were they of the great calmness that came over them all of a sudden. Instead they nestled into each others' arms and were surprised because in no time at all there was a faint knocking at the door. They had slept all night and there was Esther looking slightly put out, hungry and ready for breakfast.

CHAPTER 7

Two months have gone by with much difficulty for Marc even though he was extremely busy contacting programmers both in Europe and in North America to persuade them that his film, for which he was now seeking an eye-catching title, was worth watching. One or two Italian programmers had agreed to see his film as had also a few in France. He discovered that film festivals existed in practically all historically and architecturally important towns. Quite a few showed interest and promised to talk to festival organizers to show the film and even one promised to have a meeting with a big film distributor but it remained to be seen whether this would in fact happen.

Luckily Marc was able to use Skype for his calls to North America and he naturally focused his efforts on California and especially the Los Angeles region. He spoke to various programmers and learned that nearly all the pretty towns in the region, often in ideally situated surroundings, had their own festival, often connected to universities. However, he really did want his film to be viewed in that region in order to be near Emma whose presence and touch he now missed extremely. She lived in Hayward's awe-inspiring mansion perched in the Baldwin Hills with a wonderful panoramic view. He was able to speak to her most evenings on Skype which had the advantage of being connected to a webcam. Emma had her own suite in this huge house and Esther spent most evenings after school with her even though she had her own bedroom.

Hayward's film was now practically finished and of course as he was well-known in the business it was almost certain to be screened for one or other of the festivals. He would probably start with a small festival and then move on to a larger one with bigger audiences or if the big distributors were sure of a box office sell-out he would not have the bother of going through the festival filter system. For Marc it was completely different. He was unknown to distributors, yet alone film companies, so his film had to be exceptional to get anywhere and the programmer, if he found one, had to be exceptionally discerning and on the lookout for originality and quality of acting, a good plot keeping an audience on tenterhooks waiting for developments in the story, historically plausible not to mention shooting professionalism (good angles, innovation, precision ...).

So this was a frantic time for Marc. He had several contacts that seemed promising but were taking time to come through so he thought he would take a short cut and take the risk of flying directly to California and of meeting the organizers of modest and relatively unimportant film festivals in person. Several footage copies of the film had been prepared by his team so he decided to take two with him. They would probably have to be stowed in the hold of the aircraft so had to be packed extremely carefully.

He had given himself one month to achieve the impossible because of the financial situation. He simply could not overrun his loans. He had found himself reasonably cheap but functional "lodgings" on the Internet – a large, very comfortable room with double bed, desk, sofa and a small kitchen and shower room with a nice view over the green hills and neighbourhoods dotted around the area. He was pleased with the rental and after allowing himself a day to recover from jetlag he pressed ahead to make appointments with programmers. He knew from the start that it would not be easy and that most people connected with films would want a commercially viable story with the usual ingredients of romance, criminality, screeching police cars and a happy ending which was not at all the stuff of Marc's film. He realized he had not even found a title for his film so he spent the first morning in his room viewing the film and turning over titles in his head and on paper. He knew the name Hortense had to figure in the title and in the end he settled on "Hortense and the blue room" knowing of course that he could change it at any time. He had decided not to tell Emma that he was close to her for the time being. He was half afraid she might take fright and that the famous Hayward would get wind of it and make life difficult for her. Lately when Marc thought of Emma or even when he was not thinking of her, an image of her face would come and go very quickly across his inner field of vision but the strange thing about it was that her black hair, which for the months Marc had known her fell straight down to her shoulders, was in these images tied back neatly behind her head in a pony tail or a bun. Her lips were more heavily made up than Marc had ever seen – in fact Emma hardly used makeup at all, just a little mascara. He was quite astonished because in one image she looked so sure of herself and yet in another so worried looking. He decided he would phone her that evening and talk about it.

The first two days of his efforts to convince programmers of the seriousness of his offer were fruitless and he went to bed feeling slightly depressed all the more so as it had been impossible to contact Emma. "Just as well, he thought, she would have perceived his lack of alacrity."However, the third day a programmer did agree to view his film or parts of it. This person seemed more culturally evolved than the first two so it looked promising.

Marc was invited to project his film on a large but not cinema-sized screen. The programmer, an intelligent looking man in his forties, introduced himself as Mr O'Brien and was accompanied by a woman who during the screening used a special torch pen to scribble things in a notebook. They asked him, from time to time, to skip chunks of the film, probably to save time but all the same obtaining a good overview of it. You could say it was the equivalent of reading an article or book diagonally. When eventually the film was over the woman asked Marc to wait 10 minutes or so while they had a short discussion.

When they came into the waiting room where O'Brian's faithful co-programmer, as she turned out to be, had asked Marc to wait, he could even see from their faces that they were not going to reject "Hortense and the blue room" out of hand. Marc stood up as they entered. O'Brian turned to him and introduced Mrs Giacomo, an attractive woman in her early fifties who was smiling quite broadly.

"Well, we can see you have put a lot of work into this film even going so far as shooting a part of it in another country. We are quite impressed by the changing atmospheres across the film and how your actors almost look as if they are not acting. You play your role very well, Mr Leboucher and Hortense is well, stunning. We believe we have seen her in another film over the last year. Can you tell us where we might have seen her?"

Marc then related how Emma was now a preferred actress in Hayward's (he referred to him as Mr Hayward) cinema group and was appearing currently in one of his films.

"Well, listen Mr Leboucher, broke in Mrs Giacomo, we think the film is good. It's emotive without being weepy, the story bowls along very nicely and we think audiences will be able to relate to the characters. This is important. There is just the right mix of good and not-so-good characters and of nuanced moods. There is also just the right amount of action to break any possible hint of boredom. We like it and we think audiences will too. We intend with your permission to screen it at a small university festival as from Friday. If the film passes muster and we believe it will, we will apply to have it filmed at the SunValley Festival of Film Discoveries. What do you say?"

"I thank you enormously. I couldn't wish for anything better; When will you be screening Hortense."

"I couldn't tell you for the moment but I'll send you an SMS by the latest Wednesday evening."

The meeting drew to a close without any further discussion nor was there any need for any more. Marc was overjoyed and as soon as he had bought himself a takeaway, taken it up to his room and put it on a low heat in the oven he punched in Emma's mobile number on his own phone. It rang and it rang but no reply. He thought he would try again in half an hour and in the meantime he logged in on the tablet he had brought with him to obtain information on the SunValley event that he had jotted down on a piece of paper. It appeared that although it was not a festival that was acclaimed throughout the United States, it was well known officiously to all the professionals in the business of film making. Screening a film at Simi, as it was affectionately called, sometimes led to making a reputation for oneself. One could only hope.

Having eaten he tried Emma's number once more and was overjoyed when he heard her voice.

"Hi Marc, how are you?"

"I'm fine Emma but missing you like mad." There was a chuckle at the end of the phrase but Emma knew he was covering up a real need to speak to her and she felt pleased and serene at the same time. "I have got some good news. There's a programmer who is willing to see me in California. I didn't have much luck in Europe –unfortunately but perhaps fortunately, we'll see. He seemed very interested in the subject of the film and impressed that you star in it. I've booked a flight and will be in California on Wednesday evening. I've given myself a day to deal with jetlag so that I'll be ready for Friday for the interview. And you, my dear Emma? Are you OK? And little Esther? How's she?"

"We're good, as they say here. Just looking forward to seeing you again. Hey, this is a very good line, isn't it? It's not usually so good." She sounded bright and the energy in her voice was a tonic to Marc's ears.

"Yes, isn't it? He felt his heart beating uncomfortably fast. Tell me then, how's your film doing with Hayward? I expect you must be almost finished by now?"

"Yes, almost finished. He's got all the resources of the biggest film producers so it goes very fast but, Christ how exhausting it is. He thinks it's going to be a box office sell-out. But then he's always like that. He thinks he's the best. He's been a little difficult lately – a bit nervous, I expect. He always treats me well. He's convinced he's gong to win me in the end. Don't worry, Marc, you have nothing to fear. I don't let him get anywhere near me except for character positioning in the various sets. What I don't like is that he is quite offhand with many other members of the cast and that's making them a bit hostile to me – not in words but I can see it in their expressions so I have to go out of my way to repel his tentative advances. But no matter. Yes, Esther is OK. She loves living here and I must say that Hayward does treat her quite well. Good job because I don't know how she could exist without him. She'd be back with foster parents or in care if she wasn't here. She's lovely but needs constant attention and reassurance. When shall I see you?"

"Saturday should be good or even Friday evening. I suppose you have the right to leave the estate?" Marc coughed a little as he said this showing he was not at all pleased with the way Emma was, to all intents and purposes, confined.

"Well no, Marc, I can do what I like when I'm not on the set and I do occasionally take a taxi into town but it's nice here. I have everything I need and Esther is often by my side. It's true, I eat out with Hayward from time to time but Esther nearly always keeps us company. Please don't worry, Marc. You know I love you – there I've said it. But I wanted to tell you something – it's very weird – I have pictures of a face zooming through my brain lately. The face is yours but in one picture, can I call it that? your hair was quite long and in another you were wearing a beard. I don't quite know what to make of it ..."

"You're not the only one, Emma, the same thing has been happening to me with you as the image. There again, it's your face, no doubt about that, but your hair is not at all how you wear it. Do you think we will find an explanation for this enigma?"

"Frankly, Marc, I don't know. What I do know is that as long as I can hear your voice often and that I can see you – and we're seeing each other this weekend –that's great – I prefer to try to forget these psychedelic phenomena. They do put me out a bit but perhaps it's our brains reminding us quite simply that we both exist and not to see hidden causes behind it. What do you think?" Her voice was gentle and reassuring but Marc, knowing Emma very well now, could sense a certain tension.

He decided to relieve her of her anxieties."You're quite right. We'll speak no more about it unless it worries one of us more than usually. These visions, I'm sure they will disappear and they're just waiting for us to be together in the long term, if you see what I mean?" He chuckled as he said this;

"I do indeed and I think you're right. Ooh, I feel better already! Hurry up Friday or Saturday. I have to go now. *Bisous*, Marc."

"Lots of *bisous*, too, Emma."

He thought afterwards that it was strange that Emma had for the first time since they had met used the French word *Bisous*, meaning a kiss on each cheek. He was touched but at the same time felt a little guilty that he had had to tell a fib of omission in respect of his whereabouts. Still, it had been done with the best intentions. He would tell her afterwards in any case.

CHAPTER 8

The showing of Marc's film at the modest film festival at a local university went well with O'Brian and Giacomo saying that it was a good sign for the Sun Valley Festival of Film Discoveries which was scheduled to take place from Sunday 21March to Saturday 27 March 2010.

Marc had not told Emma that their co-production, Hortense and the Blue Room, was to be screened at the SVF which was just as well because Hayward's film was also scheduled for the festival. That was going to make it difficult for the jury. He was now very impatient to see Emma and in the end he found he was free on the Friday evening. They agreed to meet at the Glendale Springs Inn in Glendale at 8.30 p.m. What she told Hayward to "justify" her absence Marc never knew but it must have been convincing because when she arrived she was shimmering to Marc's eyes in beauty. Her black hair had grown to below shoulder level and glistened in the sunshine framing her face in sheer happiness. Her eyes too, as twinkling and attractive as black diamonds, could not disguise her joy at being with Marc once more. They met outside the inn at Glendale and immediately fell into each other's arms and caressed the other's hair followed by a long drawn-out, beautifully sensual kiss, or rather a series of kisses. They just did not care who was watching them and when they did eventually open their eyes were astonished to see a group of people standing around them and gazing at them in wonder. This group of people then applauded as one, almost silently, daunted by the beauty of the scene. Both Emma and

Marc then stood back astonished at the spontaneity of what had just happened and Emma whispered to Marc, "Bow" which they did together to further applauses from the group. Then Marc said to the onlookers. "It's not for a film," which made them all laugh.

They spent a very enjoyable evening together and were even able to confer a sacred seal on it by spending an hour together in Marc's hotel room before Emma had to return to Hayward's domain.

Hayward had now been told of Marc's presence and he was not at all pleased and sought out all sorts of ruses to prevent Emma from seeing him. He reminded her that she had signed a contract with him but when she pointed out that the contract was only in respect of the film he said very pointedly; "Did you not read the small print in the contract?"

"What was the point, asked Emma, the small print is only significant in the case of litigation."

"Well, apparently you did not see that Esther will be obliged to return to care if you are no longer here to watch over her," he said triumphantly.

Emma was completely flabbergasted and realized that she was practically trapped and obliged to remain with him. "You can't do that. Esther is happy here and she knows that I will be returning to the UK after your film is screened."

"Well I think I can and I have told her that you will probably be staying here for quite a while."

She realized now that poor Esther had just been a ploy in Hayward's determination to have Emma as his wife. She was deeply disgusted by his behaviour because she knew she could not allow herself to abandon Esther. Not only did she genuinely love the child but she also saw that she had a duty by her. She was not yet aware that Marc's film was to be filmed at the festival.

Hayward now said something that was auspicious, in Emma's eyes, for the improbability of its happening. He said maliciously. "You starred in a film by your friend, Mr Botcher wasn't it? Well, he must put his film against mine and many others of course at the Sun Valley Festival of Film Discoveries and if he gets a better rating from the critics than mine I will keep Esther with me and cater for all her needs. There, that's a fair deal." He was laughing sarcastically when he said this as he believed that his own film was practically in the bag and that Marc's film had not the slightest chance of being listed in the festival. He did not even know that Marc was in California and that his film had already received acclamation from the two programmers. Emma felt completely crushed and left the room without uttering a further word. She had no idea that Hortense and the Blue Room was listed and it was only later that evening when Marc phoned her that she became privy to it.

They now had roughly two weeks before the SVF and as Hayward's film was now practically in the roll-out stage Emma and Marc were able to spend quite a bit of time together. It was however becoming increasingly difficult for Emma to leave the "estate" without getting Hayward riled and in the end she had to tell him of Marc's presence in California.

"What is he doing here? he almost shouted. It was plain he was exceedingly put out. Anyone would think he was here to have his film nominated for the Oscars. He laughed sarcastically. I can tell you he has absolutely no hope of getting nominated for any of the festivals in California." He said this knowing nothing about Marc's film, especially the fact that O'Brian and Giacomo, whom he knew personally very well, had given the film a high recommendation.

"I don't know exactly why he's here, she lied, except to see me."

"Well, listen to me Emma. I don't want you to be getting ideas into your head about this man. You know I admire and love you and will not let you go without a fight ... and ... remember, he uttered nastily, there is Esther to think of."

Emma was disgusted by this remark but as she realized with absolute clarity that he was blackmailing her and had in any case expected it to happen at some time, she knew that Marc and herself had to play their cards with extreme dexterity. As she could not countenance the type of remark Hayward had made, she started leaving the room saying "I know ..." slowly but with insistence.

As Hayward was absolutely convinced his film would make it to the top as most of his films did due to the immense resources thrown at them, he now declared something that had he known "Hortense" was also to be screened at the SVF, he might have forborne from saying.

"If your hopeful young film maker beats mine at the festival, he's all yours and I will guarantee Esther's future here." Here again he laughed but this time heartily because even had he known of the possible nomination of Marc's film at the festival, he would have found it ludicrous that it could be a contender for an award that he just knew was already won by himself and no other.

The conversation, if it could be so called took place in the spacious living area where there were a long dining table, several sofas, reclining chairs, a large TV screen on the wall, a bar of course, books and flowers everywhere and a large hatch to the kitchen. Twenty of so people would have been comfortable in this palatial setting. However, (could this turn out to be his undoing?) he had installed several high performance microphones in strategic spots in the "room" because it was inherent to his character to trust no-one and he always wanted to know what had been said about him or his films by anyone anywhere in his domain. Emma knew about the system because a maid called Zelda while doing her maid's work had accidently knocked a microphone to the floor when she was cleaning something or other from a pair of steps. As she liked Emma and Esther very much she had divulged her discovery to Emma thus warning her not to say any thing she might regret. Emma immediately stored Hayward's last mockery of Marc's film in the back of her mind and thought that perhaps it might become handy if she was pushed into a corner although she was fairly sure, just as much as Hayward, that "Hortense" could never be a box-office winner. She might have thought differently had she known what Marc told her two days later when they again met for a meal and a cuddle but this time at Marc's hotel. She could scarcely believe her ears. So what if, contrary to Hayward's view of any work other than his own, Hortense became a finalist against Hayward's film? It suddenly became a strong possibility and Emma was dumbstruck.

"Marc, my love, do you think there's the slightest chance we might come out on top?" she asked when her head was settled in its comfortable, newfound position on his shoulder and her body firmly settled against his.

"Before, I could never have envisaged that possibility but my two programmers are convinced there's a good chance and I can tell you that they know their job inside out. In addition, they have promised not to let Hayward know of our film before the night. That's normal practice – discretion is an important part of their job."

"Gosh, I can't believe it Marc." She raised and shook her head as she said this. "But I must say I am a bit muddled. I'm in two films and of course I want to get a good press for both but I shan't be disappointed if Hayward's film doesn't make it to the top as long as yours does!" she said with a sort of hint of challenge in her voice as the tone mounted.

"Hey now my love, calm down, we are not there yet and perhaps never will be. Be patient and perhaps luck will be on our side."

Emma returned to her apartment in Hayward's mansion. She was legally free but there was no point in anticipating his ire which might or might not arise, depending on the outcome of the festival. While she was returning she was turning over in her head a method of recovering the recording made earlier in the day in which Hayward had said laughingly that he would ensure the well-being of Esther if Marc won the SVF "Swan" award for the best film. She determined to speak later that evening to an electronics/IT expert she had made friends with when working on Hayward's film. The expert was a young woman of her age and one in whom she had absolute trust. They had often laughed together behind Hayward's back at some of his idiosyncrasies. She realized that if Hayward got wind of Marc's film nomination he would remember what he had told her about ensuring Esther's care and future. For the moment he had no idea of the threat that was being posed so she knew that action had to be taken very quickly.

CHAPTER 9

The week of the Sun Valley Festival of Film Discoveries had now dawned and all the film producers, celebrities and everyone involved in the numerous films to be screened were getting excited. Hayward's film that was described as a highly realistic science-fiction film describing how a group of beings from a very advanced civilization living deep down under the surface of the earth for centuries almost succeeded in making a huge section of the earth's surface (an entire country) and their citizens their slaves had it not been for the fantastic actions of the hero and heroine (Emma). In fact it was a fairly typical science fiction story but with splendid cinematic video and sound effects that would be an instant success with the young. It would certainly be given a good rating partly because of Hayward's reputation (how could he not get a good rating?) and partly because good box-office receipts could be reasonably anticipated. The film was due to be shown on the Wednesday, a day chosen by Hayward because he knew it was the best day of the week for attendances. As for Marc's film, that was scheduled for the Friday.

So the day arrived for the screening of Hayward's film. This was the day Emma arranged with her IT friend Johanna for her to seek, find and make a copy of the tape of the sound recording Hayward had not given much thought to when he made his reckless, hubristic offer concerning Esther. Emma had given her the access code to the mansion and had warned the maid and Esther about the operation. As the initial information about the recording system had come from the maid there was no need for alarm from that direction and Esther being highly intelligent was certain to be discreet, too.

So here was Hayward, dressed up in an expensive suit and bowtie with Emma sitting on one side of him and his artistic director on the other. Emma looked very attractive but not more than usual. She had always refused to use more than very basic makeup and this event was no exception to the rule. Her hair was loose about her face and she wore a blue sweater (expensive-looking all the same), black slacks and non-high heel shoes. Hayward looked very pleased to be showing her off. Emma did not feel at all the same. She wanted the whole affair to be over. She wondered how Johanna had fared or was faring.

Hayward was still not aware that Marc's film was to be screened later in the week as the list had only been completed up to and including Thursday, the day after. For the introduction to Hayward's "Far-under" film, he himself the film producer, the film director, the main male actor and of course Emma walked proudly together up to the rostrum where the usual round of introductions, short speeches and joking took place as is cutomary on such an occasion. Hayward strutted about like a peacock and made hardly disguised allusions to his prize-winning film as if the award had already taken place and indeed in his mind it had. Even to a casual observer it was manifestly obvious that he was sure of the outcome of the festival. Emma, on the contrary, made a very short address saying how she enjoyed her role in the film but made no claim to greatness and for anyone listening with any sensitivity at all to what she said the words were remarkable for their modesty. There were the usual applauses after each speech before the "team" returned to their "executive" seats to actually now watch Far-under, Hayward's two hour-long feature film.

That evening, back in the Hayward mansion, Far-under's producer received an email containing the list of the remaining entries for the festival. He was sitting back with a cigar in his hand and a gin or vodka on the low table before him on which was placed his Apple and looking very smug when suddenly his jaw dropped, he stood up in rage and shouted. "Emma, here at once if you don't mind ..." Emma was in her apartment so could not hear his rants thus obliging the maid to fetch her.

Emma knew of course or rather correctly guessed what had happened and adopted a demure, demoiselle-type stance. "Yes, Hayward how can I help you?" She uttered without the slightest sign of sarcasm. "Oh dear, you look as if you've had a fit. Sit down now and tell me what's on your mind." Indeed, Hayward did look as if he had had a sudden attack – his face was deep red, his arms were waving insanely and his eyes were as expressive as the projectiles used against citizens in his film Far-under.

"You did, did, did ... not...not tell me that your... your Frenchie guy was showing a film at SVF ..."

"I only knew yesterday and in any case, she said with the faintest of smiles, you are perfectly confident about the outcome of the festival."

"Yes, he said, suddenly lowering the tone, I have nothing to fear. I think I can clock up six or so votes even before the jury comes to its final decision. When my film was screened today I was told that it was in the running for first place. Have to see if your Mr Lebotcher guy can do any better." He laughed with a strong tone of irony in his voice. He was now reclining in his chair, all traces of anger having vanished. This was clearly due to what Emma had inferred from her brief phrase.

Emma was relieved that she had asked her friend to recover the recording which was now on a USB key and on Emma's mobile phone. She might need it or perhaps not. Saturday 27 March, the day of the announcement of the award winner, would decide whether or not the recording was necessary. She sincerely hoped it would be, mostly for the sake of Esther but also for Marc. He deserved a prize after all the work he (and she) had put into "Hortense and the blue room".

CHAPTER 10

We have now arrived at the day of the attribution of prizes, Saturday 27 March. Most of the 9 members of the jury arrived in the early evening. The deliberations had taken place in the morning and early afternoon in two sessions. The jury had come to their decisions with a certain degree of difficulty but this was only to be expected at such deliberations as the futures of several film directors and film producers were at stake to some degree. All those present had partaken of light refreshments (no alcohol – that would wait until after the ceremony) and were waiting for the very large cinema projection room to be filled with the invited spectators, that is anyone connected in any way with the films that had been screened during the week. As with any film festival the ratings or rankings of the films were appraised in line with a series of categories. The most important category would be the film most appreciated overall by the jury – not a very precise category but one which if obtained meant that the reputation of the film company would be boosted and its future profits assured. The other categories would include the production, the quality of the scenario and photography and the level and originality of the performance of the main actors and actresses. There were also awards for best foreign films and non-English speaking films.

People were now settling down in their seats waiting for the start of the ceremony. One could call it a ceremony but it would be more like a show with dancers, singers, orchestral interludes and other gems of the entertainment world decided by the organizers. So the music started up with a bang with snippets of several musicals played by the 20 musician strong orchestra. Gershwin music included Porgy and Bess, an American in Paris and so on. This was all fairly typical of a film festival award ceremony.

Some ten minutes later when the beat of the music had slowed and when it eventually came to an end, the jury president came on to the scene accompanied, naturally enough, by an attractive young woman star, a winner of a past ceremony. The organization of these ceremonies often banked on the surprise factor and this was no exception. The president announced first of all the winner of the photography category which involved neither Hayward nor Marc. Next came the production and Hayward was unexpectedly announced the winner of this category. Details of each category were debated before the public by various members of the jury who were now all on the podium. The scenario award was won by another film director and the best male performance by the main character in Far-under. Hayward should have been more than pleased up until this point but of course what he was looking for was the jury appreciation award because it embraced the qualities of most of the categories in one single appraisal. All the main categories were broken down into many sub-categories and these were awarded right, left and centre so that most of the producers and directors involved in the SVF, not to mention the actors, actresses and technical teams, would leave the ceremony with something to be pleased about.

Hayward could now be seen scowling almost openly although in fairness to the man he did applaud all the winners but just could not hide what he would have called attacks on his professionalism as one after another of the categories escaped him. Although this was just the name of the game in the aggressive world of film festivals he just could not understand why he was denied success. However, anyone even remotely connected with this environment could have told him that the type of film he had produced was no longer in the running even if it was extremely well produced.

And so when Emma was chosen as the best actress - not in Hayward's film but in Marc's - it was almost, but not quite yet, the last straw. The last straw of course was when "Hortense and the blue room" was the film most appreciated overall by the jury. There were differing opinions among the members of the jury but there was only one person who voted for "Far-under". Each film, one after the other, was acclaimed by a show of hands and effectively Marc's film was the only one that gained five out of the nine potential votes.

Hayward could stand it no longer and he stalked out of the venue as if he was trying to avoid being stung to death by a swarm of bees. Indeed, he was thrashing his arms about and cursing loudly to the extreme amusement of nearby spectators. Hayward tried to take Emma with him but she refused and when the man had finally left the building she beckoned to Marc who much to the further amusement of spectators sat down in Hayward's vacated seat. He whispered to her that he had just had one of his micro-second visions and this one appeared to be a wheeled sword of all things that disappeared from view in a flash across the horizon. Emma was flabbergasted because she also had had a similar image rushing across her inner field of vision. The phenomenon seemed to unite them as nothing else could and their mutual gaze with no words uttered gave them a deep sense of unity.

Marc was then invited to mount the podium and the five members of the jury who had voted for him explained their reasons. One said that the historic setting for the film was done in such a way that the spectator had no trouble in feeling entirely in his or her element in the ambience and decor. Another appreciated the performance of Emma who was, it must be admitted, outstanding in the role of Hortense while yet another extolled the virtues of Esther on the scene.

The above ceremony was naturally enough followed by an aperitif party in honour of all the winners where everyone discussed everybody else's films. There was one exception to the revellers and his absence was widely but discreetly discussed. The winning male performer in Far-under made a point of moving over to be near Emma and Marc and even he could not help but laugh at the way Hayward had behaved.

There was now left one very sore point to be sorted out and that was quite obviously Esther. Emma knew that Hayward would apply pressure on her to keep her to himself but she had no wish to broach the subject herself. She was certain that he would open a broadside on her quite soon. It would probably be on the morrow when he would have got himself together again after his disappointments at the festival.

And so it was. Emma sometimes ate her breakfast served by eastern European maids in the company of Hayward who had effectively sent an invitation to her room for this purpose. She knew that this was going to be a very difficult moment in her life but she also felt that she had the resources to deal with it. Was this because of some inner strength that she harboured and was unaware of or due to the visions she and Marc had experienced the day before? She shook her head with a feeling of defiance and decided that for the sake of Esther and for the love she felt for Marc she could tackle anything.

So she came into the vast living area where a low table was adorned with all that was necessary for a good breakfast including fresh fruit juices, cereals and milk, croissants, different types of jam including marmalade and of course a steaming coffee pot. She approached the low chair where Hayward was seated and practically beamed at him, knowing that this was going to be her moment, not his. One could see that he was visibly put out by this exterior sign of nonchalance but he quickly hid such a show of weakness that he could not abide in his own behaviour and his eyes narrowed while he said. "Come and enjoy a good breakfast with me. I have something to say to you …" The last phrase was uttered slowly and with deliberation.

"Oh yes, what could that be I wonder? and by the way I congratulate you on your wins yesterday. You should soon reap the benefits of them. Well, I'm listening ...?" Emma said this with a smile and while looking Hayward directly in the eyes.

"Emma, he said staring at her like some disgruntled schoolmaster, you do now realize that you and Esther will now be living with me permanently as we previously discussed. I have your written consent for that."

"Hayward, you have been instrumental in getting my career launched and for that I am very grateful to you but I have my own life to lead and career to pursue. I will be returning now to the UK or France and I will with great pleasure welcome Esther during her holiday periods but I know you will do the right thing by Esther and ensure her well-being and education. You know that without the special care she obtains due to your initiatives she would become exceedingly unhappy and unable to deal with life due to the handicap she suffers from." She said this without changing the tone of her voice and with the maximum of amiability.

"Look Emma, and she could see that the real Hayward was about to reveal itself, I cannot look after Esther except with your help. I know you will do the right thing and stay here with us both." His serpent-like nature was now once again revealing itself and it was obvious that he expected Emma to agree.

"I'm very glad, said Emma in a dead pan voice, that you will continue to do right by Esther. She could not tolerate a life in care as you know well. But as for me I shall be leaving for Europe as I just told you and I think your last condition deals with that entirely."

"My last condition, what are you talking about? If you stay here, Esther has nothing to fear."

"I would remind you, dear Hayward that you wagered that if Marc won the jury's approval for overall best film I would be free to lead my life as I wish and that you would guarantee Esther's well-being in your house. You must remember that so I think there is no more to be said."

"I never said such a thing, Hayward almost shouted in obvious bad faith, and even if I had how could you prove that?"

"Well, my dear Hayward, just listen to this" and she extracted her mobile phone from her handbag, twiddled with various buttons until she had found the necessary application and then pressed "Recording N°xxxx, time and date"

Hayward was completely mesmerized by this turn of events. He now stood up and contrary to his usual way of behaving just opened his mouth and gaped. He did not know what to say so Emma said it for him.

"Whenever I detect that you are going to say something disagreeable or inappropriate I just press the button on my telephone in my pocket or in my handbag. I have made quite a few recordings but I erase them almost immediately as a general rule." She lied perfectly glibly not wishing to incriminate Zelda in any way.

He eventually sat down and regained some of his usual composure. "Ok, it looks as if you had no intention of honouring the agreement you signed. Well, we'll see about that. I shall be contacting my lawyer. I strongly believe, and here he did not sound at all convincing, you will have to keep to your side of the bargain. I shall let you know the result of my contact with my lawyer but don't think that just because you have the recording you will get away with this. For the moment you will stay here with me in this house." He said all this hesitantly and looked absolutely flattened as if he could see a tsunami bearing down on him.

"Listen Hayward, you have the charge of Esther and I will come and see her quite regularly or she can cross the Atlantic to visit me (she avoided saying "us" instead of "me") and in any case if you need me for another film I will make myself available. But you must let me be free to change parts of my script and you must consult me on the subject matter of the film. Your film this year is very good but it is not what people want. They want something that has a bearing on their lives. Of course they still love car chases and physical fights, cops and robbers but even in those areas they still need to find a connection, albeit tenuous, with their own lives."

He still uttered nothing at all so bewildered was he at the turn of events. His mouth opened and shut several times. He had nothing to say.

"Hayward, I must leave you now. I promised to take Esther for a walk in Culver City Park. We won't be going far but I wanted to point out some very important aspects of Nature to her and perhaps by talking together she could form an opinion as to what sort of future she wants for herself. We shan't be back late so we can dine together this evening. Zelda will be preparing something for us to eat at lunchtime. I thank you so much Hayward for your understanding. Let me know the result of your meeting with your lawyer but I'm sure you will come round to my way of thinking. There was not a hint of irony in her statement which was accompanied by a perfectly normal, non-concocted smile.

Hayward said nothing and just scowled at her. He was sitting back in his chair and was patently not the Hayward that Emma had known up until that point in her relationship with the man.

She left him at that point to see Esther in her room to discuss what she had been doing trying not to show her anxiety to the girl who due to her autism had extrasensory perception in respect of the moods of the persons closest to her.

CHAPTER 11

Unknown to Emma but later related to her by Zelda, Hayward had phoned his lawyer friend who fortunately was a reasonable sort of fellow and who had the good sense to come to the mansion straightaway to try to sort things out a little. They had a scotch together and during the ensuing lowering of tension he persuaded Hayward that he needed a break to be able to relax and think things over. The latter had to be pushed a little but in the end accepted his friend's advice and booked a flight to Florida to a club where he sometimes spent his vacations. He said nothing to Emma but just left the next morning very early to drive to the airport.

All this would make the subject of another story altogether but the upshot was that after two days of sulking and being generally unpleasant to the staff of the club he happened to meet Sydney King, an Afro-American jazz singer and as she recognized him as a relatively well-known film producer they had drinks together, a meal together, danced together and then ... no matter! She succeeded in talking sense to him and apparently as they hit it off together – both intelligent and at the same levels of success in their chosen professions – she agreed to accompany him back to his mansion after they had spent a week together at the club.

Hayward only let Emma know of his return the day before by SMS. He also contacted the maid by telephone and gave her certain instructions that would become apparent in the evening. Hayward and Sydney left Florida early and arrived in the mansion at about 4 p.m.

Emma was astounded by the preparations that were taking place. The maid, Zelda, was even seconded by a young man who managed all the comings and goings connected with getting a fine dinner ready for the evening. Emma was of course now contacted directly by Hayward who asked her and Marc to be his guests that same evening. Esther would also be invited.

Emma and Marc entered the vast living area each one holding one of Esther's hands and were amazed to find Hayward dressed as if he were attending an official occasion with trim suit, bow tie, beautiful calf shoes and beaming to welcome an important foreign magnate and his wife. They were also surprised to see a very attractive Afro-American woman at his side dressed in a long white clinging gown and a degree of cleavage. Her shoes could not be seen under the long flowing dress but high heels could be imagined because she appeared to be an inch taller that Hayward.

"Please let me introduce Sydney King to you. You will remember her recent album entitled "Honey and Moon" – a huge success, eh Sydney? Sydney, Emma and Mark, you will remember my telling you, are my favourite actress and film director, and this is Esther, he said taking her by the hand, my favourite foster daughter." Esther managed a shy smile;

"Hayward, said Emma, Marc is spelt a 'c'."

"Oh yes, you're French aren't you, Marc? Well I wouldn't have believed it. You have no accent."

"Thanks a lot for the compliment Mr Hayward."

"Oh, just call me Hayward like all my friends …Well come and make yourselves comfortable all of you and we'll ask Zelda to serve us aperitifs. What would you like Emma and Marc and Sydney?" There's everything from whiskey via gin and vodka to fruit juices, if you prefer that. Esther, would you like a coke or a fruit juice?"

"A coke, please."

"A martini for me, Hayward, thank you," said Emma while Sydney opted for a fruit juice.

"…and a gin and tonic for me," said Marc, now visibly dumbfounded at what seemed to be a transformation of character and behaviour on the part of Hayward compared with what he had seen of him until then and from what Emma had told him. He was now just waiting to see what was round the corner because he could see very well that this was a sort of introductory show to impress the young couple for whatever reason that might be. The answer was not long in coming.

Hayward started very slowly. "Have you everything you need? Olives, nuts, raisins, pickles? OK then, great. First I want to say something quite difficult for me. I expect you have seen me as an overbearing, aggressive and selfish person and I believe that up to a point you were right. I admitted all that to you, didn't I, Sydney." She nodded. "I also admit that I left here in a bit of a huff after the festival but I had the good luck to meet Sydney and she was able to persuade me to relax and instead of lashing out at fate to relax and think positively about my position and ultimately about yours, Emma and Marc. Sydney has very good advice to offer." The latter here smiled appreciably. "I took a bit of time to assimilate her advice but it eventually percolated into my thick skull." Indulgent smiles to all three and even to Esther who looked mystified but was probably able to see that things would be changing for the better even for her. "Since yesterday I have turned things over in my mind and have come to realize that I cannot oblige you, Emma, to do my bidding. It's true you are a very talented and attractive young woman and I would have liked to have you by my side on a permanent basis but there is such a thing as free will and I was attempting to make you abandon that by a form of blackmail and for that I am extremely, yes, really extremely sorry. I can guarantee, Emma that I will take great care of you, Esther, turning to her, and you can now take me for your uncle, if you wish (she nodded but slightly puzzled by the turn of events). You already have a foster mother, don't you – that's you Emma – and I think you will know how to make the most of your life. I have already noticed a difference in you, my foster daughter since you, Emma, entered your orbit and of course you will be free during your school holidays to go to Europe to see Emma and Marc."

Esther now exited with Zelda at the latter's behest as the maid realized that more serious matters were about to take place. She had glanced at Hayward who had now assumed an official type of expression.

"Well, that's part of my *mea culpa* (Emma and Marc were nodding and smiling indulgently) but I have a proposal to make you to do with film making. Marc, I have not yet seen "Hortense" although I will make sure I do, but to have gained the best rating from the jury at the festival means you must have great talent in the domain of film directing. Not only that but I have learned that you yourself wrote the scenario and took the main male actor's part. Quite something! So the proposal I will now put before you is not pie-in-the-sky but based on concrete achievement. This is what I propose."

"I plan to set up a subsidiary of Hayward Studios in Europe somewhere. That's where you two can help me - that is to find a good location – but not only that, I want to make you the studio producer, Marc."

"Hey, wait a minute Hayward, said Marc very discreetly, it sounds wonderful but I have to tell you that the production side of filmmaking, even though for Hortense I was obliged to be everything from funding agent via producer, postproducer to director, it was I must admit, sheer slog and the only side I enjoyed was directing the film. So frankly, Hayward, I cannot accept the post of producer although if you offered me the job of director I would look at it very closely and even in that case I would continue writing scripts as I am passionate about that side of things. As for finding a location, if you agree to what I have just said, I might be able to help as I had to do a great deal of research for my own modest affair."

"OK Marc, fair enough, I should be able to find a good producer with whom you can work but what about you Emma? Would you like to participate in the venture? There will be quite a few jobs available. You will obviously be offered roles in films as you are such a brilliant actress but there will have to be a set designer which is of course a very responsible post and perhaps that could be attractive to you. I saw how you made suggestions in Far-under. Listen, for the moment we will leave it at that. You can chew it over together and we can continue the discussion tomorrow, if that suits you. But I would like to say again how sorry I am that I caused both of you a good deal of uncertainty and unhappiness. Frankly, I don't know how it happened but the kick in the teeth I received made me sit up for once, (not straightaway I will admit), take notice of what I was doing to myself and others. It's amazing to me how different I feel. Even the personnel have started smiling at me and that, I can tell you, is a situation I have never known until now and it's due to you two and of course Sydney. Thank you all so much, I feel a different person. I hope I'm not embarrassing you?"

"No Hayward, you are not embarrassing me, and I am very pleased to see you, how shall we say, are more comfortable with life? Your offer is enticing but I do feel like a little break from playing roles in films. I think I told you that I am passionate about history and especially the history of my own family. I plan to study a little and probably start having a family. I could be free, say in a couple of years to take on a role but we'll talk about that, as you suggested, tomorrow."

Esther then rejoined them and during the meal they discussed everything and anything unconnected with the film festival and the atmosphere was like that of a typical family gathering. All five relaxed and Emma and Marc felt that life was taking on a definitely positive appeal.

They rounded off the evening dancing, Hayward with Sydney, Marc with Emma before changing partners. Esther also danced, and very well too, with all four of the adults in turn.

Esther was taken by Zelda to her bedroom but not before everyone had cuddled her and complimented her on her dancing. Then Hayward returned to his suite with Sydney while Emma and Marc decided to spend the night at Marc's hotel although not before informing Esther that Emma would be back in the morning. She still needed reassuring.

At the hotel, once in the bedroom, they wound their arms around each other and indulged in the longest kiss in history as they tentatively suggested afterwards. It was certainly the most all-absorbing and the most mind-lip-tongue joining experience either of them had ever undergone in their lives. The kiss, or was it more than a kiss, seemed long but was it? They looked at each other intensely but with great desire and intuitively knew what the other felt. They did not have to discuss anything. Their relationship was, so to speak, anointed and was now unbreakable.

Their lives from that point changed intrinsically. They bought a semi-decrepit former wine-grower's house in the South of France in a village called Gabian with wine cellar located on the ground floor and it was Emma's huge delight to convert it into a delightful house where one could be at peace with oneself yet entertain a fairly large number of people at the drop of a hat. The work was going to take years but she was not at all in a hurry to finish it. Marc, not surprisingly now with Hayward's support found a distributor for his film, was able to reimburse his debts and took on the direction of a new Hayward financed film. Apparently, it was again connected with space and time travel but involving ordinary mortals from past centuries, not invading monsters from the future. Yet another science-fiction film but apparently convincing! Marc was also able to find time to write a script for a film based on a classical Greek theme. Like Emma, he was engrossed in history. She meanwhile spent much time in libraries and on the Internet searching for records of her father who had fought with the French Resistance. She and Marc also travelled by train to Anjou from time to time to visit the family and to carry out some research into the latter's family history. They enjoyed this joint research work enormously. Emma sometimes travelled to Los Angeles from France. From time to time she would accept a role in one of Hayward's films which would enable her to see Esther. As for that fair maiden, she had made great strides in combating her autism, helped it should be said by Hayward himself and some very effective psychoanalysis professionals. She also accompanied Emma and Marc from the States to Gabian at least once a year.

So the years rolled by with the ups and downs of professional work interspersed with periods of homemaking-cum-house-making, travel between Europe and the US, not to mention the bouts of research into family history. They also became the virtual parents of Esther enabling her to blossom, finish her schooling successfully and embark on her university studies which she decided would be in France and probably Montpellier, not far from Gabian. Hayward continued to be her "uncle" and provided everything she needed as a young woman setting out in life.

CHAPTER 12

We have now reached the year 2019. Life for Emma and Marc was fairly rosy with the usual ups and downs of any existence on this planet. The 1st and 2nd floors of the house in Gabian had been entirely renovated over the previous seven or eight years offering 2 comfortable but not luxurious apartment suites. They lived on the first floor leaving the second floor for visitors such as their parents, friends (who were now numerous) or Hayward and any friends he cared to bring. Esther had her own room on the same floor as Emma and Marc.

Emma was now forty and Marc forty one. Professionally their lives were fulfilled, Marc having directed several of Hayward's productions and a few of his own. Emma, likewise had appeared in a good number of films and usually obtained a good write-up in literary magazines and newspaper articles.

However, an unexpected event took place in the late Autumn of 2019 fairly late on a Saturday evening. From an unknown Web address – tempspace@bihfr.com – Emma received the following email which was backed up by an SMS carrying the same message. It was in French.

"Dear Mrs Jameson. First of all be assured that this message is not junk mail. We are an entirely respectable organization whose main aim is the detailed study of ordinary people's lives in the past and through the social media we have heard that you are seeking recorded information on your family. We think we can help you but we need your acceptance for a phone call we will make to explain everything. All you have to do is tick the "yes" box and the date and time frame that suits you. Please do not delete this message. It could be important for you. We thank you sincerely for the attention you have given us."

Emma was completely nonplussed when she received the message but from mere curiosity she read it in full but did not either bin it nor tick the requested boxes. She had to think deeply about it but felt convinced somehow that it was neither a con nor a hoax. It touched something, she could not say what, in her inner being. It was nearly time to turn in so she would sleep on it. However, Marc noticed her strange silence and asked her if there was anything wrong. She did not want to tell him because she felt sure that with his pragmatic nature he would dissuade her from answering the email.

Well, after a bad night's sleep, continually thinking about the message and the subtle reaction of her mind and soul thereto, she decided that answering the email was the only action she could take to set her mind at rest. She did this when she was alone in the bathroom after breakfast. She ticked a time frame when she was almost sure that Marc would be engrossed in one of the films in which he was ceaselessly involved. This was nearly always in the late afternoon or early evening. Having taken the decision and acting on it Emma promptly forgot the message although three days later on the Tuesday following her response the telephone rang and she was startled to hear a woman with a charming, melodious voice introducing herself. She had a very slight American accent.

"Oh Hello, I hope I'm not disturbing you. My name is Anastasia Prokovich and I work for Tempspace. Are you Emma Jameson?"

"Yes, that's me."

"Oh good. I sent you an email the other day and I was very pleased to see that you answered it. Are you there …?"

"Yes I'm here. Just a little perplexed …"

"I'm relieved you haven't hung up on me because it's quite delicate and difficult to explain why I, or rather we, need your help. I will start with a fairly simple question. Do you agree to answer? It's nothing personal, I can assure you."

Emma, now fully on her guard and ready to hang up if she found any question(s) inappropriate replied. "Well you really have piqued my curiosity but I warn you, if I don't like it I will indeed hang up…"

"Please do not worry. That will not be necessary. The question is simple but requires some thought and just a one-word answer. The question is this. Do you recall the main events of your life since you were eighteen years of age? Think carefully and I just want a yes/no answer – nothing more. Take your time."

Emma effectively found that she could only remember some very notable events in her life – the wedding of her one and only sister back in the year 2000 and a mountain hike a year later.

"Yes and No. I remember a few things but I have a photo album which enables me to pinpoint occasions in my life."

"Ok, Mrs Jameson, we'll leave it like that for the moment. Think about what we have said – very little, I must admit, but important – and on a day of your choice, I will call back. If you really don't want to talk to me, just don't answer - I will understand – or if you like just call me at any time during work hours. You have my number displayed on your phone."

"Yes, OK, I will think about it and let you know the best time to call me if I decide I want to go further. You have aroused my curiosity, it's true."

"We'll leave it like that then for the moment. Goodbye, Mrs Jameson" and she hung up.

Emma knew perfectly well that she would continue the discussion, if it could be called a discussion, simply because the woman, Anastasia, had provoked her into opening a sort of Pandora's box, the difference being between Emma's version and Pandora's was that nothing came out of the box and all was left within. She realized she must have subconsciously pushed most of her experiences since the age of eighteen and until her meeting with Marc from her mind. She rushed to her photo album and tried to associate ideas, thoughts and sensations with the various photos. For some, like the mountain hike, she remembered having seen the valleys glowing ethereal in the evening sunshine but now wondered if even those feelings of awe could be ascribed to images from a TV documentary or perhaps a feature film and not to her memory. She decided that if Anastasia could enable her to extract what was in the box she had no choice but to go along with her but she would say nothing to Marc for the moment.

Marc, when he came in eventually fairly late after a hard day directing Hayward's new film, another science fiction work (didn't he love them?), looked quite unlike his normal self and what is more, he was hungry. Luckily there was something Emma had prepared that just had to be placed in the microwave oven so that task was soon relieved but even when he was rounding off the meal with an apple and was sipping a coffee he looked irritated and even irritable which did not at all resemble his normal behaviour.

Emma came up to him while he was still seated, stroked his hair and waited for him to say something. She waited patiently but finished by sitting down on the chair facing the table at 90° from his and looked into his green/grey eyes with the hint of a smile about her lips to try to calm him.

For some reason or other Marc did not want to relate what was irritating him and indeed after his meal and glancing through his postal mail he calmed down sufficiently to give Emma a timid smile and then a hug. "It's nothing. It's a small issue with the film so I intend to forget it."

Emma, intrigued, said nothing knowing or rather hoping that he would tell her of the problem and maybe seek her help as was so often the case. But no, he said nothing more about it and although he took great pains to hide what was on his mind by being, for instance jocular, she could see that it was not natural, a little overdone, but still she said nothing just waiting for the right moment.

The following morning when Marc had driven off to his film set which was conveniently located just one hour's drive from their home, Emma telephoned Anastasia and asked her what the next move would be in unravelling the tantalizing question of her memory.

"Well, first of all Emma –we did agree to call each other by our first names, didn't we? – you will have to go by car to a place called Super Besse in Auvergne. It's a 3 ½ hour drive. You'll find a hotel called SuperSejour where you will be given a nice room overlooking the valley or the mountain. You will have nothing to pay and your petrol will be reimbursed. When can you come? It's entirely up to you."

"Just a minute, Anastasia, why can't you just tell me on the phone why I'm having difficulty with my memory and above all how could you, a complete stranger, know anything about it?"

"I know perfectly well that it's strange, Emma, but I just ask you to trust me and you will have your answers after two days. Two full days will be enough and you will be able to return home feeling relieved and, I believe, much happier. Do you think you could make it in October?"

"Yes possibly but I will have to tell a friend when and where I'm going. I can't just leave like that." She did not want to say that her partner would not be told about the visit. She would in fact tell him that she was making a visit to her mother's place which was long overdue anyway. Her parents were divorced.

"That's OK. You can tell the gendarmes if you like", she said laughingly. "If you would just give me the two days you will be available as soon as you can and I will send you your bookings by email."

"I have already thought about a convenient time and for me the 2nd and 3rd of October will do very well. That's next week."

"Well, to tell you the truth Emma that's a bit short notice for me. Could you make it the 9th and 10th?"

"OK, but I would like to ask you a question, can I, or is it secret to that extent?"

"Go ahead, you're entitled to ask questions."

"I just want to know if I shall be alone or with other people."

"That's fair enough, Emma. A good question. There will be a few other people present in the same situation as you. I hope that sets your mind at rest."

"Well, it only partly answers my question and it doesn't really set my mind at rest but it enables me to start putting the pieces of the puzzle together a little – just a little. I see I will have to trust you, so trust you I will. Are you 100% sure that I will recover my memory after the visit to your establishment?"

"Yes, I am absolutely sure about that. There's no doubt at all about that but I cannot tell you any more for the moment. As I have already told you, you will not be disappointed in the slightest."

It was strange, thought Emma, but simply talking with Anastasia gave her confidence. She knew now that she could fully trust the woman. There was something about her voice, the intonation, emphasis on certain words that made Emma believe she was not talking to anyone ordinary. She even smiled to herself.

"OK then for the 9th and 10th."

"Thank you, Emma. You will receive all the necessary documentation tomorrow very probably. I must leave you now," and she hung up. There was no unnecessary

"Goodbye" nor "Have-a-nice-evening" with Anastasia and Emma appreciated that very much.

When Marc returned home that evening Emma could see that he was not his usual cheerful self. She asked him the same question as she had the evening before but he was just as loquacious as then – zero explanations except to say yet again that there was some little problem with the unfolding of the film but he did say that he would have to be absent for a few days very soon but could not say exactly when. Strange, thought Emma. She took the opportunity of telling him that she intended to visit her parents on the 9th and 10th but he said that he would unfortunately be unable to accompany her due to his work. That was a relief for Emma who was now feeling a little awkward herself. She decided to play it cool and after the meal even though it was dark and the outdoor temperature quite low, she asked Marc if he would care to take a little stroll with her which he accepted unhesitatingly.

They donned duffle coats and scarves and set out from their lovely abode along a lane towards the long time abandoned railway station at the top of a slight rise. The atmosphere between them immediately improved and they talked about Esther, Hayward, their present lives and even the idea of starting a family was raised. Nothing was said about Emma's visit to her mother's nor about anything else connected with their planned breaks! It was as if they were each perfectly aware of the other's projected expedition so had no need to discuss it. This was of course ridiculous but the understanding between them was plainly tacit. They walked, paused, held each other tight, kissed, chattered about nothing in particular – the stars, the sound of the tramontane blowing briskly about their faces, the village where they lived, the neighbours, anything at all that lightened the atmosphere. When they returned home they nibbled some biscuits, drank a herbal tea, continued chatting a while before turning in, relaxed and cuddled lovingly without actually making love – that would come later during the night but that is another matter altogether!

CHAPTER 13

Emma was now getting ready for her visit to SuperBesse and the SuperSejour hotel which entitled her to a very nice room for 3 nights. She had the choice of a room giving onto a lake or on the other side of the hotel onto a fairly steep hill. She preferred the hill side as it looked so peaceful and unencumbered. Unencumbered was indeed the word and the adjective applied almost as well to the lake side of the hotel for the simple reason that access to the hotel was at the end of a tree-lined drive, about 300 m long.

She finally arrived after asking her way several times as the GPS system flew in all directions. She decided to speak to Anastasia about that as she would about other details of the visit and even the hotel itself seemed a little weird. It's true there were a few ordinary middle class people to be seen including a small family in the lounge but the hotel staff although perfectly polite were somewhat detached in the way they went about their jobs and there was very little noise of any kind. There was a small restaurant in the hotel but she was given the choice by the receptionist of eating in the restaurant or in her room. She chose the restaurant because she wanted to keep her eyes open and see if there was anything unusual going on. However, she soon came to terms with her tendency of being suspicious about everything and told herself not to be stupid.

She had just chosen her starters, a simple walnut salad, when she saw a tall, lean woman entering the restaurant and asking the person in charge of the register some question or other. She saw the girl pointing in her direction so she rapidly turned her gaze to her mobile phone on which she was following news events. Emma knew instinctively that the woman was Anastasia. As she came closer she saw a dark haired woman with a slightly pear-shaped face and large, dark, lively eyes and wide lips without makeup. Her introduction to Emma was a gracious, joyous a large smile and "Hello, Emma, you must have guessed, I'm Anastasia. Are you comfortable in your room and well looked after?"

Emma simply nodded pleasantly and gestured Anastasia to sit down at her table. "I am totally amazed at my own behaviour. If someone had told me that I would be talked into going away for two days and three nights to a destination that I did not know and above all for a reason that would seem completely surrealist to anyone normal ..."

Anastasia simply sat on her chair looked pensively at Emma with the glimmer of a smile about her eyes and lips. "You know, Emma, you are not entirely wrong about your surrealism comment because there is an aspect in your - can we call it an adventure - that cannot be effectively placed in a known category? I can't tell you more until tomorrow but let me assure you I will be at your side or very near throughout the two days. Can you be at the reception desk tomorrow morning at 9? You will of course breakfast in your room. Reception will phone you at about 7.30 so that you can place your order. You should have time like that. Now, I must go as a few other persons like you need to be reassured. I wish you a very good night's sleep, Emma, and I am more than happy to have made your acquaintance. Let me tell you very earnestly, Emma, that you will not regret these two days, I can assure you. And, by the way, I have not forgotten about your search into your family history. When the two days are over, I will do all in my power to help you unearth your lineage. I have contacts. Bisous." And off she went leaving Emma partly reassured but partly frustrated. There were many things left unsaid but that had been the case since the SMS she had received. She continued with her meal but decided to call Marc to find out more about his "urgent" trip for the film. He was not answering so she left a message on his mobile. Some ten minutes later he phoned back, asked how she and her mother were faring and explained that he was in London.

"I left yesterday, he said, and will be staying two more nights not far from Notting Hill, remember the town? There's some technical lighting problem and I have to be there to do some trials and order the equipment if it's suitable. It's nothing really but it's annoying and during these two days I am unable to make progress with the film. It's about time travel and I do not feel very convinced about it. It's just one of those things." His voice was a little strained and he did not sound terribly natural but Emma decided to put that out of her mind. She was undoubtedly a little perturbed by her own situation and decided to say nothing other than a few trivialities and then to wish him good luck and a good night. That mutual but slightly unpersuasive polite exchange, lacking the usual tenderness-imbued quality then ended as each of them hung up. Emma guiltily thought she was no example to Marc as she was effectively hiding the real reason for her departure but on reflecting further returned to her previous conviction that he would certainly have dissuaded her from attending the invitation, or was it a summons? So, she just sighed, finished her meal slowly but thoughtfully and retired to her room.

She was awakened in the morning by some pleasant music emanating from somewhere but when she picked up the bedside telephone it stopped and a pleasant voice asked her what she would like for her breakfast. She wanted something simple and easy to digest so she ordered orange juice, two croissants and a pot of coffee. Some ten minutes later the room service attendant knocked on the door and when invited to enter carried a special bed tray laden with Emma's order and on her invitation placed it on her bed in front of her. She thanked him profusely and he disappeared. "This looks nice" she thought and almost without thinking of the reason for which she was sampling this luxury, tucked in and enjoyed the fine, tasty croissants and delicious coffee.

One hour later she was waiting in the vestibule for the arrival of Anastasia and noticed that there was a young man, perhaps of her age more or less who was also apparently waiting for someone. She took it into her head to move towards him and offer a courteous "Good Morning" and after greeting her in turn he instantly seized the opportunity of asking her nervously. "Are you waiting to see Mrs Prokovitch?"

"Yes, indeed I am. I had almost forgotten her surname as I call her Anastasia when I speak with her."

"In fact she wanted me to call her Anastasia, too, but I prefer keeping my distance. I hope I'm not being indiscreet but are you here for a question of memory? "

Emma did not have time to answer because at that same moment Anastasia appeared crossing the hotel entrance swing doors and moved swiftly towards them both with a wide, candid smile on her face and her arms held apart, palms upwards, in greeting. "Hello Emma, Hello Bertrand. I trust you both had a good night's sleep. I see you have already introduced yourselves and yes, you will be in contact with each other throughout the day. Well, first things first, we must go to our appointment at 9.30, so if you will follow me, off we go." She said cheerily and practically all in one breath.

CHAPTER 14

She led the way, very surprisingly, not to the hotel entrance where Emma expected to be taken by taxi or car to some nearby venue but to the lift where she pressed the -2 button. The lift arrived in a small brightly-lit vestibule in which were arranged flowers and books. Anastasia turned to her two followers and said gently. "So far, so good but the next part might surprise you. Don't ask questions for the moment. I will explain more to you shortly at the conference. I say conference instead of appointment because we will meet an expert or two who will know something about our particular problem and will answer your queries." She pushed open a massive door and the atmosphere on the other side was a complete antithesis to that in the vestibule. The light was faint and when Emma and Bertrand got used to the gloom they could see the start of a low and narrow tunnel bending slightly to the right some fifty meters further on. What was more surprising was that laid on the floor of the tunnel was a railway on which stood a dark, open vehicle in which was installed two benches each designed for two people. Anastasia ushered them gently up the step into the wagon and closed the small, low door of the vehicle. She then picked up a phone that was fitted inside at the front of the wagon and simply said. "OK, we're ready."

The vehicle, wagon, Disneyland-type ride, call it what you will, then lurched forward and rattled slowly along the track negotiating two bends before arriving at its destination which looked just like the point of departure. The ride, or whatever, had taken five minutes.

They descended from the vehicle, went through a door similar to the one at the departure point and found themselves in an adequately lit anteroom where Anastasia announced the following.

"We are now entering the nerve centre of the complex where everything involving you is installed. There is a special room behind that door containing six consoles, one for each person. Your four colleagues, or comrades shall we call them, are already in place just waiting for you. I see you look mystified for the moment and that is perfectly understandable. There is just one thing to remember and that is that you all have an interest, some even a near obsession, with history. We will go further with that if we have time after a video that you will now be viewing, so let's go in, meet your comrades and make a start. My colleague, Ernst, will be taking you through the routine. There is another group that will be carrying out the same routine as you but later."

She pushed open the door and behind it was the room she had partly described. It was obvious that they were inside the mountain or hill but it was equally obvious that they were not too deeply below the surface as there was a yellowish, natural light descending from the roof in which a myriad of very small windows could be seen if one glanced upwards. Nothing could be seen beyond these windows except a green hue, presumably grass or undergrowth or similar which would have been protected from walkers or skiers by a grid system above. Six consoles were set inline and four of them, as related by Anastasia, were occupied by four other persons, two men and two women in their thirties or early forties.

A door behind the consoles now opened and a white-haired man came through and Anastasia introduced him. "May I present Ernst to you? He is one of our experts. I shall be on hand to help you. "

Ernst spoke with a German accent. "Good morning, my friends. Thank you for coming. We are now going to view photos and short videos of life in the past. Each of you will view a different filmed document and that is explained by the fact that you were all interested in different facets of the same periods. Each person's show - shall we call it that? - is aligned to their particular interest and algorithms did the rest. So I suggest we start. I should say that there will be nothing to alarm you but certainly you will be intrigued. That, I can promise you," he said with a large smile but very reassuringly. You will be able to ask questions afterwards.

Emma sat down in front of her screen and without any explanatory title or announcement of any kind the short stretches of video and many photos, each of only a few seconds in length, passed in front of her eyes. One could at least more or less set the period of the scenes to the early 19th century simply because there were no cars or even proper roads, no trains or only antiquated steam locomotives, men in top hats, women in long dresses held tightly at the waist, large mansions and village fairs.

At first Emma felt nothing in particular, just slightly bored and annoyed that she had been brought here simply to watch this hotchpotch of images. However, when some 45 minutes of this unfurling of pictures had passed, she suddenly felt a throbbing in her chest, her sight became blurred momentarily and she felt hot about the face. This lasted just a few seconds and jolted her into trying to concentrate more on the screen. The showing continued in the same endless, what seemed like footings for a film, although much shorter, like the fast turning of pages of a photo album. Towards the end of the 90 minute sequence she felt the same symptoms as before – slight pains in her chest, blurred sight, perspiration and a momentary feeling of being out of breath. As before, this lasted only fleetingly and she had just the time to put the experience (what was the adjective to describe the experience? – surprising, pleasant, unpleasant, upsetting? – she could not say.) to the back of her mind when the showing terminated as abruptly as it had begun.

Ernst, accompanied by Anastasia, now led them without a word to a neighbouring room with the same lighting but arranged as a lecture room with a board in front of which Ernst stood and a dozen or so desks and chairs arranged somewhat haphazardly in the room. The six "viewers" took their seats. It was she who spoke first.

"What were your reactions to what you have just viewed? I'll take you in alphabetical order. Say exactly what you want. It's in the interests of everyone that you say exactly what you think. If it did nothing to you, please say so. Well now, let's see, Mr Abbot, you're from the UK, are you not? It you wish to speak in English I will interpret for you. Now then, what was your reaction to the viewing?"

"I can just about manage in French, Anastasia, as I have studied the language and lived in France for a few years. Personally, it did not do much to me except twice I started to have a headache but it lasted only a few seconds. That's all."

"Thank you John. Now it's your turn Anne Delaunay." Anne Delaunay stood up and said briefly. "It was the same for me although I had a slight pain in my side like a cramp. It happened twice but was not really painful." She sat down.

"Emma Jameson, can you tell us what you experienced?"

"Well, like John I found it very boring at first– I'm sorry but that's what I felt – until there was a throbbing in my chest and my sight went blurred for a second. That was the first time, and like the others it happened twice but the second time I also felt slightly out of breath. How can I say it? My mind was bored but my heart was moved by what, I cannot say."

"Very interesting, Emma," said Anastasia. "Those reactions are fairly typical but you will learn more about that tomorrow. Now, Martin, Bertrand and Cécile can you tell us what you felt?"

When the latter had finished their short lists of minor ailments Anastasia declared after glancing at her phone."There has been a slight change of schedule. We were going to show you another set of videos and photos this afternoon but that will be postponed until tomorrow. We have one other group to manage and we slightly underestimated the time it would take to manage the two groups but after the second viewing tomorrow we will explain everything to you. Then there will be a meeting of the two groups together, all twelve of you. Both groups have six participants. You are free this afternoon to do what you wish but please keep the reasons for your visit here a secret – I mean if you are talking to anyone in the hotel or village, just say you are here for a history conference. Please, it's important. It would jeopardise the whole project if the local press were to hear about it. Tomorrow, I promise you, Ernst and I will explain everything and a great weight will be lifted from your shoulders." The six participants looked at each other questioningly at this declaration but Anastasia continued. "Yes, I can really reassure on that score. You will feel you have made progress in your lives. So I will take you back to the hotel now and we will meet again tomorrow morning. The time of your meeting will be sent to you by SMS and email. Let's go, shall we?"

They made their way back to the hotel on the same vehicle as before and as soon as Emma reached her room she phoned Marc. He did not answer but sent a reply by SMS saying that he was in a meeting but that he would call her later that afternoon. She lay back on her bed feeling slightly drained but after 30 minutes or so decided to take a walk to the village. She was just leaving the hotel when she saw Bertrand (the man she had met that morning while waiting for Anastasia) in the drive a few meters in front of her typing something frantically on his phone. She walked very slowly in his direction. She would have liked a chat with him as he seemed empathetic and what is more she would have liked his real impressions of the morning's showing. She was about to walk past him while offering him a smile when he closed his phone and said. "My wife does not seem to be available today. That's very strange."

Bertrand had a swarthy appearance, lots of dark hair and a generally calm and agreeable personality. He looked a little discouraged.

"You know, Bertrand, I'm having the same problem. Tell me, did you tell your wife the nature of your visit here because if it's any consolation to you I had to invent a pretext for my partner? I told him I was visiting my mother..."

"Well ..., said Bertrand with a long pause which gave one to think that he was wondering whether to answer the question frankly but then he eventually declared, I must admit that it was the same for me. But that doesn't explain why she isn't answering."

"I expect there's a very reasonable explanation, Bertrand. But I wanted to ask you, is it true you cannot remember anything for a certain period of your life because that is indeed my case? For some twelve years of my life I have to rely on photos to bring back my past and then when I talk about it I have to invent things. Weird, eh?"

"That is peculiar because inexplicably I have the same problem but we must have done something in the past to have warranted all the palaver of being talked into coming here and watching crazy videos and stuff that have no sense. What do you think - Emma, isn't it?"

" Yes, Emma is my first name, I know it looked ridiculous what we saw today but I'm willing to bet that tomorrow we will see things differently – and I'm sure your wife will call you back."

All this time they were walking slowly down the drive but suddenly they both realized that they had to return to the hotel for lunch as it was close on 1 p.m. When they reached the hotel they entered by the main entrance and were directed to the dining area where they found themselves seated with the other four members of their group.

During the meal they chatted together talking partly about the morning's happenings but as this was limited in scope they branched out into anything – jobs, interests, children – almost as if they had known each other for some time. They all decided to go for a stroll together in the afternoon. Emma was about to retire to her room when, on an impulse and being of an inquisitive nature, she decided to scout around the ground floor of the hotel. There was nobody on duty so she ventured through the double doors that were situated to the right of the reception desk and at which there was usually a porter stationed. The door that gave onto the dining room and lift to which Emma and her group had access was on the left of the reception desk. No-one today, not even a receptionist. She opened the door, slipped through and cast an eye around. Very strange. There was another dining room and another short corridor to another lift but what was more surprising was that the whole area seemed to be a mirror image of the part of the hotel where Emma was lodged. She slipped back into "her side" of the hotel. In her room she decided to call Marc but apparently he was unavailable. This was not at all like him. The film set he was directing must be a very intense affair. Still, he would probably call back shortly. She sat down in a comfortable armchair and in next to no time was fast asleep. When she looked at her watch she found she had slept for an hour or so but Marc had not called back and she suddenly remembered that a walk had been arranged starting in just ten minutes. Time to tidy up before meeting the others in the vestibule.

She found herself naturally enough side by side with Bertrand at the start of the walk and asked him if his wife had called back and when he answered in the negative she felt she had to tell him that it was the same story with Marc. They both agreed that it was simply a coincidence and nothing to worry about without being really convinced.

The walk was enjoyable, there was sunshine and it was noticeable that the six "conference" participants remained as three couples practically throughout the stroll. After walking for about an hour they decided unanimously to slake their thirst at the village cafe. Here, there was a better mix and Emma found herself next to Anne and a man with whom she had not spoken until then. She questioned them on the memory issue raised that morning after the viewing and it was obvious that both of them were very impatient to see how things would pan out. Emma did not mention the lack of contact with her partner, preferring not to know or perhaps fearing to know what the responses would be.

However, that evening after dinner with the others she retired to her room and was almost amazed later in the evening while she was watching the TV to hear the jingling tone of her mobile phone. It was indeed Marc who apologised for not being able to return her calls but was in the thick of it or shall we say that was how he described it. He asked after her mother and they chatted about nothing in particular for the rest of the conversation. Emma found that he was very cheerful and in complete contrast to how he had been before her expedition to SuperBesse. This was inexplicable but she decided that there was a good reason and she did not suspect that he was in any way indulging in an "extra-marital" affair. Her thoughts were cut short by her telephone once more but this time it was Anastasia who requested her to be in the foyer the next morning at 7.30 as the day, for her and Ernst, promised to be fairly frantic. Anastasia told her very sincerely and Emma found that she did indeed sound sincere, that many questions would be answered at the end of the morning session but that at the end of the day, after the second but final viewing, all participants would have the occasion to pose all the questions they wished. She took this at face value and set her alarm for 6 a.m.

CHAPTER 15

The next morning after being accompanied to the IT room once more they were asked to turn their chairs away from their screens because Ernst apparently wanted to explain something and it went something like this.

"Good morning, my friends. I'm sorry to have got you up so early but today is very busy for us and we did not want to keep you here a further day. First of all, you are now going to see a series of photos and videos that reflect life in Europe at the start of the 20th century and I didn't tell you yesterday but the same principle applies today. You will not recognize anyone in these photos and footings because all the faces have been changed and like yesterday you might have strange feelings from time to time. It's nothing to worry about. After the showing you will go back to the hotel and following an early lunch you will return here, directed by Anastasia, for the final session when you will be invited to inspect an important facility here. After that, there will be a little surprise awaiting you but I can say nothing more for the moment except that when the day is over many of your worries should be over. So, good luck."

All six of them looked at him dubiously wondering what on earth he had up his sleeve but Anastasia was looking on as unperturbed as ever offering them all reassuring looks. As before, they took what they had been told as Gospel and returned obediently to their screens. As Ernst had told them, the scenes, videos and photos that unfolded indeed showed life from the early 20th century. Each person had their particular scenario and that was something they had discussed when they had made a halt at a cafe during their walk the day before. They had not been able to explain it but presumably all would be exposed before the end of the day.

As Ernst had said, Emma, like her five fellow viewers, experienced strange sensations and for her they were located around the heart and in the belly and she noticed that her fingers and toes tingled from time to time but bearing in mind what Ernst had said she was not anxious about it at all. The viewing lasted some 90 minutes just like the first session but this time, by dint of greater concentration, she thought she recognized in the persons who passed across the screen fleetingly certain types of ways of walking, certain stances, certain gestures of the hand but could not in any way associate the name of a person with what she saw. In any case, she thought, the associations she was making with these body movements probably came from movies so she cast these ideas to the back of her mind.

At the end of the showing all six persons stood up looking slightly put out but this lasted no more than a minute as Anastasia then took them back to the hotel for a coffee or tea. The time was only 10.30 a.m.

Emma chatted to Bertrand for a moment. "Did your wife call back? I hope so because Marc, my partner, did so eventually and all seemed OK."

"Yes, funny that, he replied, Jenny called back as well and like your Marc she seemed perfectly OK. There's something I don't understand here. Tell me Emma, did you have any funny sensations after the second session?"

"Yes, I did, faint fibrillations, a slightly sick feeling in the tummy and tingling finger tips but it lasted no time at all. And you?"

"Same. I felt stressed for a couple of seconds and my eyes lost focus but there again, just for a few moments. I wonder what's going on?"

"I agree it's strange, uttered Emma, but I trust Anastasia and I think by the end of the day all our questions will be answered. What do you think?"

"I want to believe you but it's all like a sort of dream. I can't get my mind around it. By the way, are you impassioned by history and if so what is your area of research, if I may put it that way?"

"You can indeed put it that way. Actually, I wanted to study history in depth but when I looked into the possibilities after university I decided that being a history teacher did not appeal to me and that research posts would be out of my range so I went in for acting and that's what I have been doing until now. Marc is in the business too. He's a director."

"Interesting. Actually, I am a history teacher and quite mad about the subject. I go to as many conferences as possible on the subject and I can tell you practically anything about the history of the world in the19th and 20th centuries! My wife works in another area altogether –she's a nurse – but she did at one period become very interested in the subject although unfortunately I can't remember much about it. Still, that's the reason we're here isn't it?"

"Well, Bertrand, I am going to my room now to find out how my mother is getting on to prevent any suspicious questions on the part of my partner. I'll see you very soon for lunch before the climatic end to the visit – or will it be an anticlimax?"

"Good question. OK, see you then, Emma."

So here are the six fellow wonderers grouped in the vestibule waiting for Anastasia to take them once again to the, hopefully, memory-finding procedures hub in the mountain. She was there on the dot of 2 p.m. with a very large smile on her, it had to be admitted, trust-inspiring face. You just could not feel you were in the wrong place with her, so all six trooped obediently with her to the antiquated, almost dilapidated passenger wagon on the equally "seen better days" track itself. It made such a noise as it rattled along but went very slowly so even if it had derailed no-one would have been hurt and there was a narrow path beside it along its whole length as an alternative way of reaching the destination. However, there was no problem and they arrived none the worse for the journey at the now familiar facility.

Anastasia now ushered them, not into the first small lecture room that they had already seen, but through it, along a short corridor to a second lecture room, just as small but lit up and with a folder placed on the desk in front of each of six seats.

Ernst stood in front of them with Anastasia seated beside him.

"My dear friends, you have spent until now two quite bewildering days and you must be wondering what is going to take place now and I can assure you that you will be simultaneously astounded and reassured. You have undergone already what I would call the most difficult part of the 2-day memory finding procedure. You must have been mystified and perhaps ready to throw in the sponge thinking that the whole enterprise was a hoax or even worse. But no, we are now about to unravel all the mystery surrounding this extraordinary adventure, for adventure it most certainly is. We can now without any anxiety go back seventeen years in the past. Please can you open the folder in front of you but check that it's your name marked on the cover. It is? Good! At the top of the first page you will see printed "Contract between TempSpace and ......" Your name is printed clearly in this space.

You will now see explained in the contract that due to your intense interest in history, and notably the beginning of the 19th century, you agree to take part in the adventure of finding out what life was really like in that period and then in the following century – the first starting in 1817 and the second in 1923. You will see in the document that it was not planned to leave you to your proper devices. You were to be part of a life that already existed. You would not be thrown to the lions, so to speak. So far, so good. Now I have to explain something to you that is very complex and requires plunging, just a little, into Einstein's theory of relativity. You all know that once in space, time means nothing and I can tell you that we discovered here, in this place, that the equivalent of an hour or two at the present time, here and now, could become a decade once you are precipitated into space. Some time ago, we decided to try forays into the past but there was nothing precise in our ventures although eventually with the help of modern IT science and algorithms we were able to go where and when we wanted in the past. The object was of course to be able take modern technology into the past to record certain periods that were completely undocumented to know what ordinary people of the time did and thought.

However, we were never able to overcome the fact that once one got a foothold in the past one became part of it and any equipment that we might have taken with us became unworkable and we as ordinary persons of the time were unable to fathom out what the equipment was. It was considered to be something almost diabolic and burnt on a fire. Well, that was back in the late eighties and since then we have made some progress. We discovered in fact that there was no need to lug devices back into the past. We were able to achieve surveillance from our base here. From 1990 onwards we sent teams of twelve volunteers into the past on eleven occasions. What we had forgotten with the first expeditions was that it is impossible in time to live two different lives simultaneously. We sorted that out fairly quickly by being able to suspend either the past or the present in the lives of the volunteers. I won't explain how because it is very complex indeed but just take it from me that we have completely mastered the problem." Here, Anastasia nodded with much candour.

"Now this is where you come in. I shall now take you to the control room where you were stationed for just a few hours fourteen years ago, in 2005, to be exact. Please follow me." He opened a further door at the other side of the room and led them along another dimly lit corridor until they reached double doors that seemed to be made of metal and were opened by means of a push button connected to some driving mechanism that shifted the door slowly. As the doors opened it could be seen that they were very thick indeed. They now peered into a black-looking chamber made of the same material as the doors. Ernst turned on the light which beamed from a dozen or so small lamps in the ceiling. The team of six stepped inside and peered around. Very strange indeed! On one side there appeared to be a sort of enormous control panel but which had been emptied of any equipment. All that remained was a very large frame the size of a bookcase with many cut wires projecting from it. There were pieces of solar system charts dotted about the back of the frame and there appeared to be places for three controllers (would they have been controllers?) in front of the setup. There were no seats in the facility and it was all very eerie indeed. On two other walls there were other much smaller recesses that caught the eye. The whole chamber had indeed been abandoned some time ago.

Ernst continued. "The twelve teams – you are the twelfth – stayed in the same hotel where you have been staying and came into this facility two by two, one woman and one man but in no way related either by blood or by friendship except for the first two expeditions where there was a single person. Each team of six, as I think you have been told by my colleague, is closely associated with the other team of six. Algorithms were used to team up couples in these past centuries as much as possible by giving them compatible interests. Unfortunately the first two expeditions did not have this advantage but we rectified this problem for the third and following expeditions. You are the last one as I have already told you. By the way, the documentation we obtained has become automatically dissociated from any real names and therefore there is no mention of your names anywhere. The recordings, integrated in historical documents have been destroyed – Anastasia will touch on this - so you have become part of history without there being any allusion to you – not the colour of your skin or hair, nor your height or build.

So, to summarize a little, each of you six came here of your own will fourteen years ago to discover what life might have been like in the past. One hour in the facility which you are now in but which was made non-operational some eight years ago meant you spent several years in the two past centuries. However, even if the marvellous operation of transposing you to another century only lasted, as I say, one hour, there was a result on your life in this century. You continued your lives in the normal way not realizing that after a few hours or a day at the most, what you had just experienced here was tidied away in your hippocampus for use later on but completely forgotten to your normal everyday reflective self – and that of course is why you are here. Most of you did not even realize that you had lost your memories over that relevant time frame. It was Anastasia's relentless efforts that enabled you all to come here. She has done a grand job and so have you, for trusting her and her explanations.

We will shortly be joining the other six of your combined team and I will then be able to explain how your memories will be restored. You have not met the other six members until now because quite simply the process of regaining your memory would have stopped short and your visit here would have been for nothing. Anastasia will now take you to a rest room where you can have a coffee or tea while I repeat what I have just told you to the others. You can ask Anastasia any question and she will answer you if transgressing the strict protocol we have devised here is not involved. I will see you very soon.

They were taken along an extension of the corridor that had led them to the abandoned control facility for ten or so meters. The inside of the room they now entered, although Spartan, was furnished with small armchairs, two coffee tables and a table on which were installed the coffee machine and kettle.

The six time travellers settled down in their chairs each one engaged in consulting their portable phones and looking annoyed or worried as a result. The message on Emma's phone was prosaic and neither positive nor negative. Marc had typed that everything was now going well with his time travel film, and that he would see her the following evening. She simply replied "Good." It must be said that for almost the first time since they had known each other – some nineteen years – his message annoyed her but she quickly told herself that perhaps her messages had the same effect on him. She laughed to herself.

When everyone had received a tea or coffee, Anastasia, still seated, explained to them something about the underground site. The exact original use for the underground complex was unknown, she said, but that it had been tunnelled out during Napoleon's reign and then 150 years later used by the Wehrmacht as a base and place of torture against the French resistance movement.

Then there were a few questions involving the remainder of the afternoon and Anastasia answered guardedly by saying that by 6 p.m. the whole process of recovering their memories should be over but that in the meantime there would be some surprises. Time was moving fairly fast now and the minute hand on the clock on the wall was nearing twelve while the hour hand was on three. They chatted awhile or doodled with their portable phones until at 4 p.m. precisely a swarthy man they had not as yet seen opened the door, introduced himself as Guy and asked everyone to follow him to the lecture room where the day before they had talked about the consequences of the first video/photos/footage they had viewed. When they arrived in the room they saw that there were twelve desks and chairs arranged in three rows of four and all six in the group were curious to see what the other six persons would be like. Would there be three men and three women or all women, all men, or what?

CHAPTER 16

The door opened and Ernst stood in the opening for a few seconds before turning round to face the six persons behind him saying in a nonchalant voice. "Well, take your seats and then we will be able to go a little further ..."

One can just imagine the uproar and bustle that ensued as each person in each group of six, those seated and those entering the room, discovered that they knew one person very well indeed. Six couples very quickly formed. Jenny entering the lecture room immediately found Bertrand and of course Marc coming in saw Emma straightaway. The prevailing image was arms around waists, heads on shoulders, lips against lips. Amazing! Anastasia, Ernst and Guy were beaming with pleasure to see what was obviously for them an anticipated joy but a joy all the same. The initial commotion connected with unexpectedly finding one's other half was now subsiding and the three "agents" urged all six couples to take their seats. Emma and Marc found themselves sitting behind Bertrand and Jenny. Photos should have been taken of the looks shared between Emma and Bertrand.

Guy, with outstretched arms, now succeeded with some difficulty in quietening the assembly and said they would be given five minutes to come to terms with each other's worries and grievances and indeed one could hear coming from practically all six couples expressions like: "I'm so sorry to have doubted you" or "It's extraordinary that neither of us twigged ..." or "That explains why you were so cagey" and so on.

When Guy saw that he could attract their attention he said. "Well now we come to the final part of the project but let me reassure you, eleven groups have passed before you and all unfolded without difficulty but you must absolutely follow our instructions to the letter. We shall very shortly be returning to the IT room where you have already spent two times 90 minutes viewing parts of videos / film and many photos from two separate centuries. Ernst told you that the faces of the persons to be seen on these footages had been changed. You will now see that the real images have been restored. I can see that some of you are looking restless and ill at ease because you believe you will be seeing the same 3 hours of video, film or photos once again. It's true you will be seeing those images again but shorn of the photos and the time for the showing has been divided by three. Now then, and you must listen carefully. The number of consoles remains the same but instead of a single seat there will now be a double seat before each screen. You will have the impression that the unfolding of the footage has been increased in speed but this is not the case. Simply, a lot of matter has been discarded to concentrate on the essential. The IT room will be in semi-darkness so that you can focus your attention on the screen and not be distracted. However, I don't think you can possibly be distracted and the half light is just a precaution. Now then, this is the part that needs explanations from someone convincing so I'm going to ask Anastasia to do just that. I believe most of you get on well with Anastasia. The proof is there are four or five among you who needed a great deal of persuasion. But she managed it." Muted chuckles could be heard from several desks.

Anastasia now stood up while Ernst and Guy looked on to help if necessary.

"We must not forget the reason for your visit to Super Besse – it is to extricate the memory that has been locked in your hippocampus with a key that has been mislaid. We are about to find that key to release your memory. However, please remember what Ernst has already told you; that it is impossible to live two lives simultaneously. As each sequence of film/video is displayed you will instantly recognize certain incidents and events but at the end of each sequence a green light will blot out all the images of the sequence. You will feel a tingling sensation in your head but which will not hurt you in any way. When the following sequence is displayed you will have completely forgotten the first sequence but strangely enough a small part of the memory of your real life, in this century will spring back to you. The green light cancels out all of the sequences one after another while your memory slowly but surely is recovered until at the end of all the sequences of the two centuries you will have entirely recovered your memory. This exercise is fairly exhausting; you are forewarned, but the immense relief you will feel at the end will more than compensate for it. Have you any questions?"

It was Emma who asked the one and only question but which must have been in the minds of all twelve. "Yes, Anastasia, I have a question. We have all now understood that we volunteered to take part in a sort of time travel experiment and that to some extent it succeeded. I would like to know if there is anything at all of our voyages back in time that our memories will retain. This is important for me because when Marc and I first met we had the impression of already knowing each other. We cast this aside and I think we never mentioned it again – is that not so, Marc? (nods from Marc). Did any of you other couples have any experience like that?" There were several nods and yeses from various couples.

"That's fair enough, Emma, but the process you will now experience takes account even of that and I can assure you that no memories of lives in other centuries will remain so if you have no further questions we will now proceed to the computer room.

They obediently followed Anastasia to the IT room and waited to be placed one couple before each console. This was because there were six video and film showings each one allotted to one couple and one couple only. Emma and Marc were given the N° 2 console and they sat down and waited without speaking.

There was a complete hush as Anastasia stood in from of them after all twelve had swung their chairs round to face her. She placed a finger to her lips and more or less repeated what she had already said in relation to the green light but this time insisting that the twelve viewers keep their gaze firmly on the screen.

The lights dimmed in the room as Guy and Ernst set the session into motion by turning various knobs and dials on their control board.

Emma and Marc held each other's hands tightly and waited for the first piece of footage to appear but it lasted no more than two or three seconds – the first was a horse pulling something in a field, then another horse on which could be seen seated a young woman who very much resembled Emma except for her attire– and so it was throughout the first half of the session where events of the 19th century unfolded very quickly interspersed by the green-lit screen which almost immediately had the anticipated effect on the two of them. They clasped and unclasped their hands in quick succession all the while perspiring profusely.

When the first 30 minute session was over Anastasia addressed the twelve participants by saying, "I know it is quite wearing so would any of you like a glass of water or fruit juice?" Nobody did and someone was heard to say, "Let's get on with it and get it over!" to which the general response was "Yes let's."

So the second piece of footage from the early 20th century then came into play. Here again, as far as Emma and Marc were concerned, there were extremely brief shots of various elements like a hay cart, an ancient aeroplane or high powered cars and one or two shots they were able to recognize as being themselves although so "come and gone" that they doubted the validity of their senses but frankly as the green light seemed to arrive at a much greater frequency than before, or so they believed, the reality or not of each image had very little significance. Once again, when the showing was over they felt absolutely exhausted, were wet with perspiration and just sat haggardly in their chairs as Anastasia, Ernst and Guy, seeing that all six sessions were over handed the couples cool drinks which this time they all gratefully accepted. Emma stared Marc in the face and said out loud without realizing it. "I can remember coming here the first time when I was eighteen."

"Me, too," resounded from the six consoles, all eleven voices practically in unison.

It was now the turn of Guy to address the small gathering who had now turned their double chairs to face the three agents.

"You see, there was no question of telling you a pack of lies. Everything we told you has turned out as anticipated but now I would like to add a little information about the outfit we have here. Firstly, I would entreat you to say nothing of your experiences in this place because although commissioned by the government back in the eighties, it has always been a sort of state secret. In any case, I think no-one other than yourselves would or could believe such a fantastic tale. Remember how you were when you all came here fourteen years ago. You only started to believe something when you were taken to the control room. The aspect that is hard to grasp is the fact that the hour or so you each spent being precipitated into space was transformed (because of the time/space phenomenon) into many years spent in another century and as we have already explained that is why you lost the memory of things you undertook in the present century. You should not now have any problems of memory from when you were eighteen or nineteen and when you now look at the photos you relied on to replace memory the details of the occasion when the photo was taken will spring back into your mind. I think Anastasia would like to add a few details concerning your travel back in time. Anastasia?"

"Can I thank you all for your fantastic cooperation throughout this adventure that you have all accomplished very convincingly? You will be able to ask questions in a minute but I am going to anticipate what I think will be a dominant concern for all of you. Although we have already touched on the subject it was not the right time to go into details but now seems to be an appropriate moment. You will want to know what, if anything remains in your mind of your adventures in those past centuries. Emma already raised the question before the viewing. Am I right? Everyone nodded or said "Yes." As we have already said one cannot live two lives simultaneously so it is impossible to recall what went on during your expeditions. The videos, films and photos have already been automatically destroyed so there is no way of knowing what you in fact did in those times. This has been routine procedure

374

for reasons of secrecy or mental health. However everything you lived through, your reactions, results and everything else were recorded and will be integrated in historical works for the benefit of future students. But nothing, absolutely nothing, can be traced to any of you. Now then, it might happen that scraps of your adventures could escape during dreams but you will not recognize their having anything to do with your travel in time. Feedback from the other eleven teams before you bear this out so you can be reassured on that count. Now then, are there any questions?"

"Yes, I have question, said a young woman named Nathalie. What will be the long-term consequences of what we have all lived through?"

"Very little, from what we gather from the previous teams' accounts. Most seem to feel that their daily lives have gained in strength, maturity, sustainability and a general feeling of understanding for their fellow human beings. The majority are happy to have lived through the adventure. You will see, very gradually, how the experience affects your lives. Any other questions? Yes, Gilles?"

Gilles, a very slim man of about forty years of age with long black hair now stood up and said quite simply. "We all know now that the two hours we spent in the hot seat, can we call it that? ... translated into fourteen years in two previous centuries. Nobody has asked the question so I will now do so. How on earth did we travel in time and space if our bodies remained firmly rooted to our chairs?"

"I'll hand you over to Guy for that one. That's his specialty."

Guy now stood up. "Hello Gilles, yes it's a very appropriate question to ask. It is of course extremely complicated but the basis of the issue is that your body of course stayed here while your mind or spirit, if you like, found itself in a recipient person in each of the two centuries. The person that received your spirit had been chosen using historical records, highly sophisticated technical processes and of course algorithms without which nothing would have been possible. The algorithms helped to find the appropriate person who was similar in appearance to each of you with similar ways of thinking to yours and naturally helped you meet your partner in the most natural way. Nothing was left to chance. That also explains why you lost your long-term memory in this century. Does that help? It does! Good!

I should add that when you departed from the mind of the person you had adopted to return to our century, that person continued their life from the point in time when you left them.

We will be publishing a secret document in the next few weeks in which all these details will appear. It will be available to a few scientists who work on the subject, to Ernst, Anastasia and myself and to you and the eleven teams that preceded you. However, Ernst, Anastasia and I will be available to talk to you or even to meet you whenever you like if there are further queries. Now tell me, all of you, by a show of hands if your memory has been fully restored after these two days of work. Let me see now – there is one person hesitating – but no! ...all your hands are in the air. That is very gratifying to us." Anastasia and Ernst were nodding their heads in approval. I think Ernst would now like to give you a little information on this establishment." Guy sat down.

Ernst now stood before the twelve very concentrated members of the team and declared. "This establishment or facility it is fairly obvious has seen better days especially the operational side which closed down some eight years ago. That facility, although extremely useful to us in the early days, reached the limits of its utility and became superseded by an up-to-date setup which is located elsewhere. We cannot tell you where for obvious reasons and of course we are not alone. The Americans and perhaps the Russians and Chinese have structures into which they pour resources so as to be precursors in the domain. So this under-the-mountain location which has an interesting history might well be converted into some type of museum or theme park. The access from the hotel will probably be walled up except of course if the hotel becomes part of the project.

You twelve were therefore the last time travellers through the facility and I would sincerely like to thank you for your co-operation at the beginning and over the last few days. You have been great. You will all have realized why we took great pains to keep each of you separated from your spouse or partner until the last minute. The experiences you went through would not have been valid had you known you were going to meet someone from your own era in those past centuries. By the way, two centuries were involved and not just one because we wanted to confirm the validity of the complex processes we had devised. You will all now return to your normal lives knowing that you have contributed in no small way to the furthering of historical knowledge. All will remain secret of course – we trust you not to divulge the whereabouts of this place though I doubt if anyone would believe you even if you tried! You will not remember what experiences you went through – we have already explained why – although there may be fleeting images in your dreams but from what we have gleaned from feedback from the other eleven teams the images will be entirely harmless and probably quite pleasant. Anastasia has already mentioned that, I believe. The previous teams have told us their dreams amounted to nothing more than views of the sea, of mountains, of pleasant glances, that sort of thing. That's all from me. I think Anastasia wants to inform you of something. I hand you over to her."

"Well, everyone, you now know how this rather special place here, under a mountain, has affected your lives for the last fourteen years but to us and the rest of our team who have moved to the rather more modern setup some distance from here, today is rather special because it marks the end of a long period of searching and probing into the past for historical reasons that started on a trials basis long before the first of the twelve teams started helping us. Let's try and relax now.

We will return to the hotel by the east or west wing, whichever is yours, take a shower if you feel like it and reassemble in the dining room in the west wing where we will celebrate the accomplishment of today's successful mission and the end of an era for our outfit. I believe our full team will be here this evening and a few other people who will be thrilled to see you. So, shall we adjourn for the moment and re-unite say at 8 p.m. in the dining room? The rail cart can only seat eight people so either you ride or you walk. I will walk. It doesn't take much longer.

At this moment, Emma stood up and asked if she could see Anastasia for a moment. Of course she agreed.

"Anastasia, I am or rather we are extremely grateful to you and your team for restoring our memories but in spite of your protestations to the contrary, we would like to, or rather need to, know what our lives were like in those two centuries. There must be some way to have a glimmering of how we conducted our lives in the skins of those people in the past. There must be some way!"

"Listen, Emma, as we have said there is no way of retrieving those photos, videos and film footings of your lives back then. Part of the protocol was to destroy them but of course the substance was conserved in written form and is kept in the library of our new highly secret HQ. I don't see how I can help you. We are sworn to secrecy on that subject but that's strange, everyone until now, has just been happy to recover their memory and live their lives as before. That doesn't mean that the past does not interest them. On the contrary, most people have taken up the study of history more seriously. I am very sorry, Emma but that's all I can say."

"Well, thank you Anastasia for being honest with me."

Emma walked in front of Marc to the hotel where they parted with another long kiss after the latter said he would fetch Emma at her room just before eight. This he did. They were both dressed appropriately and felt fresh from their showers. Emma's black shoulder length hair glistened and she looked delightful. As usual she wore little makeup. Marc had donned nicely cut dark trousers and a colourful shirt, casual jacket but no tie. He detested them. His fair hair also gleamed and he looked frankly happy. You could almost pluck the happiness from his face.

CHAPTER 17

They arrived in the dining room and were more than surprised to see that there was a vast table adorned with all the accessories for an important dinner and included magnificent flowers which caught the eye immediately. Once in the room they saw that many people were standing around in groups but they only recognized the people from their own group. As they moved slowly around the outside of the gathering they were intercepted by Anastasia who exclaimed. "Oh, Hi, Emma and Marc. We wanted this last evening to be a surprise and that's why you have a third night booked in the hotel." She then addressed the whole group of people. "We have managed to bring together two teams from the last two years so that makes thirty-six for the three years' groups. One couple in last year's team are amateur musicians and have kindly offered to entertain us with some dance music after the meal. Emma and Marc, please come and meet some of your predecessors at this facility. With that, our couple circulated among the guests while sipping a glass of martini. After half and hour or so all the guests were invited to take their seats at the table and be served this time with champagne. Again Anastasia at the head of the table addressed the gathering.

"As you all now know the facility here at SuperBesse has finished its active life and that is why you are all here but very soon a well-known American film producer will be here – just a minute, his name is Harvard, I believe, though I might be wrong. He used his first name Melvyn – I've just had an SMS from him. He'll be here with his stepdaughter in ten minutes –

and you will be undoubtedly interested to know that by using parts of our facility as a fictional backdrop only he is producing a time travel movie. Most of the parts of this facility you know well will have been altered for the film. That was a condition for using some of the shots. For the moment continue your meal and enjoy yourselves."

So, the festivities continued until Surprise, Surprise, who should enter the room on one arm of Anastasia but Hayward, while on the other hung Esther. Emma and Marc looked at each other in utter astonishment. What on earth was he doing here and how was it that he, Marc, knew nothing about Hayward's connection with SuperBesse and above all that the film he was directing was based very largely on the TempSpace outfit and that he knew nothing about that? Both Emma and Marc kept their heads down out of Hayward's and Esther's sight to see how events would unroll. They were soon made aware of how the situation had come about.

Not everyone in the room had a sufficient enough command of the English language to understand what he might say so Anastasia who spoke four languages fluently translated into French for him. He started.

"Thank you so much Anastasia for inviting me here today. I know it's a very moving moment for you and your team as you have built up this station over many years and you have given Humanity treasure troves of information in respect of history and especially in respect of the ordinary lives of women and men of past centuries. I came to know of your establishment through searching for an institution or organization which studied time travel and this one here in France was the only one offering access and for one good reason. It was and is still formally forbidden to access such a facility in the US and Russia and the only reason why your wonderful team allowed me here was that the technology here was ageing and the outfit was closing.

As Anastasia, Ernst and Guy will tell you I was part of the second expedition back into time and you will know that I had to go solo because that was how it was done until the following year. I, of course, just like you, have lost any recollection of what went on in those two past centuries but apparently it was far from easy being alone. So, I am here this evening at the invitation of the team and for the same reasons as you.

Now I know there is another updated system somewhere else in France but the location is secret and access to it would be just as difficult as it is in the US. But for the purposes of my film the technology and system here have been ideal. The film should be released in a couple of months. From my visits here and my talks with Ernst, Guy and you, Anastasia I was able show my film director, Marc Leboucher, what was needed."

"Did you say Marc Leboucher, Hayward?" said Guy from one side of the table. "Unless it's a pure coincidence we have a space traveller with that name and I believe he is here with us now. Are you there Marc?"

Marc was then obliged to show himself and he stood up. "Hayward, it just seems impossible that you are with us today and with Esther as well! I had no idea that the film we are making drew its inspiration from SuperBesse."

Everyone at the table looked one way and the other as the two men spoke and then were quite amazed when Esther dashed away from her uncle or stepfather and flung her arms around Emma's neck. Emma proceeded to stroke Esther's hair and hug her fondly and did not completely follow the course of the conversation. Explanations as to why Marc was unaware of Hayward's knowledge of SuperBesse and on the contrary why Hayward was unaware that Marc had a connection with the facility were lost on her but all turned out to be straightforward. Ernst, Guy and Anastasia between them gave all the explanations that were necessary to Marc's couple and to Hayward and to all the invited guests who were astounded at the turn of events. Of course, all hinged on the fact that Marc and Emma, like all the participants in the time travel venture and over a period of more than ten years had lost all recollection of their first visit to SuperBesse and only the second visit so many years later had restored their memory of that first visit and indeed of their personal lives between the two visits.

While the three agents were explaining the whys and wherefores of the situation, Hayward had moved over to Emma and Marc and hugged them fondly and the four of them including Esther kissed each other French style on the cheek (*la bise*). The positions at table were then adjusted so that the four could be together. The meal proceeded with all the exuberance and extravagance of an important celebration. Champagne was served if desired with all the courses and the meal continued for a good three hours. Then the musicians took up position and played soft, relaxing and tender music. Emma danced with Marc, Hayward and Bertrand while Marc danced with Esther and one dance with Bertrand's partner Jenny. This lasted for about an hour until it could be seen that many people were yawning and presumably looking forward to putting their heads down, Marc joined Emma in her room and the staff of the hotel put up a temporary bed for Esther who expressed the wish to be with our couple for the night. Hayward remained with a few fellow guests to chat about this and that and down a couple of cognacs before turning in. He was in his element. He was of course invited, together with Esther, to stay with Emma and Marc for a few days before continuing his film production work in the States. He planned to accompany Marc to Notting Hill on the way to see how the time travel film was going which was all the more interesting after his visit to the SuperBesse facility.

Once in bed and with her head on his shoulder Emma declared. "Dear Marc, do you remember that we both had a fleeting vision of a wheeled sword of all things when your film was rated top film at the Sun Valley Festival. It happened when Hayward stormed out of the concert hall in anger. You remember?"

"Indeed I do and I know what you are going to say now. You have seen the same vision again... Am I right?"

"You are right. I have seen the same vision again – when we saw Hayward being presented at the dinner, but it was radically different. There was indeed, as before, a bright sword attached to a wheeled affair but as it moved across my field of vision it decelerated and then stopped altogether and do you know what? – the image dimmed little by little and disappeared without moving. All that took, say, only two seconds. I really think that's the end of the vision. It's tied up with SuperBesse, that's clear."

"That was when I experienced it as well and like for you it was much slower and for me seemed final, too. Do you know what, Emma? I think we must just forget these odd occurrences. Like you I don't think they will ever happen again. Let's just lead our lives as well as we can and find our happiness together."

"I'm glad you said that, Marc because that is all I want to do and do you know what? I haven't had my period for two months!!!!!!"

...........................!!

CHAPTER 18

Sleep was somewhat difficult for Emma and she spent a fitful night going through the events of the previous days at SuperBesse especially concerning the restitution of her memories which were now flooding back to her from across the years. She also now knew that Marc had accompanied her for a decade or so in each of the two preceding centuries and of course she wondered how and why. She also knew that Hayward had been there but doing what? Had he been a benefactor to them or had he been a bad guy? She told herself that she should not exaggerate and that Marc's advice about leaving the past to itself was basically sound and the discovery that she was very probably pregnant was marvellous. She would buy the test as soon as possible. So, things were good and the future looked far from humdrum and commonplace. Still, there was another aspect that bothered her. Both she and Marc had been catapulted so to speak into the past and had assumed the forms and spirits of actual inhabitants of the day. The two of them had been obliged to quit the bodies and minds of those persons when their "mission" had been accomplished in order to move into another century. That had happened when they were whisked from the 19th to the 20th century. Now, what bothered Emma was what happened to those "real" inhabitants of the time when the two "interlopers" had left them. She would talk to Marc about it at an unauspicious moment. Best to leave it for the moment. He might well think along the same lines but it might take days or weeks. With his pragmatic mind he would undoubtedly want to let bygones be bygones.

A week later, Hayward and Esther returned to the States but not before Emma and Marc gave them a sightseeing tour of the South of France – Aix-en-Provence, Marseille, Nice, Carcassonne ...Esther was very loathe to leave but it must be said that Hayward went out of his way to reassure her. She knew that it would not be long before she was with Emma and Marc again and it was important that she returned for school. Even Hayward was quite content to be driven around but eventually, knowing that he would be returning to his newfound friend Sydney he allowed himself and Esther to be driven to Nice for a flight back to the States.

So, the days went by alone in painting and decorating their house, walking in the lovely surrounding landscapes or nosing round the shops in Pezenas, a nearby very touristic venue, until one week later when Marc was absent she could no longer accept her inaction in respect of the persons in the past and decided to phone Anastasia. She was fairly pessimistic as to the likely outcome of the call but she resolved to carry it out all the same.

She was waiting for Marc to leave for his work and he had in fact donned his overcoat – there was a slight nip in the air – when suddenly before stepping over the threshold he turned around, closed the door behind him, much to the surprise of Emma, and said simply. "Emma, there's something I would like to talk to you about ...   "

"OK, I'm listening, Marc."

"Well, I don't want to bother you or upset you and after the hectic flurry of unforeseen activity at SuperBesse I have been thinking a lot about our strange lives in the past. Somehow, it just seems too fantastic to be true but we have the proof that we have lived parts of our lives or other persons' lives in the past. We have regained our memories. I think that's a proof. If you want me to stop, just say so, but I feel somehow as if there's something missing and to be quite honest I would really like to know what we did in the past together. Anastasia more or less told us that we should and would forget about all that as the happenings had all been tied up and buried, so to speak, but she did talk about written records of the personages we possessed - can we say it like that? - but that the footings and videos had been destroyed."

"Marc, that is really weird because after the various meetings and conferences we had at SuperBesse I spoke to Anastasia along those lines. You must have seen me taking her aside before we broke up at the site. I have been having exactly the same sorts of feelings but like you I didn't want to bother you. I assumed you would not have liked to reflect on it, having better things to do – like your film – and being of a pragmatic frame of mind you would just want to cast it from your mind. It's wonderful that you think like me ..." She really did look pleased, a wonderful smile now framed about the eyes and lips and she hugged Marc tenderly. I was just thinking I would like to contact Anastasia and ask if we could have access to the historical records to which the videos, photos, films and presumably conversations were transposed. What do you think?"

"Wonderful idea but I thought we might be able to go even further ahead and build something solid onto that if ever you succeed in getting any information from her. Perhaps if we do receive any information, and I am sure if we do it will only be minimal, we could write a play script or something. I would like to get away from films for a while and have a go at theatre. Our minds might then be able to interpret what we experienced in past centuries as half truth and half fantasy. It could easily be therapeutic for us."

"Marc, that very idea was floating through my head but aimed rather at, yes, sorry, a film or perhaps a dual-author novel. I hadn't thought of theatre but that suits me down to the ground. Listen, I'll see what I can squeeze out of Anastasia first. I'm not terribly optimistic but you never know. Then perhaps we can find a troupe of amateur actors to put on a play. It shouldn't be too difficult writing the plot if we already possess the basic stories from the two centuries. It's very exciting, isn't it? I never thought that there could be a sort of golden awakening from our experiences. You're right, it could be very uplifting psychologically. Still, let's not get carried away."

"Well, my wonderful mother-to-be Emma, I must be off to finish this Hayward film. It should only take a couple of weeks now but if we have to go far to see Anastasia and hopefully the records, I will just take the necessary time off. So there, Hayward?" Here, they burst into laughter in unison and the fit of laughter lasted a good minute. They then wiped each other's tears before tenderly kissing and then separating as Marc skipped briskly, two by two, down the stairs to his car.

Emma now went determinedly into the kitchen, made herself a double espresso and then settled down at the table which was set just before the large bay window overlooking the balcony and the road.

The number rang for a good 20 seconds before someone answered. "Yes? TempSpace here, can I help you?"

"I would like to speak to Anastasia Prokovich please. I'm Emma Jameson. We know each other."

"Just a minute. I'll try and put you through." There was a longish pause with annoying music which one assumes is meant to relax you, then.

"Anastasia Prokovith speaking. Who is that?"

"It's Emma, Emma Jameson. You know, we met at SuperBesse!"

"Oh, of course, how silly of me. How are you and, let me see, ah yes, Mark, isn't it?"

"We're fine but you remember I asked you back at SuperBesse if it were possible to know what our lives were like in the 19th and 20th centuries. You said it was impossible to divulge anything but I beseech you, Anastasia, to give us the bare bones of our lives in the past. For the moment we are just interested in the 19th century part of our experiences. The reason is that Marc and I have a project in mind. Can we meet you somewhere, even at your HQ?"

"Quite honestly, Emma, I cannot tell you the location of my present work but I can tell you the name of the administrative department where it is situated. It's the Drôme. How does that help you and why exactly do you want to meet me?" She was her usual jaunty, empathetic self.

Emma returned her civilities and on hearing that she was fine followed it up with, "Look, Anastasia, Marc and I know very well that all the media baggage tied up with our escapades into the past – videos, photos, etc - have been destroyed but you did say that it had been transposed into written documentation which means that there is a record of whose bodies and minds we adopted for the period of time we were there and the manner by which we came into those persons' lives and how we vacated them. We have a project for a play and we would like it to be based on our experiences. What do you say?"

"Well, Emma, I did say that the team signed a confidentiality clause so I have no right to tell you anything but seeing your pressing need for information I am prepared to stretch a point and provide you with very, very basic information on your stay in the 19th century. The documentation that encapsules your experiences as part of our experiments into the possibilities of moving from one century to another is by no means detailed and simply shows what happened. No conversations are recorded. It is just an enumeration of events. The lives of the persons you embodied after your departure from their bodies and minds is noted but in even less detail, if that is possible, than when you were "in" them. The same goes for their birth, upbringing and occupation up until the time you became one with them. Names if mentioned will be largely fictitious. In any case there is no way you yourselves can consult this documentation but as you two were among the best time explorers we have ever had, if I can describe you like that, I am prepared to consult the dossiers myself and set out a summary of your experiences in the two centuries. As you will have gathered the accounts I set out for you will be summaries. Even doing that I am going over the limits of the occupational probity I have sworn to adhere to but it should give you an idea of your roles. I can't do any more than that but it will take a little time so be patient."

"That's great, Anastasia. We will fill in any gaps from our imagination. I thank you immensely because I have kept turning over in my head the fate of the persons we "occupied" (this word said with emphasis) even though it's well in the past now."

"Please think no more of those persons, Emma. They led their lives normally and the only impressions they might have had when you joined them would have been headaches or sudden jolts but nothing at all lasting. I'll need a little time, say a week or so, to set this out for you. I might add that I have never done this for other couples over the last ten years. Your experiences were, let's admit it, far from ordinary and stand out from the others' and they reflect the way you lead your lives today. I won't say anymore. Bye Emma," and she hung up.

CHAPTER 19

Two weeks, three weeks went by before Emma and Marc received any missive from Anastasia. In the meantime Emma joined an amateur theatrical group in Moulin-St-Mathieu, a culturally vigorous but non-pretentious town not far from Gabian, omitting the fact that she had taken leading roles in films and took part in a couple of theatrical projects where she was obliged to appear non-professional - a role within a role. Difficult for her but she needed to gain the trust of the other members. One evening during a rehearsal a girl in the group told Emma she looked very much like the heroine in Far-under that she had seen as a preview recently in Montpellier. Emma had to reassure her that she had nothing to do with the film and lied to the extent that she said she had never been to the US!! She told the girl that several people had already made the remark and that she now detested that actress in Far-under!

After their successful but uneventful integration via two plays in the troupe of amateur actors and actresses at Moulin-St-Mathieu, Marc and Emma proposed their play, still only at project stage to the director and he accepted it but subject, obviously enough, to his reading and approving it. This might not be for a few months yet.

In the course of the fourth week after Emma's conversation with Anastasia, the email from the latter arrived with a covering message repeating more or less what she had told Emma over the phone. The job now for Marc was to set out these bare bones of their adventures in the past and to flesh them out into living beings. Here it should be noted that Anastasia had been unable to cover the 20th century "expedition" for the moment for want of time. That would come afterwards if still required by the couple. However, even though of course they wanted to know something about the persons they had "invaded" in the 20th century they decided that they would have no practical use for the purposes of the play they hoped to stage. Here they would be concentrating on the lives of the "invaded" and not of the "invaders" so just one century for the moment.

The documentation on their two lives at the beginning of the 19th century was very basic, used fictitious names and fictitious time frames and dates. So, what did this tiny piece of history set out? First of all the two characters were described as follows. The male protagonist was very young, 19 years old at the start of the embodiment, the son of a French farmer somewhere in the centre of France. He was simple, kind, nicely proportioned and quite intelligent and was found by a local priest to have a gift for music which he encouraged by giving him lessons in the rudiments of music and also introducing him to French literature. The female protagonist was one year younger and the daughter of an English diplomat. They fell in love but the young woman was tacitly promised to a nearby nobleman by her family even though she did not wish to marry him. He however was convinced that she would change her mind and especially as in those days many marriages were effectively arranged. This person discovered the attachment of the diplomat's daughter for the farmer's son and challenged him to a duel. The latter had never learnt the art of duelling but was quick-witted enough to find a solution enabling him to win the duel. It was not explained why or how but the loser, although usually egoistical and one-minded, even rude, strangely enough accepted his defeat after a period and on the contrary went out of his way to further the career of the young man and did all he could to help the young couple establish themselves as man and wife.

Now Marc had to bash out a script from that, but strangely enough, the fact that both Emma and Marc had had those strange visions of a sword helped enormously. It was as if those images would become the very centre, the heart of the story, all attracted from the beginning to that magnetic centre and then repulsed by same. So, in the end Marc wrote one chapter at a time that would correspond to about a third of each of the planned three acts and Emma would check it, add details or delete others. There were of course stage directions for each scene, validated or changed with the collaboration of Emma that Marc inserted in the wide margins. This gave them a fairly good imagined and reconstructed but very approximate version of what they had experienced in their foray into the past.

They decided together to give the couple in the story the names Henri (with an "i") and Virginia to correspond as much as possible to the period and their social levels. The other names could be inserted as and when necessary after the story or when that part of the story would be completed. For the moment they would just have to be designated a, b, c, etc. The first task of course was to invent the manner in which Emma and Marc (their names would not be given, so shall we call them x and y?) came to inhabit the bodies and minds of Henri and Virginia. There were no technical explanations as they had to respect the conditions of their "time travel" detailed at SuperBesse. After discussing the point for a while they decided that what the two protagonists must have felt would have to be similar to their own impressions during the display of videos at the SuperBesse facility. First of all, though, their lives prior to the "invasion", even "sequestration" one might call it of their minds and bodies had to be described so there were country scenes where Henri might meet Virginia while hedging or ditching or whatever with ordinary run-of-the-mill dialogues. Virginia's daily life, likewise, had to be briefly presented as she chatted to her friends and made excursions to nearby uplands to practice rock-climbing, an occupation unheard of for women at that time. Their conversations would have been about possible suitors, clothes or anything outside of any patriarchal boundary of dialogue.

However, all would have changed for them both one night but unbeknown one to the other as they had not yet met. Henri was to be awakened in the middle of one night by short sharp pains in the chest, in the head, breathlessness and most of all by hearing an imagined boom like thunder so he would have put a question to his parents such as. "Tell me Mother and Father, did you hear or feel anything strange during the night? No, well I did and my head feels sort of heavy and misty this morning but it's nothing. It will pass." Virginia would have experienced the same sort of sensations but would only relate how she had been affected that night to Henri after two or three initial encounters.

However, for both of them their perceptions of the countryside and life in the countryside will have changed to some extent after that night. They would watch flights of geese with amazement and the growth flowers and trees would fill them with joy as if they had never before seen such normal but lovely manifestations of Nature. The comments they will have made regarding these entirely natural phenomena would have been listened to with incredulity by friends and family and it would be a matter of days for both of them before they became used to these wonders.

The first three scenes of the first act concerned the family circles of the English diplomat ("a" and "b"), of the farmer's family ("c" and "d"), of the priest ("e") and the church. The three scenes of the second act dealt with the deepening of the love of Virginia and Henri for each other, the discovery of their relationship by the nobleman de Groux and the sword fight. The latter event which was to be the principal part of the second act and the entire third scene, posed a big problem for Marc. How could anything but a long very hard object like a sword manipulated by an experienced wielder of such an implement be a match for a fine crafted sword held by an experienced swordsman? In the end he opted for the shaft of some hand farm tool, so in hard wood, topped by a small rounded piece of even harder wood attached to the end by very short chains to make it slightly flexible. This took time and many experiments before he was satisfied with its potential capacity. Now he had to see how it would work out in practice. In the script Henri knew a boy from his childhood from a less poor family than his own and who had received lessons in duelling when he joined the French army. He agreed to teach his friend the rudiments of the art. Of course all this had to be converted into conversational language and took time. Also, what was going to take time was the rehearsal for the duel which was the point of fulcrum for the story, so for the play. The actor was someone Marc and indeed Emma had spotted during their various rehearsals for previous plays put on by the amateur troupe. He was of medium height, nicely built, fast in movement and in the way he talked and was able to play the part of almost any male character and was delighted at being proposed the part. It was he in fact who devised the various movements, gestures and manoeuvres of the fight but Marc was not really looking forward to the rehearsals because he foresaw lots of hitches connected with the duel. However, all would go smoothly in the end.

The later part of the story explained how the nobleman came to offer Henri and Virginia a comfortable living. This was partly explained by his shame at having been beaten by a mere farmer's son but went further than that by virtue of the fact that he saw in the young man's physical and intellectual capacities the means of furthering his own interests. In any case, he argued, there were plenty of other high ranking families with daughters. To his credit, there was also a certain degree of humanism in his thinking that would have borne the designation of Christianity at that time.

With Emma's help once again, Marc rounded off the play with a scene where the two fall victim to highwaymen but overcome them through the use of a firearm held by the coachman and another held by Virginia and the use of Henri's now well-known "stick". After this incident they once again climb back into the coach to continue their journey, probably to their new house, and it was at that point that the "space travellers" would leave their hosts' bodies and minds to return to the 21st century. Virginia and Henri would both receive sharp pains in the head and become breathless once again. Virginia would then remind Henri how this had already happened to them both before their first meeting.

In the script, settings and actions of the play, Marc inserted several subplots including between the priest and Henri, dialogues by the latter's parents connected with their concern for their son's future and for their farm, the nobleman's conversations with his wife involving their wish that their daughter marry with de Groux and interactions between the various characters. There were parts in the play for the whole troupe of the Moulin-St-Mathieu drama group and nobody seemed to mind that the newest members of the group, Emma and Marc, had assumed the main roles. This was because the play was totally new in concept and had been written, or so they thought, for their group alone.

There remained the problem of translating the English script into French but Emma and Marc had a little money in reserve after their success in the US and one member of the drama group was a professional translator of English into French. The work took just over two months for Sabine the translator. She was bilingual and the script seen from the point of view of a French play director might well have been the original text and not in English as Marc had written it. It was excellent.

CHAPTER 20

THE PERFORMANCE

The small local authority community centre acting as a theatre for the play was full of spectators half of whom were friends and family of the acting troupe. A permanent rostrum was in place equipped with a basic electrical mechanism for raising and lowering the curtain and a Dolby system. As the time arrived for the start of the play people started fidgeting and consulting their programmes on which was printed a rough summary of the story in the play. The title of the play was "The adopted ones" and was described as the invasion of persons living in the early 19th century by individuals from the future.

The first scene against a backdrop of rough stylistic agricultural sketches was very basic starring a real goat on the stage on which straw had been littered and two men one of whom was much older than the other. One would assume that they were a farmer and his son. The son was raking the straw while the father milked the goat that was tethered to a stake. They could be heard chatting together but only parts of the conversation could be heard by the audience. However, the words "Henri" and "Father" could be heard from time to time so the two individuals were identified. After five minutes or so a woman in her fifties perhaps, dressed in the long ample attire of modest country women of the time came on scene to beckon the husband and son to the main meal of the day. This was therefore an ordinary day in the life of Henri, a farmer's son.

The decor was swiftly changed without the curtain being lowered and became by means of the backdrop a wealthy bourgeois family's lounge of which the foreground on the stage formed part with the armchairs and table that were now installed. Onto the stage came yet again a "middle-aged woman", very elegant this time with unmistakably English clothes. She sat down and started to read a fairly thick book and had hardly started her book when her daughter it would seem arrived on the scene and sat down in her turn. They smiled at each other. "Virginia, I would like to talk to you about your future. You are now 18 years old and you must soon think about a convenient marriage with a suitable partner in France. You speak very good French. We have noticed that you have had the attention of de Groux for a number of weeks and ..."

"Mother, de Groux is wealthy, quite handsome and just right for some young lady but I must admit he does not attract me in the least and for him to attract me he would have to save my life or something similar ..." She broke off into peals of laughter.

"But Virginia, you know that there are not all that many young men in this region of France who are of your standing, with your education, your artistic achievements, your good looks – and if there are some, they are all betrothed or about to be from what I've heard from our neighbours."

"Alright Mother, shall we leave the subject for a moment. I want to take my horse, meet a few friends and do a little rock climbing. It makes me feel really relaxed and wonderful and not at all like a kitchen or salon-bound lady, more like a man. There, I've said it. I want to feel free to choose my spouse ..."

"Oh, Virginia, you will never learn but do you have to go rock-climbing? It's not at all a young lady's occupation." Here she received a withering look from Virginia who simply rose from her seat and left the room.

Scene 2 of Act 1 was rather unusual as the decor was split in two with a partition across the middle of the stage from front to back. In each was a bed with, on the left Henri in apparently a very basic room judging from the backdrop of that part of the stage with an attic window behind which could be seen the moon. He was wrapped in several blankets and seemed fast asleep.

On the right could be seen Virginia, also in bed but in more than a basic environment. One could see on the backdrop a period wardrobe with costly garments hung inside and on a real chair next to the bed some costly undergarments. She also was fast asleep.

The church bell tower could be heard in the background through the Dolby system ringing out midnight, then one o'clock, two o'clock and then three.

At that moment the two sleeping forms pulled themselves up frantically to sitting position, held their hands to their ears as if they had heard some loud noise, rubbed their eyes frantically, then their heads and looked, to say the least, quite frightened. However, they apparently decided, both at the same time that it was just a bad dream and while still rubbing their eyes, gently this time, they settled into their beds and fell asleep once more. One could just see figures busying about on the stage changing the decors (still two) when the light dimmed and then brightened to reveal a basic farm kitchen to the left and a rather sumptuous dining room to the right.

Our two protagonists were revealed each of them in turn partaking of their first meal of the day, breakfast for the one and *petit-déjeuner* for the other, both with coffee, Virginia first, then Henri, again on their particular side of the split decor, asking their mothers if they had heard anything in the night and then dismissing the subject. But each then went to the nearest window, looked out, and made ecstatic declarations on what they saw. Henri saw a deer not far away and said to his parents. "Mother and Father, look at that lovely creature. How wonderful is Nature." They both looked at him as if he was totally out of his mind, shook their heads and carried on eating and sipping their coffee.

The same brief scenario unfolded in Virginia's parlour when she made a remark about some horsemen to be seen in the near distance and a flight of swans as if she had never seen such sights before.

These were but the high spots of their otherwise humdrum morning relationships with their families

Scene 3 showed the backdrop of the interior of a church with the church bell ringing to attract worshippers. At the front of the stage were set out several rows of what seemed to be real church pews. Beyond this foreground was an altar probably of cardboard covered with an altar cross. There were candles, flowers, a crucifix and all the paraphernalia of a catholic church. Behind this quite convincing glimpse could be seen the side view of an organ, there again almost certainly in cardboard. A male person could be seen sitting in front of the structure with arms stretched as if playing the instrument and indeed some church-like music, perhaps Bach or Handel, pervaded the scene. There were several members of the church choir behind the altar but in front of the organ. There was also a female violinist. After a few minutes, the "congregation" (the rest of the troupe together with a few people they had roped in for the scene) took their places on the pews but it could be seen that three places were left vacant. The church bell then chimed 10 o'clock and shortly afterwards the priest arrived on the scene dressed in all the regalia of a priest - chasuble, cassock and stole - with hands held together in a sign of respect towards God and when he reached the middle of the scene he made a sign of the cross towards the crucifix. The music from the organ changed to slow liturgical music and the choir started singing something in Latin, probably the Kyrie.

At this precise moment horses' hooves could be heard and shortly afterwards the English diplomat, his wife and daughter Virginia took the vacant places. Anastasia had said that there was a priest involved in Henri's love for music so Marc decided that here was the occasion for the two budding lovers to see each other for the first time.

Indeed, from time to time when the choir shifted position as people do when standing still holding partitions for relatively long periods of one to two hours, the organist could be seen. He looked very young, unusual for an organist, in wonderful health and exuberantly happy as he churned out not particularly gay music but music all the same, music he had painstakingly learnt from the priest. Whether it was the fact that he was happy with his musical achievements, like someone who has scaled a great height with great difficulty or perhaps because he had noticed the arrival of the three English persons and especially the very young woman with her auburn hair almost hidden by a large brimmed hat bearing coloured stuffs and several bright false flowers. From time to time when he was not playing he looked in her direction and each time saw that she was looking in his. Anyone near him would have noticed that he blushed profusely, so much so that at one point when playing he missed the measure and was chastised by the priest's annoyed look. But what could the young lady have been thinking in seeing a well-complexioned lad who she would have seen rather astride a thoroughbred than playing the organ? Perhaps schemes were forming in her head, who knows? Anyway, the mass ended "and that" said Henri to himself, but out loud, "is that".

CHAPTER 21

ACT 2 Scene 1 was in sharp contrast to the previous scene. The stage was set as if at the side of a hedge in a field. The hedge was again concocted of cardboard and fabric materials and part of this same hedge was neatly laid and flat at the top while the other half was wild and uncut. The grass in the immediate foreground was represented by a wide green carpet. The person apparently responsible for the neatness of the hedge was of course Henri but as the curtain was raised he could be seen sitting down, very relaxed and chewing on a baguette containing some sort of cheese and ham.

This scene was quite elaborate because the backdrop was not this time merely a reflection of the time and place where the action was to take place in the form of stylistic drawings or paintings. No, this time it was a screen showing a photo of a country view and at the same time on the stage in the foreground Henri could be seen eating his lunch with two or three hand implements including a sickle laid on the ground beside him. The sound of a horse's hooves could then be heard and the screen changed to show Virginia seated on a steed. This videoed scene had taken quite a while to arrange with the help of a local stable but made one catch one's breath as it unfolded on the screen. The voice on the screen was of course recorded but Henri's responses were not, so the farm hand had to show proof of precision when talking to the screen. The lady suddenly said. "Good day." (She could not say "Good day, Sir" for he was a mere farmhand). "Good day, Madam", said Henri standing up looking a little foolish.

"When I saw you I immediately recognised you as the organist at the mass on Sunday. What a surprise! Do you mind if I talk with you for moment. No, then I shall tether my horse so I can talk to you"

"No, not all." Henri started brushing himself down with his hands.

The screen then changed from a video to the former photo of the country view and Virginia walked onto the stage in person. This was indeed surprising to the audience and some of them clapped at the sheer artistry of the scene.

"I hope I'm not interrupting you. I'm terribly curious about everything. I cannot understand how a professional musician can be seen working in a field ..."

"That's no problem at all. Firstly, I'm not a professional musician, but the parish priest who is a wonderful person taught me himself to play the instrument. He also taught me to play the violin. He said it could come in useful. I practically know all the sacred organ scores by heart as Fr Templeraud started teaching me some ten years ago. But in reality I'm just a farmer's son and most of my time is spent on the farm."

"That's amazing. Mr ...?"

"Delaunay and Henri is my Christian name."

"Well, I'm Virginia Clifford and I live not far from here with my parents. My father is some sort of diplomat but what he does doesn't interest me. What interests me are the people in this world and also, strangely enough since the other day, I have discovered that I like nature, something I took for granted until then. But sorry, I'm boring you," and she shook her handsome face which made the bun behind her head become slightly undone leaving wisps of auburn hair about her face. She laughed causing Henri to come out of his forced reverie and to laugh with her.

"That is strange, Miss Clifford, because I have lived and worked on the farm all my life and like you, I have only become aware of the wonders of Nature since the other day or night, rather. I mean, look at that buzzard over there and the flowers starting to bud everywhere. I wouldn't have given them a second look until now so that makes me more than happy to be laying this hedge."

"So you are laying a hedge. It looks hard work to me but I'd love to help you but my mother would be scandalised. Yes, isn't that stupid? Well, I must not hold you up. Perhaps I shall see you here another day,"

"Oh yes, this will take me the week and then I shall have to do some cultivating work in this field." Henri was smiling almost from head to toe and looked dashing with his fair hair cut short about the face but long behind the head.

Virginia made off and it could be seen that her steps were made with great reluctance. The soundtrack of the horse moving away then filled the makeshift theatre but at the same time a man's irate voice could be heard offstage and the word "cow hand" could be distinctly heard uttered with great contempt.

Act 2 Scene 2 is made up of two more hedge-side meetings between the two young people at the last of which the *curé* Fr Templeraud makes an unexpected appearance and suggests that Virginia could go to the annual village fete, called a *bal* in France or village ball, which would present the opportunity for the two of them to dance together. He would have been aware of the problem surrounding the marriage pretensions of de Groux. He said he would visit Virginia's mother (her father was rarely at home) and persuade her to allow Virginia to meet the village people and become acquainted with country life in France.

Permission given by Mrs Clifford duly obtained allowed her daughter to attend the *bal* and dance with several young men including Henri. The latter also played his violin (lent by the priest) at this event. To cut things short, the two young people made a rendezvous for the next day in Henri's father's barn. The trouble was that de Groux followed Virginia to the meeting place and challenged Henri to a duel. The latter knew nothing of the art of sword fighting but agreed to the challenge thinking he could find a solution which he did with the help of a friend who also played the part of de Groux the baron in the play. This was set out above.

The nobleman, thinking he could in no way be beaten by a mere cowhand as he called Henri, visited Virginia's mother again relating his discovery of her daughter in the arms of "that cowhand" and more or less telling her to order her daughter to come to her senses and marry him. This was logical to the mother because she could not bear to think of her daughter marrying below her station. One must not forget that she was inculcated with all the prejudices and customs of the day. He omitted to tell her about the sword fight. When Virginia eventually returned home there was much heated dialogue between herself and her mother. Virginia did not talk about the duel either.

CHAPTER 22

Act 2 Scene 3

The backdrop, a large photo on the screen, is now of course inside the barn, the location for the duel. It is badly lit naturally enough because the sun has just started to rise but little by little the light steals onto the setting, cleverly done by the lighting technician. The impression is that the slowly improving light comes through the barn's opening, the two large doors.

In the version of the story we know already from the invaders' point of view the duel lasts no more than ten minutes at the most. In this version the outcome is the same but is seen to take place at the rear of the stage so is indistinct at first getting clearer as the sun rises. When Henri has the nobleman at his mercy on the ground the sun's rays (spotlights) shine directly on the unhappy, defeated de Groux.

What did not happen in the invaders' version was that Virginia (Priscilla in the first "real" version) had entered the barn very discreetly and had watched the whole scene.

I, the author, must now try to explain something which seems unbelievable but it's the absolute truth. The spectators will have noticed a gradual difference in the performances of both Virginia and Henri from roughly their second meeting behind the hedge, via the *bal* and even more so after their lovemaking in the hay in this same barn. Let us not forget that they are Emma and Marc who had taken over the minds and bodies of Virginia and Henri but who had been here before, unknown to themselves.

By slow degrees during the play Emma and Marc felt they were indeed becoming the two persons they had invaded and this became more and more obvious to the spectators who now saw two persons actually living the incidents and events and not simply acting them. One could see the said audience completely spellbound by the performances of our two protagonists. They were leaning forward. Some were clutching the backs of the seats in front of them.

Not only that but the slowly maturing mood of Emma and Marc (I should say Virginia and Henri!) was now spreading to all the actors – the farmer and his wife, the diplomat's wife, the priest and above all to de Groux and his acquaintances. Their performances on the stage became astounding, magnetic and absolutely convincing.

Act 3 Scene 1

The diplomat's house.

Virginia, completely bowled over by the outcome of the duel even though she somehow thought it was pre-ordained went home discreetly and said nothing about it to her mother who found it extraordinary that her daughter had been out riding so early in the day but she did of course notice that she looked ravishingly beautiful and happy. The conversation with her mother did nothing to dispel the latter's belief that Virginia would eventually have to marry de Groux but Virginia just laughed enigmatically when the name was pronounced. Her mother was left amazed, mouth wide open.

The farmer's house.

Here, the scene was similar with a very happy Henri eating his breakfast with his parents. They noticed he had a cut above the eye and his mother tended to it with devotion. They also noticed that he gave out an aura of great confidence and friendliness. They in turn adopted this new mood and talked together for some time in a way they had not done for years. The four of them suddenly seemed happier together.

Act 3 Scene 2

As the curtain is raised we see we are now in the church presbytery. Sitting opposite Fr Templeraud in the comfortably austere room in which books painted on canvases are shown everywhere is a man of whom only the back of the head can be seen. The man of some 40 to 45 years sounding particularly distraught suddenly stands up in a frenzied way and we hear him say. "And you are absolutely sure nobody has talked to you about the duel?"

"What duel my dear Sir de Groux? You did say something about it as I let you in but I'm afraid I didn't understand what it was all about."

"Well it was with that farmer's son who plays the organ. I challenged him to a duel because I was more or less betrothed to Virginia Clifford. Her parents wished me to marry her but I discovered she had a secret relationship with that lad. The duel was to close the affair in my favour ..."

The priest raised his voice. "You mean you actually fought him in a duel. I sincerely hope you didn't kill him or severely injure him. I need him here in my church. How could he have had any hope of beating you? He knows nothing about anything connected with war. You surprise me and you must realize that what you have done constitutes a grave civil offence but also a serious sin. I feel you should leave me now but I will hear your confession when you wish. Good afternoon, Mr de Groux" and he started pushing the man towards the door.

"No, no Father, that's not what happened. I agree that I should never have challenged him to a duel. It was wrong of me but I didn't succeed in beating him. He won the duel using a mere stick. I could not believe it was possible. (Here you could see the priest turning his head away from his interlocutor to smile) I imagine you would be one of the first persons to know about the duel in the parish and you are telling me that you have no knowledge either of the duel or of the result?" His voice here rose in bewilderment and could that have been a strain of slight hope to be heard in his voice? "He is a man whom I underestimated completely. If he told nobody about the duel then he has a truly noble heart. Father, of course I will confess my sins to you. I suddenly feel like a piece of dirt faced with a young man of such high moral integrity. Please, could you arrange a meeting between the lad – Henri is his name I believe – and myself, here preferably if possible? I wish to offer him my apology and also a comfortable position running my estates. He is a young man of enormous potential. I see that now."

Well, de Groux I will see what I can do to arrange a meeting. Please leave an exact address and I or someone else will deliver you your reply. But let me say that it does not surprise me in the least that he told no-one. He tries always to place himself in the shoes of the person he is dealing with. That's probably why he does not attempt to leave the farm. He knows his father needs him."

"Between you and me, Father, I will arrange for someone to take his place free of charge for his father if he will accept my appointment." He now looked pleadingly at the priest but with a smile that although still wry showed a hint of benevolence.

The reader should understand that in all these scenes, I as the author can only set out the essential or substance of any conversation or dialogue. Any one of these scenes contains a large proportion of matter which although interesting from the point of view of human relations does not further the story or plot. So, for instance in the example of this scene which now closes, there could have been remarks made on the priest's sermon, the music and choir and even perhaps on the weather! From the reader's point of view this is padding but all depends on the way the padding is presented. Expressions are almost as important as words and in this scene expression is not at all lacking.

Act 3 Scene 3

This scene which is relatively long winds up the story for Emma and Marc in the skins and minds of Virginia and Henri. There is first of all the abject apology made by de Groux to Henri and his offer of an important position together with the assurance that his parents' farm would be tended by a man appointed by de Groux to replace Henri who would now have to vacate the farm and set up house with Virginia. The relationships between Henri and his parents and between Virginia and her parents would be broadly described but it should be emphasized that Emma and Marc still feel that they really are Virginia and Henri in person and not just the stage roles of those persons. That goes for all the characters because as mentioned above the two main protagonists' stage performances pervaded all the characters – a phenomenon hitherto unknown by any of the troupe and indeed by any of the spectators. It was astounding to hear them speak even to the extent that their accents changed to conform with the accents of the region and time. One spectator especially was astounded. She went out of her way to speak to Emma and Marc about this during the *vin d'honneur* after the play.

For the moment, all this has now passed. We have reached the final crucial point in the play. The backdrop is now the screen once more and we see a horse and carriage in which our hero and heroine can just be made out inside. We as spectators are riding alongside the vehicle for several minutes. The vehicle disappears from the screen and suddenly a shot is heard.

The lighted screen goes blank and the curtain descends and then rises to reveal a cardboard cut-out of a horse and carriage on the left with Virginia and Henri standing firmly on the ground. The rough painting on the cut-out shows the coach door open behind them. The driver is still perched on his driving seat at the top of a suitably disguised stepladder.

A rough voice offstage from the right calls out. "Hand over all your valuables and you can leave."

"Not on you life," calls back Virginia quite unperturbed. She is holding one of her father's handguns, a caplock which is loaded and cocked. We then see three men, two of whom are holding firearms.

"We'll see about that" says one of the ruffians, obviously the leader and makes towards the pair but stops short as a shot is heard. It is the coachman who has fired a handgun into the air. The gang leader beckons to his accomplices to move to the right and left of the pair while he himself unsheathes a heavy sword and heads for Henri. Now the latter, as he explains later, carries his mock-sword as a good luck token whenever he travels and when the gang leader laughs in his face he simply points it upwards and flips it down at great speed to hit the adversary on the head. He reels under the attack while his two accomplices are about to shoot at the pair. But just too late. The coachman fires and one of the attackers falls, a bullet in his leg. The second highwayman also fires his firearm either at the coachman or at Henri and the latter effectively hears the bullet whistling past his ear. The leader, now recovered from the blow, lunges at Henri with his sword who nimbly steps aside and gives the other another terrific blow on the head with his "stick". This time he falls to the ground.

"Is the interview now over? asks Virginia with just the amount of sarcasm necessary for such an occasion, because we would very much like to be moving along." The three villains were now retreating, one hobbling, their buccaneering mood thoroughly squashed.

The curtain descends and rises and we see the coach moving off into the distance on the screen. Then over the Dolby system we hear Virginia say. "Henri, my head feels terrible and I can hardly breathe. What's happening?"

Henri does not answer for a while then we hear him say. "My head is the same but it feels empty. I don't know what's happening." This was gasped rather than said but a few minutes later one after the other declared that the incident had been a close thing but that now they felt better and not to think anymore of it. Both the ambush and their physical reactions to it had brought them closer together. They expressed concern, tenderness and admiration (for their reactions to the menace) one for the other and continued on their journey after thanking the coachman for his intervention – all this was entirely vocalized, no more images.

The curtain falls for the last time.

It must be emphasized that the play was drawn from the summarized documentation from Anastasia and from Marc's imagination but when Anastasia came to have a word with the two during the *vin d'honneur* half an hour after the play she conceded that the plot as shown in the play was not so far from the truth. She congratulated the couple, the actors playing the parts of de Groux and the priest and said that during the play she had really felt she was back in the past. She then asked Emma and Marc if they wanted any documentation on the second excursion in the 20th century. They were both exhausted from the last months' events and with a new member of the family on the way they had decided, as one, that they wanted to forget the distant past, think of it as a period when they were seeking some sort of significance in their lives but that now they wanted to get on with the job of living today. So when Anastasia posed that question they replied in unison. "Definitely not!"

THE END